"Did I Not Say Ye Are Gods"

~Jesus

REVIEWS OF WAKING GOD BOOK I:
THE JOURNEY BEGINS

"New Novel by Maine writer co-creates a theory for everything but could ignite a religious backlash that could make the *Da Vinci Code* look like a church hymn."
David Farmer, *Lewiston Sun Journal*

"I read *Waking God*. Then my computer crashed. I don't think those two events are connected...A fast moving story with thriller aspects, interspersed by serious religious discussions...there is real thinking here. **A provocative novel, part thriller, part religion. It should make you think.** A worthy novel."
Piers Anthony, New York Times Bestselling Author and Nebula and Hugo Award Nominee

Waking God is fiction with a mission. Doe and Harris run down the field and tackle the big questions in Waking God/Book One/The Journey Begins. Herein the world's biggest culprits become the heroes as they battle not only the religious institutions, with their dogma and hellfire, but the very angels and gods themselves.

Truth is a slippery slide, but the novel's protagonist, theologian Dr. Andrew, is determined to get it, as his internal battles manifest in an all too real life war of cosmic proportions. It's refreshing to read a book that is about something. Whether one agrees with the assertions the authors put forth through this medium of fiction or not, the discussion is on the table. They've not pulled any punches. An entertaining and provoking book on many levels.
Jesse S. Hanson "author of Song of George: Portrait of an Unlikely Holy Man

Wow! Waking God: Book One - The Journey Begins is definitely a spiritual thriller. If you read between the lines, many mysteries and secret codes, The Tarot Code, are revealed which provides readers the opportunity for profound thinking.
Ann Churchman

The American Constitution dictates separation of church and state. After reading "Waking God", I'm wondering if it's possible. The key word here is 'wondering'. If the intent of this book, and the ones to follow in the series, is to provoke critical thinking, it's a huge success. Calling it provocative is an understatement.
Susan Haley, Author, *Rainy Day People - A Novel Fibers In The Web*

I like that for once, someone has had the kahuna's for lack of a better term to make people *really* think about life, their beliefs, where and how we came to be…
Katrina Stiles, Alternative-Read.com

"WAKING GOD is not an easy book to pin down in a couple of words. It's a thriller, but doesn't seem quite comfortable in that category. It's definitely a religious book, but not of any of the established religions, and in fact quite opposed to them. It's likely to appeal to many of the Da Vinci Code fans, but it's not a copycat. The back cover identifies it as "Speculative / Thriller." I think I would only change that to "Spiritual Thriller" to give a clearer idea of where it fits, but of course any label will be oversimplifying the matter.
David Ausema, OnceWritten.com

"Every so often, a new and sensational idea causes humanity to question the fundamental principles of our existence and being and catalyzes the notion that not everything is as it appears. In the new and exciting novel, *Waking God*, American University Alumnus Philip Harris and co-author Brian Doe take a look at a series of these groundbreaking and revolutionary ideas and tickle our imaginations through a journey of discovery and meaning that enlightens one on the very foundation of morality and truth.
Howard Perlman, Staff Writer for the AU Eagle Metro/National Section, Article Head: *Book by Alum Asks Profound Questions, The Eagle Online* **10/12/2006**
(http://media.www.theeagleonline.com/media/storage/paper666/new s/2006/10/12/2006/TheScene)

"Ancient prophecies coming to fulfillment. The end of days drawing near. Cataclysmic events working themselves out as if scripted. Fantastic beings appearing to Humans, and interacting with them, as one more speculative fiction tale utilizes the classic morality play format...no, wait a minute! That's where this book leaves other works in its apparent genre behind, because this is decidedly not a morality play.
Nina M. Osier, Author of *Sagarmatha* and 2005 Eppie Award Winner

"*Waking God* is at once captivating, deeply thought provoking, and spiritually inspiring. **Marvin D. Wilson, Author of *Beware the Devil's Hug***

"What if every Truth you had ever been told was really a mosaic of falsehoods? What if every religious institution that preached salvation was actually an agent of oppression?

"Epic in scope, *Waking God* is a fast paced supernatural thriller that blazes across mystical locations and panoramic scenery. There is action and intrigue, yes, but there is also a challenge to the reader in this book. *Waking God* introduces a new way of interpreting reality. The book provides an alternative contextual understanding for mythical creatures like werewolves, vampires, angels and demons, as well as taking on the weighty issue of the nature and existence of God.

Christopher Friesen, *Book Pleasures.com*

A fascinating journey through the world of religious theory, it is a work that will bring questions to believers and non-believers alike. Doe and Harris have offered an alternative view of "God," of the foundations of all organized religions and the evolution of the world itself. In a work of breathtaking depth and scope they have proposed an alternative theory that binds brilliantly with the current events of our world. It destroys the allegiances of man to churches that promise safety in return for blind obedience. It offers a world where man must accept his own personal actions and the choices he makes.

"This book delves into the realms of religion, mysticism, mythology, and magik. It unfolds layer after layer to expose the inner locking patterns of development and changes in man's quest for understanding. It is a cornucopia of information and speculation on items as varied as Tarot cards, Masons and crop circles. The authors' gift is to open the minds and curiosity of their reader.

Barb Radmore, *Front Street Reviews*

WAKING GOD

Book One: The Journey Begins

Philip F. Harris & Brian L. Doe

ALL THINGS THAT MATTER PRESS

WAKING GOD
BOOK ONE: THE JOURNEY BEGINS
3rd Edition
Copyright © 2011 by Philip F. Harris & Brian L. Doe

ISBN: 978-0-9846297-5-6

Library Of Congress Control Number: 2011920281

Cover design by All Things That Matter Press

Published in 2011 by All Things That Matter Press

Published in 2006 by: Star Publishing
Published in 2009 by: Literary Road Press

To Kelly,
Always,
Venus rising…
Ab Aeterno.

&

To Deb,
Forever;
Here we go again…
Fiat Lux.

Acknowledgments

As with most philosophies, we do not claim to have originated all of the ideas presented in *Waking God*. Truth is ancient and is the underpinning of all rational thought. Then again, there are those who say that there are no original ideas. Nonetheless, we have done our research, and find ourselves indebted to those who have gone before us in an effort to divulge to the world some kernel of universal truth. We invite the reader to review the multiple books now available dealing with the *Dead Sea Scrolls*, as well as the *Rosae Crucis* publications, *Mystical Life of Jesus* and *The Secret Doctrines of Jesus*. Moreover, we learned much from Pagels' *The Gnostic Gospels*, Suares's *The Cipher of Genesis*, Hall's *Old Testament Wisdom*, Wood's *Genisis*, and Devi's *Son of the Sun*. Of course we could not deny the timeless wisdom of the *Bible*, the *Qabbalah*, the *Gospel of Philip*, and Arthur Waite's work on the *Tarot*. To these and all conveyors of wisdom, we are forever grateful.

And lastly, because of their devotion, support, and ceaseless desire to see us succeed, we are most indebted to our wives, Kelly and Deb. They have withstood not only our countless hours of debate, but also have remained strongly beside us through the stress, confusion, and struggle to make our ideas accessible to the reader. Without them, we have no audience and no true understanding of our universe.

INTRODUCTION

Welcome to the Third Edition of *Waking God: The Journey Begins.* The 'journey' of this trilogy began in 2006, and since that first edition was published much has transpired. Book I took on the air of prophecy as the world has been catapulted into economic, environmental, and even religious turmoil. Book II, *The Sacred Rota,* was prelude to even greater changes that have seen political chaos, continued environmental degradation and climate change, further collapses of world economies, and interesting discoveries in quantum physics that may yet be humanity's saving grace. The third book of the trilogy, *The Second Coming of Humanity,* will show the possible, perhaps even the probable, outcome or world events as we approach the infamous date, 2012.

The *Waking God Trilogy* is not about the doom and gloom that organized religions would have you believe. It is not about an Armageddon style 'end times' that pits good against evil in some final battle where religious dogma is triumphant. Yes, there is a final battle of sorts, but as Mantrella says, "It is not about saving humanity, it never has been." You will have to read the book to find out who Mantrella is. The struggle of good versus evil is a myth perpetuated by religions to keep the masses in tow. There is no good. There is no evil. Are there positive and negative forces in the universe? Of course! Do people do horrible and reprehensible things? Yes. But is 'up' good and 'down' evil? No. The manifest universe is polarized. This is essential in order to even have a manifest universe. Without the negative, there would be no positive and the universe would simply exist as 'potential' without any physical presence. It would be a concept, bereft of reality.

While the *Trilogy* comes down hard on organized religion and its 'worn out dogma,' it is not atheistic. Instead, it totally rejects the idea of some schizophrenic super-being that loves to punish and reward its servants, and recognizes a Universal consciousness of which we are all a part. It acknowledges that within each of us there is a 'god seed' that is waiting to experience an awakening brought on, as in any major evolution, by not only environmental, but also social, economic, and political stress that will help to create a spontaneous evolution in humanity. Or, if allowed to remain dormant, this same seed will be our undoing. The prophecies of 2012 all speak of a choice. Nostradamus, the Hopi, the Mayans, the I Ching, the Riddles of DaVinci and the Tarot speak to a time of choosing. Hidden codices, books of revelation, and ancient sacred texts also speak of this time of choosing. That time is upon us. The elements are all there. From bursts of energy from the center of our galaxy to the scientific discoveries about the true nature of our reality, the puzzle nears its completion.

In the new editions of *Waking God*, we offer images of the sacred places that are a part of Adam's mystical journey. The places are real and their histories have been well documented. We speak of current events as they lead us to a spiritual Armageddon. We turn the world of good and evil upside down in the hopes that you will gain your own personal revelation as to the inner workings of the universe. We offer you mystery, fantasy, action, adventure, intrigue, conspiracy, a little sex, insights, revelations, and clues to the sacred in order for you to truly understand the ancient prophecy which says, "All that is hidden shall be revealed." The answers lie between the lines!

But surely, THE AGE OF 'WORN OUT DOGMA' IS COMING TO AN END.

Lucifer \\'lü-sĕ-fĕr\ *noun* [Middle English, the morning star, a fallen rebel archangel, from Latin, the morning star, from *lucifer* light-bearing, from *luc-, lux* light + *-fer* –ferous...]
—*Merriam Webster Dictionary*

"And I will tell you about the Kingdom, which no eye of an angel has ever seen."
—*The Gospel of Judas*

PROLOGUE

Mist hovered ghostlike in needles of green, fresh pine. Eager trees, tall grasses, and newly blooming flowers in open meadows, vibrant in pastel colors of an emerging rainbow, spread toward the liquid sky, as if attempting to grasp the very fabric of the blue heavens. Air, still and warm, all of thriving nature appeared washed in an amniotic sheen of morning dew. Burbling waters of a crystal brook had attracted a naked figure—a stranger—flesh clean, bangs of his long, slick hair hanging in his face as he knelt to drink. The perfect definition of the virginal form was expressed in the flexing of the finest muscle fibers as the man leaned over and lapped voraciously at the water.

A terrifying screech, and he reeled from the brook, bolting upright and flailing his arms as he turned frantically in every direction. He angled his face toward the sky, toward an opening in the canopy of leafy branches through which a solid band of sunlight rippled, splashing across his cheeks and forehead. He could feel its warmth, its subtle vibration of everlasting energy, but he could not see the light. His eyes were closed; they had always been. Even as the lids twitched open, barely and only for an instant, he remained blind to all that was around him.

The shriek came again, and he became more afraid. He had no name for the sound, no understanding of it, and he instinctively jerked his head and ducked at the noise beating through the treetops. Then the world was still again, silent but for the brook water that continued conducting its symphonic existence. He grew tired, his body numbing, as the morphine of exhaustion compelled him to sleep...

***

You can dream about life...or you can live it... Soaking his hair, sweat trickled down the sides of Andrew's face, dripping into the orifices of his ears and dampening the bedsheets. He trembled as every muscle in his body finally relaxed and he felt himself awakening. The voice was still there, easing him into consciousness—an echo, a whisper, in his mind: "I offer you the world and all its glory..." His eyes opened and he stared into the darkness. "I offer you knowledge of all that was, all that is, all that will be..." Breathing deeply, he held the stagnate air in his lungs, held it until his head swelled to dizziness. He was awake; he sensed this somehow. But..."I offer you the experience...the experience." The concept rang in his head, like silent words shouting back again. Sitting up, he swung his legs off the edge of the mattress. Beneath him, he could feel the bed sheets, wet with the sweat of the early morning's dream, with the intensity of the feelings, of the visions, of the...experience. The headache was lessening, but at his shoulder the mesmerizing vibration of the chant continued softly, almost subvocally—"Fear not, for I will be with you always." Face in his hands, he hadn't the strength to fight the voice. It hardly startled him. He only listened, half absorbing the words, while the grogginess of awakening leaked out of his soul, coming slowly, as if rising from the dead after centuries of sleep.

***

The alarm clock howled from the nightstand; his heart jumped, and a jolt shot through his body. *"Holy shit!"* he breathed, quickly slapping at the snooze button to silence it. Wincing with the stiffness in his back, he stood, went to his desk, and turned on the lamp. Pen held weakly in his hand, he wrote on a clean page of an open journal:

> *And he agreed, and from Him was taken the Vessel, the Chalice, which was to contain all that was created. With this taking came the knowledge in the form of Wisdom, and from Wisdom they went forth and multiplied. When It saw what had happened, It said, "This is good." And It placed a fiery pillar before this place of rest that none should disturb the slumber. If he awoke, all of creation would thus end and Wisdom would be lost. Being the seventh day, It rested.*

He closed the journal, not bothering to read the words he'd written. He knew the idea by now, was familiar with the message, though he comprehended none of it beyond an academic capacity. He only needed to find some way to understand why it was happening, and what in God's name it had to do with him.

CHAPTER 1

Two floors below the earth's surface, a lab technician waited for DNA results. He had no idea why the blood sample he'd been told to analyze was so important, nor did he completely understand the gravity of the results. He was to look for a sequence; that was all—a particular order that must *exactly* match the code entered into the computer two hours earlier by a man he hadn't recognized, but who wore the credentials of *Dr. L.M. D'Italia* that bore the hospital administrator's personal seal. Had it not been Christmas Eve he might have sought clarification on the matter from his direct superior, but he was alone in the lab and his supervisor wasn't answering pager or phone. And since the stranger had been sent, it seemed, from the administrator herself, he thought it was in his best interest to perform the test without contention.

The computer chirped, and the technician turned his attention to the monitor. Cool blue light washed over his face as he studied the left side of the screen, where a three-dimensional image of a double helix twisted in a frame like a barbershop pole. The colored spheres embedded within the strands clearly showed the specific pattern earlier entered into the program by the doctor. In a frame to the right of the image was a continuous stream of data from the blood analysis, as the software struggled to configure a second three-dimensional double helix.

A moment passed and the new double helix appeared in the frame to the right. The technician typed in a command from the keyboard, before double-clicking the new image with his mouse. The computer overlaid the three-dimensional double helix images. The combined frames immediately flashed red, indicating an exact match.

"Perfect," the technician breathed. He pulled a handheld computer out of the pocket of his lab coat and fingered for the stylus. Tapping the contacts button, he scrolled through a list of names and telephone numbers, searching for the extension Dr. D'Italia had instructed him to call as soon as he obtained the results of the analysis.

At the telephone on the opposite wall the technician entered in the extension number on the keypad and waited for someone on the other end to answer.

"D'Italia," a man's voice answered.

"I've just gotten the results of the blood analysis."

"And?"

"There's a match."

"An *exact* match?" the doctor's soft voice demanded.

"I would say so."

"For your sake, I hope you're correct."

The technician felt perspiration bead on the back of his neck as the muscles along his spine tightened. Though not outwardly threatening, something in the doctor's tone frightened him. Visions of the man who entered the lab two hours earlier loomed before him like a holographic projection rising out of the white tiled floor. He could see Dr. D'Italia's silver eyes burning into his face as the undulating shadow of the man's tall, slender body slid across the tips of his imitation leather shoes. The technician even remembered the oddly shaped pin shining on D'Italia's black silk tie as he imagined him standing there, his presence imposing and menacing. The angles of the doctor's chin, cheekbones, and nose were sharp and clean, as if his face had been finely chiseled out of marble, and the nails of his long fingers had appeared perfectly manicured, moving nimbly over the keyboard as he deliberately entered the DNA sequence into the computer program.

"Send the *complete* report in a *sealed* envelope. Someone will be arriving at the laboratory within the hour to remove all data pertinent to this matter from the system's computer. I would suggest that you take your dinner break as soon as they arrive."

The technician closed his eyes to make the haunting figure disappear as a bead of sweat ran down the left side of his face and leaked into the corner of his mouth, but the image of the doctor was branded into his memory as a reminder, perhaps, or a warning to perform as asked and never falter. Even though the computer confirmed an exact match, the technician silently prayed the results were accurate, for his own sake, whatever that might be.

"Yes, sir," the technician answered, his voice and hands trembling. He placed the telephone receiver into its cradle, and did as he was told.

***

Nine floors above, Jana Fashir held a newborn infant in her arms. Her husband, Abdel, elbows pressed into the bedside, leaned over his wife and peered, smiling, into the tiny baby's face. Only hours old, she was beautiful by all standards—face and head perfectly shaped, pink skin supple and evenly colored. Her weight was healthy, and blood counts normal. The Fashirs could not have felt happier or more profoundly blessed.

"What will we name her?" Abdel asked quietly. The infant lay swaddled in a white cotton changing blanket, calmly cooing on her mother's chest.

Jana gently brushed her hand over the baby's bald head, pausing momentarily to feel the blood, the life, beating in the soft spot of the newborn's skull. "What I dreamed," she replied. "I want to name her after the little one in my dream."

Abdel reached for his wife's face and kissed her slick cheek. "Mara," he said. "We will name her Mara, then." He looked into his infant daughter's eyes and called her by the new name. "Mara." Taking her tiny hand in his, he placed the little fingers against his lips.

At the end of the hall, a set of elevator doors slid open and three men in black suits stepped onto the maternity ward in a triangular formation. At the opposite end of the hallway a pair of men in gray trench coats rounded the corner and marched toward them. In smoothly synchronized movements, the two men reached into their trench coats and withdrew pistols equipped with silencers. One of the pair fired at the lead man in the triangle, striking him in the chest. The target spun against the wall, his body exploding into a quasar of brilliant light that blasted through the ceiling and into the night. His comrades continued toward the pair as if nothing at all had just transpired. The second trench coat fired, hitting a black suit, and he, too, burst into a flare of white light, his soul released from his body like his leader's, taking the same path as the first. With only one man of the triangle left, the elevator doors opened again, and another triplet of men in black suits invaded the maternity ward.

The hallway had been quiet, the Christmas Eve skeleton crew of nurses and doctors now ran for cover, screaming and crying. Over the intercom, a metallic voice called for security; alarms sounded, doors closed and automatically locked, sealing off the ward. Stainless steel carts were knocked over sending aluminum trays sliding across the tiled floors. Jana Fashir, the only patient in maternity, was left unprotected as the third man burst into light with the dull pop of a bullet forced through a silencer.

The new triplet of men in black suits weren't quick enough to beat the trench coats to the room where the newborn baby cooed contentedly, unaware of the strange commotion only yards from the security of her blanket. Nor did she realize, in the blindness of her baby gaze, she was the objective.

Jana Fashir screamed, the trill pitch of her frantic cry echoing through the hospital corridor. Within seconds of having entered the room, the trench coats appeared in the hallway again, one of them cradling the newborn in his arms like a football, while the other fired at the three black suits rushing toward them. In a moment, the two men and the baby were gone, fading down the hallway, smashing through the sealed doorways as if unobstructed.

Two of the black suits broke off and pursued them. The leader, however, entered Jana Fashir's room. The commotion in the hallway behind him grew more frantic at every moment. Electronic voices panicked in speaker boxes, and doctors and nurses flashed by the open doorway as blips of white.

In the room, Jana sat up in her bed. Her cheeks were red and wet with perspiration. On the floor lay the father, bleeding from a gash in his temple. The obstetrician was slumped against the heart machine, moaning. Wild-eyed, the mother whimpered and pulled her knees to her chest.

"My baby," she stammered. "Where have they taken my baby?"

He could hardly contain the smile. "We'll find her," the man said softly. He reached out to wipe the sweat from the terrified woman's brow. "Soon enough."

Backing away, he stopped in the doorway and surveyed the chaotic scene in the hallway. He smiled again, then turned toward the new mother as he reached inside his suit coat. "Soon enough, dear," he said, withdrawing a 9mm. "Don't worry."

He shot her in the forehead.

***

Racing through the parking lot, the baby robbers far outmaneuvered their two assailants as they wove around the parked cars to the clearing on the other side. Realizing their disadvantage, the black suits halted to withdraw their pistols. Bullets exploded into the night, tearing through the mist, but the pair with the baby were undaunted. At the grassy edge of the clearing, they lurched forward morphing into wolves. The lead wolf gripped the swaddled package between his fangs, careful not to harm the newborn life within, and disappeared into the night. Halfway across the clearing, the other stopped and threw back his feral head in a terrifying howl. The two still in the parking lot, fired wildly at targets they could no longer see.

CHAPTER 2

With his head in one hand, Andrew lifted a spoonful of Cheerios to his mouth with the other, while his eyes worked over a *National Geographic* story of the Brazilian rainforest. The author of the article, a photojournalist who had spent months in a sweltering, insect infested region with local foresters, claimed that the natural world was regenerating itself in a miraculous and terrible way. He cited the story of a man known simply as Fernando, who had been the head of one of ten crews working to clear the rainforest in the south of Brazil...

Like most of the peasants in his position, Fernando had read many stories about the importance of the forest, and after all, he and his family had received medicines made of roots, bark, leaves, and even insects, from the local shaman. Whatever had cured his wife's cancer had been found somewhere among the bromeliads and orchids, cat's claw and figs. Nonetheless, Fernando had known that when the trees and plants of the rainforest were finally gone, the medicine, too, would vanish. Many locals in Fernando's village had already been killed in landslides as deforested hillsides washed away and thousands were buried in seas of mud. Still, he and many others had little ones to feed, and the job paid. Going to the city to find work was not an option. Too many had fled the rural paradise in search of wealth in urban squalor only to end up condemned to tin shanties with little food and no medicine.

"All the world's woes," he whispered, flipping the page while the noise of his jaws pulverizing the whole grain O's, droned in his ears. Scanning the text, he sought the end of the story, curious enough to want to know about Fernando, but intolerant enough to want to avoid all the inflated prose leading up to it...

According to the village mayor, who was present in the end, Fernando whispered "Madre de Dios" as he dropped to his knees and made the sign of the cross. A radiant being of white light emerged from the forest. With each of the being's steps, the decimated parts of the forest were rapidly renewed. Roots appeared on the dark, rich soil, and trees sprouted everywhere. Fernando turned in abject terror as the swiftly-growing wall of green seemed to be on the attack and the onslaught roared toward the workers. Panic-stricken, the men scrambled to their feet and dashed toward their trucks and wagons, but they could not outrun the rushing vegetation. The forest overtook them, their bodies speared and crushed by the exploding biomass. Fernando, too, attempted to run, only to join his team, impaled on the limbs of the very trees they had come to slaughter.

He blinked once, then closed the magazine. "That was an interesting twist," he sighed. "Superstitious people and their superstitious beliefs." He was not exactly in the mood to entertain the notion that a forest had attacked and murdered a bunch of Brazilian lumberjacks. Then again, he'd never fancied himself an environmentalist, but if these jackasses were going to venture into a land as precious as the rainforest and decimate it, there certainly would be no more fitting consequence than to die by the very trees they aimed to kill.

A radiant being of white light? He wasn't so sure that he bought the idea, not because it was implausible, but because in certain circles it might be too possible.

Distracted and a bit nauseated, he dropped the spoon into the bowl and rose slowly from the table. At the sink, he dumped the milk and the last of the soggy cereal bits down the drain and then leaned against the counter, staring absently into the living room.

"Just another day," he told himself. "And another and another…over and over again." He considered the thought. "And still no closer to the truth." Closing his eyes, the opening lines of the lecture he was to deliver to his graduate class later in the morning ran through his head. "Maybe someday they'll give me something I can use. Some real piece of insight."

Precipitating events—the subject of the day.

He smiled, half amused, somewhat disgusted. An ache tapped at his forehead, spreading deliberately into his temples. The day could go one of two ways, he supposed. Either he'd be successful in killing some of the deeper convictions that his young scholars still maintained, or he'd be impaled by the very wisdom he wished them to understand. He was, however, confident, if only half-heartedly, that they would get at least something out of it, and he hoped that the favor of the moment would not find him in Fernando's predicament.

Chuckling, he pushed himself away from the counter and headed to the foyer to get his coat. By the time he reached the couch, the pain in his head was strong enough to force him into the cushions. A noise blared in his ears like a wailing baby. Closing his eyes, he gritted his teeth, as a series of images fired into his brain. He winced with the pulsing color and twisting visions blitzing his conscious mind, and yet only a single one was vaguely comprehendible—an infant, wrapped in a blanket, being carried away in the jaws of a wolf. Then, as if hit with a taser, his body jolted and the image was gone. He sat sweating, his head heavy, though suddenly free of all but a lingering ache.

"My God," he muttered, wiping his face. The single vision had been so clear, so real, rushing on him and rushing away. He waited on the couch for his heart to quiet, for his senses to remember again the familiar surroundings of the apartment. When his body had finally accepted the calmness that enveloped it, he walked unsteadily into the foyer again to get his coat.

The image was still there, though its clarity was quickly being overcome by the countless other thoughts that had permanent residence in the young professor's mind. Slowly sliding his arms into the coat, he gazed at the green tiled floor of the entranceway, lost it seemed, in the admittedly bizarre experience. Shaking his head, he threw off the numbness and tried to focus, telling himself that nothing had happened. Nothing at all had occurred. Yet, just in case, he'd better remember the feeling. Yes, it would be wise to remember it, whatever it was.

The vision grew ever more intangible as the seconds passed, as if he had been meant only to experience it and not to commit it to memory. He still had a piece of the baby, of the wolf, nonetheless, as he hurried to the den to retrieve his journal. He would write it down, whatever he could recall.

As he stood, hunched over his desk, pen in hand and journal spread open before him, he found himself bewildered. He had, after all, forgotten just what it was that he had intended to write. He had blanked the thought out altogether as he turned his dry eyes to the ceiling and listened to the faint crying of an infant breathing down from the apartment above.

CHAPTER 3

Beneath the sallow light of a pregnant moon, a midnight-black stretch limousine rolled to a smooth stop behind the twin glass towers of the ultra-modern New Life Evangelical Church.

In all, over 200 million dollars had come into the temple during its twelve-year existence. Every Sunday morning hundreds of the faithful New Life flock lifted their eyes to the crystal, marble, and gold they had helped to amass in glossy columns and rounded archways. Prized were the luxuries of cushioned pews, high-tech surround-sound systems, low-glare, super-efficient lighting, plush carpeting, and, above all, an intricately carved pulpit of the finest grain, imported from the Yucatan—only the finest gifts for their sequined god. All of this had been made real, simply through the generous gifts and donations of the sheep, whose cultic adoration for their silk-suited shepherd took the sting out of the financial hardships their faith continued to cost them.

Monies exceeding three million dollars had been willed to the institution by wealthy patrons of the born-again way, and rumor had it that millions more would be granted to the faith with the passing of some of its current, more financially secure members. Poor and rich, young and old alike gave freely and abundantly to New Life. After all, the Reverend Mr. Victor M. Woolgrabb, who was raised up from the dusty trailer courts of southern Georgia to the pulpit of the Almighty right here in Atlanta solely through the power of divine inspiration and providential guidance, was their salvation. He had been, as a little boy, ordained a member of the elect who had been promised heaven with the hiss of a serpent's tongue.

Or so he claimed.

From small-time street-corner preaching as a teenager, Rev. Woolgrabb made his way through the ranks of born-again religion on the heels of his predecessor and master, Rev. Stanley Duke, moving the old man's backyard congregation to his own finished basement, then later to a refurbished barn. As tithe revenue built—all tax-free—Woolgrabb's aspirations grew. Soon ground was broken for the New Life Evangelical Church. Duke's ashes were spread over the foundation hole, and an empire was born; its gut made fat with the unceasing contributions of the lonely and ostracized figures of humanity, whose weaknesses sought not individual liberation but collective salvation—and Woolgrabb fed on them.

Three years later, New Life went global. NLTN, *New Life Television Network*, "The channel God watches," brought the slippery image of the good Reverend—complete with salt-and-pepper mutton chops and fold-over hair—into the welcoming living rooms of the invalid and the needy, the old and the unemployed. Eventually, mail order tithing constituted a respectable percentage of the institution's income, and Rev. Victor M. Woolgrabb ascended the ranks of notoriety on a national scale. Benefit dinners and public charities of all kinds featured the religious celebrity, brushing elbows with the most powerful evangelists in America. He even posed for a photograph with the Dalai Lama, only hours after delivering the blessing at the United States president's second inauguration.

The sudden onset of witching-hour rain drew mist from the warm pavement that rose like steam around the limousine. Rev. Woolgrabb passed through the shower on his way to the car, umbrella spread open above him. Though the puddled water in the parking lot had gotten his fine Italian shoes wet, he shook off the notion as he closed the umbrella, handed it to the chauffeur, who obediently pulled open the back door for him, then disappeared into the vehicle.

Inside, darkness obscured Woolgrabb's sight, but he could feel the company of another body sitting across from him. A scratch of flint and a lighter ignited, softly painting the narrow chin and high cheekbones of the shadowy passenger as he tilted his head to light a cigarette. When the flame died, the darkness rushed on them again, save for the glowing cherry of the cigarette.

"So Hollywood," the stranger softly quipped.

"Hollywood?" Woolgrabb replied, staring at the burning end of the cigarette.

"All of this," the stranger continued. "Middle of the night, stretch limousine, lighter and cigarette. This scenario is so Hollywood." He paused to chuckle. "The will of the imagination still astounds me."

Woolgrabb smiled. "We can have anything we dream of, really," he said in his thick southern accent.

The stranger leaned toward him; the reverend could feel the breath on his face, smell the smoke in his nostrils. "And of what do you dream?"

"Serving God."

The breath was gone. Woolgrabb could hear the body settling back into its seat. A moment passed, then the stranger erupted into laughter.

"Serving God," he mocked. "Yes, yes. All very sincerely, too, Reverend Woolgrabb." The laughter stopped as suddenly as it had begun. "Everything is in place," he said, a subtle command in his speech. "Now you are to do it."

Holding his breath for an instant, Woolgrabb collected himself from the insult. "Why me?" he asked at last. "You've never answered that for me."

"For fun," the stranger answered frankly. "I couldn't think of a more perverse notion than having you do this for us. Besides, you'll never remember doing it. You'll simply wake up one day far richer than you already are, and we will have begun what so badly needs to be done."

"And my kingdom?" Woolgrabb muttered.

"Oh, yes, your kingdom." Silence descended on them for a moment. "The kingdom promised to you will be granted to you, my faithful minister. You shall receive an ironclad kingdom, fit for one of your stature."

The reverend felt a hand on his shoulder, heavy and clamping, then his blood slowed and the sound of his heart beat vaguely in his ears. He was getting drowsy, unable to resist the compelling voice. The orders reverberated in his brain: "Seven days…nine o'clock flight to Rome…car waiting with everything needed to do it…in and out…Swiss bank account…ironclad kingdom…"

CHAPTER 4

"Hallelujah!" the choir bellowed as their hands slapped together, their scarlet robes swaying to the beat of the drums, guitars, and keyboards.

"Hallelujah!" the congregation of hundreds answered in refrain, their hands in the air, bodies entranced with the music and the power of faith.

"I say, Hallelujah!"

"I say, Hallelujah!"

A thin black man in a tailored suit stepped behind the podium, his face glistening with sweat, his mouth turned up into a smile of great praise, and beaming white teeth. He clapped his hands high above his head, the microphone picking up the sharp sound and sending it out over the heads of the sheep.

"Hallelujah!" the choir sang louder, their collective voices vibrating the glass ceiling.

"Hallelujah!" the congregation answered obediently, marble columns reflecting the notes.

"Now, ladies and gentlemen," the speaker called out as the music continued at full volume behind him and the choir resounded with his words, "I give to you The Most Reverend…"

"The Most Reverend!"

"The most special…"

"The most special!"

"Our very own ambassador of the one true Holy Lord…"

"Holy Lord!"

"Our father and shepherd!"

"Oh, our father! Oh, our shepherd!" the choir celebrated, the cadence quickly gaining speed. *"Oh, our father! Oh, our shepherd…"*

From the other side of a stained glass partition suspended by golden chains at the back of the stage, the reverend appeared, hands waving and aged face bright with joy. The silver flecks of his double-breasted suit sparkled in the crystal light burning down on him from above. The congregation yelled out *"Hallelujahs!"* and *"Amens!"* as the shepherd made his way to the podium and stood, basking in the glory of his faith. With one hand he brushed back his wavy white hair, and with the other he gestured for the crowd to quiet and the choir to end their entrance hymn.

As silence unfolded in the ultra-modern temple of marble, glass, and gold, the reverend smoothed the hair of his mutton chops and surveyed the wonder-filled eyes of the faithful who made the weekly pilgrimage to gaze once again on the man and his self-made mountain to the born-again Christian God.

"My people," the reverend began slowly, powerfully, the words dripping with the slant of deep southern dialect, "you have returned again to *Jeeesus!*"

The congregation shouted out its praises, some clutching at their hearts as they threw back their heads and closed their eyes.

The reverend held up his opened hands, as if fixing to raise Lazarus from the tomb. "Now is the time, my sheep, to sing out the power of Christ and the goodness of *Goddd!*" He smiled confidently as the crowd grew more entranced, as if his speech flowed forth from the mouth of Moses himself.

This was his forum, the act in which he reveled. Often, when standing above these lost souls who crawled away from the horrors of their own ill-spent lives to take refuge in the material wealth of God, he thought of how proud his mamma would be of him. *The cancer that had ravaged the old woman's body to dust was bitter repentance,* he thought, *for a life of abuse, and sweet salvation from an existence of squalor.* The limelight of religious infatuation, too, took him far away from the humid sweat of his bedroom, where nightmares of his father whipping him with barbed wire vexed his mind night after lonely night. But in the end, it was all a part of the training, he believed; of the suffering a man must endure in order to find salvation.

"You have heard of the great dissent in the world," the reverend continued. "You have heard of the plan of the devil to bring down the steeples of faith. There is danger in messin' with the Lord!" He paused to absorb the concessions of the flock. "But remember, my children," he blustered, a bony finger pointed to heaven, "Jesus turned, and said unto Peter—'Get thee behind me, Satan: thou art an offense unto me: for thou savourest not the things that be of God, but those that be of men.'"

Clenched fists rose like whitecaps in the ocean of the audience, and they called out words damning the blasphemers.

"Now, my people, we must stand *strong*," he insisted, moving away from the podium to center stage. "We must be *resolute* in the face of such iniquity! For what man of faith, no matter how many men he commands or hearts he misleads, would look the Lord between the eyes from his Roman palace and claim that he has the *secret* of all God's creation? What man, I ask you? Dig down deep into your hearts and tell me if you don't feel the power of Satan in this holy man's outrageous claims. Why, he is not the Son of God himself. He is no *prophet*. Only the faithful and just will *ever* know the nature of *Goddd!*"

The congregation spread their arms wide, stomped their feet, and reaffirmed their undying allegiance to God's great faith—a religion only the reverend could deliver to them.

"People, hear me. I don't *need* to point fingers. I don't *need* to mention names. I only *need* to show you the graven image of the devil with miter and staff, big ol' rings on his fingers, and walls of ol' blood-soaked stone *risin'* all around him. That's the face of *evil*, my friends. And from the black hole of its mouth, it dares to invite the wrath of *Goddd* down upon us all lest we *fight*, my people. Fight 'til the Lord comes to *raise* us up again!"

Cries, moans, screams of exultation for the reverend twisted into the air, and the windows screening the clean white sunlight falling into the massive hall, trembled at the noise.

The shepherd stood proudly at the edge of the stage, his lanky form floating above the flock. "The devil tells us that *his* faith holds the truth," he said. "That *his* church possesses revelations beyond the scope of human understandin'. What gives *him* the *right* to speak such *heresy*, ladies and gentlemen? What god fell on him and bestowed *him* with the knowledge of the world? We *already know* the truth, my people. Let me hear you scream '*Amen!*'"

"*Amen!*"

"Let me hear you yell out the name of your *savior!*"

"*Oh, Lord Jeeesus!*"

"There is only *one* God, my sheep, and the faithful shall know the *truth* on judgment day. *Shame* on those who think they know what they have not prayed for. Shame on them."

"*Shame on them!*"

"To *hell* with the many who think they hold the truth when their truth is but the shadow of *Satan...*"

"*To hell with them!*"

"Speak out, my children!"

"*We hear you, oh Lord!*"

"Commit yourself to ridding the world of such abominations!"

"*We fight for you, Lord Jeeesus!*"

"Of the glory-seekers who'd steal the attention away from the work of God's *true* disciples! Of homosexuals who'd have you believe they can know no other way! Lesbians and gays, parading around our streets as agents of the devil! Whores and gossips, my children, are in *league* with this *unholy* man, this mitered *demon*. Our faith must remain strong and our hearts resolute, for the good Lord *himself* has put each one of us on a mission, and we shall surely succeed in the errand..."

As the congregation settled into convulsions of divine possession, the reverend rubbed his hands together, as his loyal attendants distributed brass offering plates throughout the crowd. If one idea was certain, he loved the commerce of God, and seethed with hatred for anything that would threaten his livelihood.

***

Andrew stood outside O'Neill Library, briefcase in hand and plaid tie lapping out of his overcoat, in the early morning breeze. Across the square, he watched a vagrant stumble onto campus, with a cardboard sign that read "Warning," and listened to the gray-haired, soiled man yell out his sermon to students and faculty scuttling to class.

"You must believe!" the tattered old man insisted through rotting teeth. "I have opened myself to condemnation!"

He switched the briefcase to his other hand and leaned against the building, strangely interested in what the preacher had to say. Almost immediately, he'd become conscious of the intellect writhing in the dirt and the stink of the would-be prophet's mortal disguise of flesh, blood, and clothing.

"This has always been their tactic," the old man declared. "Offer a truth different from their own and be labeled as the *evil one* or in league with the devil. I have tried to offer you guidance, but *they* will not let my words reach you without their censorship. The true demons of this world are hiding behind halos, cathedrals, little white steeples and onion domes. Now do you see why I will be condemned? They will cast a dark shadow upon the light I offer. They will call my story blasphemy'! But it is *they* who blaspheme my words and teachings. This they have done since the beginning of time…"

Checking his wristwatch, he decided that he'd better get to class. There was much to talk about today, and he wanted to finish the semester on a strong note that would make his graduate students really think over the summer term. Still, he found himself considering the vagrant's words for just a moment longer.

As if he'd sensed the young professor studying him, the vagabond suddenly swung his head toward the onlooker, their eyes meeting only long enough for the old man to mouth, "You will believe."

Vaguely unnerved, he glanced away, shaking off the experience as the vagrant continued to yell at the others in the square.

If anything, he was becoming more and more aware by the moment that his universe was beginning to wobble. This day couldn't possibly get any stranger. Stepping away from the library, he told himself that later he'd have to find out who *they* were, what light might be offered, and what god it was that whispered revelations to a homeless old man from the bottom of a *Smirnoff* bottle.

CHAPTER 5

"For the remaining minutes of this course I want to discuss an idea that will be very new to you. In our increasingly complacent society, the common refrain is that one person, or one small group, cannot make a difference. You often hear, 'Why bother to vote? My vote won't make a difference.'" He grinned at the confusion on the faces of his students. "Yes, this is a lecture on theology and not political science, so you need not be looking at each other, wondering if you're suddenly in the wrong classroom or if I've been hit on the head and forgotten the title of this course," Dr. Andrew said lightly to a Boston College lecture hall, packed shoulder-to-shoulder with graduate students.

Quiet laughter eased through the terraced hall.

"Theology and politics have had a long historical and parasitic relationship," he continued from the microphoned podium. If anything marked the tenor of his lectures, it was his affinity for co-mingling religion and politics with any social or environmental issue. His outspoken nature earned him both respect and disdain from his colleagues, and adoration from his students.

Born and raised in a small New England town, he was the youngest of six children. His father was a truck driver and rarely home, leaving the childrearing primarily on the shoulders of his waitressing mother and two sisters. Naturally inquisitive, he was frequently forced to leave his Sunday school classes because of his disruptive nature—he asked too many questions and often found himself giggling at his overly-obese

Baptist minister. His first real religious confrontation came at the early age of seven, when a priest told Andrew's best friend that he could not attend craft classes being held in the basement of the Baptist church because good Catholics might be subjected to Protestant ideology. The young Andrew went to the priest himself and tried to explain that the craft classes only involved making baskets, learning to tie knots, and drawing pictures. The priest asked him if they recited the *Lord's Prayer*, and Andrew assured him that they did.

"Ah," Father Malley nodded triumphantly, "the Protestant version of the prayer is quite different than ours, so your Catholic friend obviously cannot attend your little Baptist craft classes." He patted Andrew on the shoulder and skittered away into the rectory. This single moment sent the young boy on his spiritual journey and formed the basis of his bias against institutionalized religion, which he would later in his academic life term *churchianity*—a concept that he would apply to all organized religions.

None of Andrew's siblings went to college, and only one even graduated from high school. The pressures of blue collar life resulted in his two sisters being "knocked-up" before either of them had reached the age of eighteen. One brother was killed in a back road drag race—too much alcohol and too many curves in the road. The brother that did graduate went into the armed services and remained a low-rank "lifer."

Regardless, Andrew had a happy childhood. Despite his relative poverty, his mother went out of her way to cater to his wants and needs. To achieve this feat, she worked long hours, leaving Andrew on his own to explore the intricacies of life. Five years separated him from his next sibling, so he frequently found himself on his own, staring at ant hills, examining spider webs, or lying on his back watching the clouds. He instinctively knew that there was more to life than working in a dead-end job or having kids before he was ready to grow up. And whether they were real or imagined, he frequently saw lights in the skies that he just knew were alien spaceships.

Among his frequent journeys to the beach—their one, if not only, family activity—he found himself on the rock jetties thrusting out from the shoreline. He would sit there for hours enjoying a sense of peace and reverence. He took comfort from what he would much later learn were the five great elements: air, water, earth, fire, and the human spirit. For the boy on the beach, feet dangling in the water, all of these elements clicked together. As a young adult, he was taught that the world's great cities were on bodies of water for commerce, but he had come to the belief that the real reason for their location was that humans needed the proximity of water to balance their inner spiritual desires. The pentacle, although he felt the symbol greatly misunderstood, spoke of a truth that was basic to human existence.

In high school, Andrew was academically superior, but hardly an athlete. While he was big-boned and tended to be on the heavy side, he simply didn't care to spend his time on a football field or basketball court. He loved to read, a practice that consumed much of his free time, the remainder being given over to publicly and privately arguing religious and political issues. He was not handsome in the way society viewed beauty, nor was he homely by their standards. "Average" was the word he liked to use, but his one outstanding quality rested in his piercing blue eyes, where all of his emotions, thoughts, and desires swirled. But while the gaze of many people were immediately drawn to his eyes, eye contact was rarely maintained with him. It was as if people were uncomfortable looking into the crystal blue of them, perhaps afraid that their very soul would be scanned. Few could take such scrutiny.

As a college student, Andrew became obsessive about academics, spending all of his waking moments on his studies. His graduation from Yale was a surprise only in that his financial background proved inconsistent with the moneyed heritage of his classmates. Tuition had been paid through academic scholarships and part-time employment. While this income deficiency and lack of "blue blood" prevented his entrance into the famed, although secretive, *Skull and Bones*, Andrew found himself sought out by many "connected" classmates for assistance with writing term papers and running study groups. The young scholar had a knack for pre-guessing test questions, and this reputation garnered him favors from the more well-to-do students.

His academic standing and the favors owed him enabled him to complete his Masters and PhD at Boston College. His doctoral thesis, *God's Evolution as Reflected and Guided by Man's Religions*, earned him great acclaim from scholars, and scorn from the clergy—*all* clergy. In his argument, Andrew put forward the idea that what humanity called "God" desired to understand Its own nature and to experience Its own existence. To do this, he claimed that It created, or imagined, the manifest universe, or universes, as a means of holding a mirror to Itself.

"Since time does not exist to God," Andrew wrote, "because He *is* all time, the manifest universe is like a book or a history of God's existence, which It desired to read. Just as any novel contains its own past, present, and future between two covers, one does not experience the concepts therein until one chooses to read each page."

The point he wished to make was, for that time, somewhat extreme, especially in the area of theology. Comparative religious studies had only touched on what were deemed as "strangely coincidental" themes and "possible" multi-levels of sacred text interpretation. But Andrew was, in his novel analogy, promulgating what he believed to be a basic truth of the universe and organized religion. He premised, "What is read now quickly becomes the past, and what is to be read becomes the future, yet the entire story exists in the now." Subsequently, man's religions and their evolution told the story of how God actually evolved and became what It was now and what It always was.

To Andrew, all religions were but a history of God and contrary to their own beliefs. Institutions of faith were required to change since God's story changed, even though God was considered both immutable and ever-changing. However, the conservative nature of the world's churches refused to bend. Religion, Andrew offered, was like a chapter in a history book that simply resisted and did not want to become the next chapter, because it felt that if it became "history," then it would no longer exist. He went on to argue that "human genes show us that history is still alive and makes up a part of what mankind is today and what it will be tomorrow." In other words, a book with missing pages just didn't work. The existence of previously "read" pages was integral to the story, and its continued existence was essential to humanity's complete understanding—and God's understanding—of the whole story, the whole Self.

The clergy, and those tied to *churchianity*, didn't like the notion that they represented only a small and incomplete page in God's Great Book. They found themselves instead caught in a master paradox: they existed in the present, and yet claimed to know Truth. To know Truth, however, one must have read the entire book. To have read the entire book, one must have been *outside* of time in order to have escaped the "now." Since the known world had "apparent" limits, Andrew insisted that it would seem impossible to read a "limitless" book while being manifest; therefore, religion was but a few pages in a four-billion-and-counting-page volume.

Nevertheless, Andrew's apparently complex thesis gained him notoriety in the heady world of theology and comparative religious studies. He learned quickly that notoriety was not necessarily synonymous with acclaim, as the controversy over his work made him a much sought lecturer and popular icon among "New Age" thinkers.

"I want to introduce you today, in the final lecture of the semester, to the concept of *precipitating events*," Dr. Andrew explained to his graduate students. "This concept will give you something to think about over the summer break."

He waited for the dull ripple of feigned chuckles to cease before continuing.

"I know the idea of thinking during the summer is heresy, but you may be required to write about this topic for your first term project next fall."

Moans and groans welcomed the idea of next fall's projects for aspiring theology graduate students, though there existed a silent understanding among them all that Dr. Andrew was *the* professor to study under if any desired to be considered freethinkers in the academic theological world.

"Every major point in history can be traced back to a precipitating event," he began. "This event is the immediate cause, but it is also itself an effect. Let's consider some examples. The American Revolution: the precipitating event was the 'shot heard 'round the world.' World War I: the assassination of Ferdinand. World War II: Hitler invades Poland. Civil Rights: Martin Luther King is killed." He paused for a moment, then added, "Christianity: the Crucifixion.

"These events are obviously not the underlying cause of great historical moments, but rather are the final straw, if you will—that which precipitates the next great event. Consider the American Revolution again. One can make a long list of causes, or reasons as to why there was revolution—the tax issue, no representation, unfair commerce laws, indifference on the part of the King, et cetera. All of these causes built a pressure in the colonies. That pressure was released when the first shot was fired in Lexington. Likewise, pressure built around Martin Luther King; pressure built in Germany, in Iraq, in czarist Russia. Finally, in each case, an event occurred—*a precipitating event*—that allowed the pressure to be released. Such events are frequently attributed to one person—the assassin for example—or to a small group of people. Those who blew up the World Trade Center, for instance. In other words, millions of people may well be affected by the event, but they do not participate in the event itself.

"Wondering what this has to do with theology?" he asked wryly.

The heads in the lecture hall nodded almost in unison, as if on cue, and for an instant, the professor felt their sycophantic relationship with him.

"Well, then, consider this: What is the precipitating event that created God?"

Several pens stopped writing and others were held suspended in the hands of their users. The students glanced at each other, then away. Many stared into their notebooks, perhaps fearing to be called on to make an attempt at answering such a perplexing question. Finally, heart beating bravely, a single student in the shadows of a far corner dared to ask for clarification.

Andrew, chin held high in proud acknowledgment of his challenging question, smiled slightly. "What is the event that caused mankind to create God?"

The same student answered, "Isn't that a little backwards? I mean, didn't God create man?"

The professor's smile widened. "Which god, sir, are you talking about?"

A murmur rushed through the crowd, then was gone, lost to the raising of Andrew's hand.

"Let's go way back, shall we?" he said. He moved away from the podium, his voice strained but clear, now that he no longer made use of the microphone. "Ra, Osiris, Isis in Egypt." The names echoed in the vaulted ceiling as if called down from the mythological skies by the hails of the ancients. "Zeus," he continued, "Ares, Diana, Poseidon, the entirety of the Greek pantheon of gods; Danu and Lugh from the mists of Ireland; Odin, Thor, Loki of the Norse; Doondari, Etu, Anansi of Africa; Moon, Sun, Earth Mother, Great Spirit; and on and on." He paused, knowing he had more than made his point about the importance of specificity in academics, and especially in theology. "Are these the gods that you say created man?"

Andrew turned slowly toward the student hiding in the corner. No response. But the professor would not be daunted. "Sir, are these the gods that you say created man?"

A lull of silence replaced the fading reverberation of Andrew's voice, and the shadowed student shifted uneasily in his chair.

"No," he answered hesitantly. "I meant *the* God. The *real* one." Stifled laughter met the reply as Andrew nodded emphatically and chuckled. "The one in the *Bible*," the student continued, an air of defiance in his words as he strove to squash the reactions of his classmates.

A glance at the clock on the back wall reminded Andrew that he didn't have the luxury of extra time left to decimate this young man and his "real" god. He had yet to make the students understand.

Instead, he asked rhetorically, "Before the 'real' God came, why did man begin to believe in a god or gods at all? Everyday ancient peoples saw the sun rise, the phases of the moon take shape. They experienced rain, thunder, and lightning. Trees were no strangers to them. The natural world was not only a part of early man's life, but also the very *center* of it. Why did the notion of divinity even arise? These were everyday elements of their lives. You have all grown up with televisions, radios, computers, cars, rockets, and so forth, but you do not call these things divine. The idea would never cross your minds, and you already have at least a concept of the term 'divine.' Do you think that after seeing the sun rise a few thousand times someone said, 'Gee, I think the sun is simply divine and I'm going to worship it as a god, whatever that may be?' Or, six thousand years ago, did some random Greek get up in the morning and ask, 'Why am I here? I bet some god by the name of...of...of...Zeus (that's a good name!) made me and I'll be rewarded if I'm good.'"

Though they smiled, it seemed that the students felt the earnestness in the professor's voice, and didn't laugh. The power of his words, as ridiculous as they sometimes sounded, trapped the noise in their throats.

Andrew took a deep breath and returned to the microphone. "I want all who are returning for the fall semester as continuing students of theology and comparative religious studies to gravely consider the following points. Before your 'real' God appeared, where did the concept of divine, holy, godly, come from? Why were divine attributes given to everyday occurrences? Why did every culture on the planet develop these concepts? And finally, what, if anything, was the precipitating event that gave rise to heaven and hell, and to the college of gods?"

As the students madly transcribed the questions of his lecture into their notebooks and laptops, he cleared his throat and checked the time on the clock once again. 9:57 a.m. Almost over. His head ached with the questions he asked because they were questions he struggled with since the moment he'd discovered theology. These students would be no further ahead in understanding the divine nature of the universe at the opening of next semester than he would be at the end of his career, he believed, and the ignorance toward the profundity of the discussion Dr. Andrew was proposing would hardly suggest to the most serious and devoted of students, that they would also wrestle with these ideas for the rest of their academic and religious lives.

"In closing," he said finally, "remember that while I have spoken about events on a societal scale, these same types of events also occur at the personal level. Only at that level might one understand the term 'epiphany,' 'breakthrough,' or even 'crisis.' This summer, watch for both personal and societal precipitating events, and be prepared to revisit the subject in September."

The round of applause barely lightened the weight of thought Andrew found himself slipping into as he considered his own words and the troubling questions he had willingly shared with those also struggling to understand. He had, without their permission, planted a seed that might haunt them from this moment on. No one knew the absolute truth, he conceded in his own mind. No one had yet discovered the true nature of divinity.

Nodding, he collected his notes from the podium, and slid out the side door, safely escaping the throng of groupies heading for the front of the lecture hall to inundate him with demands for further clarification or guidance. He could not entertain them today. He had far too much on his mind.

CHAPTER 6

The mist moved slowly off the cliffs, leaving in its wake a sweat-like sheen of moisture on the ancient stone walls of the castle. In its glistening silence, the rough citadel appeared as if it had just been stillborn of the fog and left in all its majesty to guard forever the open sea. The crisp air offered little hope of a mild spring, but even with the absence of sun and warmth, the birthday girl's little heart was filled with happiness. The nine-year-old had grown "like a sunflower," according to her stepfather, since last summer, and now she stood an even five-feet tall weighing fifty-eight pounds. Tall and thin, her most striking features were her long black hair and deep green eyes. Already a Middle Eastern beauty, her copper complexion provided a stark contrast to her probing crystal eyes.

The child enjoyed her regular Saturday visits to Edinburgh Castle for brunch. On this particular morning she was insatiable, quickly consuming fish and chips and a Scottish egg. Unfortunately, she had been limited to only one Scottish egg per visit by her stepfather, who never let her forget how her past indulgence led to a messy stain of vomit on the backseat of the Audi.

Finishing brunch, she now wandered away from the outdoor terrace, in search of her favorite spots on the castle grounds. It didn't matter to her that on her birthday the morning gloom held a heavy foreboding. The weather never spoiled her childhood wonder or curiosity, and it certainly would not keep her from marveling at the massiveness of the structure, or at the view of the surrounding areas from the castle's high position in the central city.

Moments later, her stepfather called after her, and the two, hand-in-hand, made their way back to the black Audi parked on Princes Street. An older man, her stepfather was kind, but stern. Tall with white hair, and thin gray eyebrows, the chiseled angles of his face and small silvery eyes often cast a gaze that held the attention of those who encountered him. For many weeks his handsome, yet arresting appearance had scared her, and only by the kindness in his manner toward her did she come to trust him. Most of all, she loved him for the trips to Edinburgh and for his genuine desire to be with her, as a father should love his daughter.

The Audi eased onto Princes Street as they headed for the airport, to the private airstrip where a jet was waiting to take them on a short holiday to London. She didn't journey to London often, but she liked the occasional excursion into the big city to visit art galleries and museums.

Her stepfather turned the car at Junction 1. He glanced at the little girl, a smile curling in the corner of his mouth, and she grinned back at him. Suddenly, his head slammed into the headrest of his seat and a spray of blood washed the windshield crimson. The car careened across the airstrip, striking a steel drum before crashing into a storage hangar and coming to a sudden stop against the building's back wall.

The car jolted to a halt thrusting the screaming child forward. The slack in the seat belt allowed her slender body to slam against the dashboard. She lay broken on the floor of the vehicle, fighting to stay conscious. She could hear footsteps and the groaning sound of the damaged passenger door being forced open. The smell of burning stung her nostrils as she felt herself lifted out of the vehicle…

Then her world went black.

The police arrived to find the Audi engulfed in flames. Forty minutes later, the fire was extinguished, and emergency personal extracted two charred and steaming bodies from the wreckage.

Miles away, the little Middle Eastern beauty was on a private jet soaring high above Europe.

CHAPTER 7

The morning lecture proved more rousing to Andrew's spirit than he'd anticipated, having set out to taunt his students with a profound idea. They were only just now, after four semesters of comparative religion courses, beginning to grasp the theory of precipitating events. The concept, on a very superficial level, was comparable to the accepted notion of cause and effect, but to the consternation of his superiors, his courses were never really focused on comparative studies, regardless of their descriptions in the syllabi.

In spite of his controversial nature, Andrew attracted students, and students meant endowments. Much could be tolerated when large sums of money were involved, even with funds apparently sourced from obscure groups and organizations. Occasionally, he would try to track down the huge sums donated in support of his work, only to come up against dummy corporations and headquarters with nothing but postal box addresses. He didn't dwell on the issue often, though he wondered about the nature of his secret backers. As far as Boston College was concerned, as long as the checks were valid and there were no signs of impropriety, the true identities of signatories were of little concern.

More importantly, Andrew was on a quest. Behind his theory of precipitating events, he also sought to develop a unified theory of religion. While physicists were exploring a more real world theory of a unified universe, Andrew felt that such a hypothesis would never truly answer all of life's greatest questions. Intuitively, he knew that quarks, neutrinos, packets of photons, vibrating strings of energy, dark matter were but half of the "grand equation." What science was discovering about the nature of the physical was, in his mind, old news. Ancient texts had long since postulated the vibrating essence of an energy-based universe, but when the mystics spoke of etheric matter, nous, planes of consciousness and spirit, the scientists scoffed. What was different, he often queried, between the transcendental notion that an event in one part of the universe rippled throughout all of reality, and the current quantum string theory? How did any of this differ from the biologist's "web of life"?

He rejected the clichéd notions that the origin of religion was based on some amorphous, and oftentimes demented deity. The debate as to whether Jehovah, Zeus, Brahma, Allah, and Odin were prime movers, or even one and the same entity, Andrew left to sanctimonious theologians. There was something much greater than that issue. The precipitating event of *all* religion was locked in some secret temple, text, or myth of the ancients. There were just too many recurring stories, too many shared symbols and numbers, too many similar pictographs and concepts that could be attributed to cultural diffusion. Yet even diffusion could not be the answer, because too many areas were isolated and too much had happened at the same time.

This was his quest: To discover the unified secret, both lost and perhaps conspiratorially hidden, that lay behind man's spiritual existence. If he could close the circle, science and religion would once again merge, and the serpent could swallow its tail.

It was in this mindset that Andrew cajoled, berated, and hammered at his students, but he never acted out of spite or cruelty. Deep inside his psyche, he was uncertain if he had what it would take to complete his vision quest. As a result, he felt that if he pushed and prodded and even bullied his students, one of them might offer an insight, a different perspective that would inspire his own searching mind to solve the true riddle of the Sphinx.

Andrew returned to his apartment later that evening, exhausted. A frigid wind was blowing from the harbor, threatening to suck the energy out of all who dwelt for any length of time in its grip. The wind chill was frightfully low for this time of year, and anyone with a shred of intelligence sought the warmth of hearth and home.

He tossed his black overcoat onto the couch and headed straight for the gas fireplace, which, thanks to the modern marvel of thermostats, glowed in the otherwise darkened room. After he adjusted the knob to maximum, he watched as the flames burst higher in a *poof* of sound. Extending his hands, he tried to wick the heat into his frozen body. He glanced at the phone on the Parson's table behind the couch and saw the red light on the answering machine blinking. It was Friday, and he suspected that the message was from his newly-wed friend Eli, who was probably hoping to drag him out to the area's pubs, since his wife still let him have his night out with the boys once a week.

Tonight, however, Andrew wanted no part in bar-hopping—he had a pounding headache. *Another* headache—coming on as suddenly as they always had, and lingering deeply in his temples. Nothing from over-the-counter drugs to meditation could force the dull pain out of his skull any earlier than it wanted to dissolve itself.

When the warmth finally reached to the tips of his numb toes, he walked the short hallway to the bathroom. His first thought was to take a relaxing whirlpool bath but the idea of running water and taking off all of his clothes sounded like far too much work. Instead, he swallowed four enteric-coated aspirin and an extra strength *Zantac* for his recently acquired acid reflux. Quickly splashing some hot water on his face, he dragged himself into the living room to the soft Italian leather recliner, where he kicked off his shoes and plopped into the chair. He pushed the little black button on the right side of the recliner, and with a slight creak of leather his feet were instantly raised from the plush maroon carpet.

From the chair he could still see the blinking red light on the answering machine. In fact, he fixated on it and began to count the blinks. He always counted. He would count how many steps it took to get to his car or to walk down a hallway. He would count the seconds it took to fill a glass of water or for a bartender to fill a draught. While eating lunch in the quad on campus, he would count people and sort out the number of blondes from brunettes. He hated doing it, but he could not escape what he called "the curse of Count Dracula" from *Sesame Street*.

At one hundred and fifty two he stopped, strangely unsure if he was awake or asleep. Low rolling thunder grumbled in the distance, a strange phenomenon on this unusually cold evening. Then he saw lightning.

"I must be dreaming," he said aloud, drowsily. "I must be dreaming..."

"Andrew..." The name, unexpected, came softly on the wind.

"Andrew," it came again, whispering through the rumbling that vibrated everywhere as flashes of lightning became more powerful and frequent.

Who are you? his mind replied, lips unmoving.

"Mantrella." The voice was male in tone, but with a feminine sweetness. "Here are my names so that you may finally know me..."

In the blindness of a dream, Andrew reached for paper and a pen.

The voice continued. "I am Mekek Taus, the Peacock, the Flesh of Kadir, Mazadan, Gradale, Jami-Jamshid, the Spear of Destiny, the Holy Rood, Lapsit Exillus, Hathor, Murrugan, Sanat Kumara, P'an Ku, Amaru, Enki, the Fisher King..."

With each name spoken, the tone of the words oscillated from male to female, hard to soft, light to dark. Andrew recognized most of the epithets from his academic research and experiences. He felt the formation of a tear at the corner of his right eye that slithered slowly down his warm cheek and stopped briefly at his chin before dripping onto the paper bearing the names he'd scribbled over the blue lines. While the voice entered his mind as a ripple on a quiet pond, it exited with the roar of a tidal wave. The lightning and thunder were sucked into a breath-stealing vortex ending in a large *pop*. Then, in a stillness reminiscent of the eye of a hurricane, one last name was quietly uttered.

Andrew bolted upright, slamming the footrest back into its nest at the base of the recliner.

"What the hell?" he choked. Once again the blinking red light commanded his attention, and trance-like he stared at it for an extended moment of time.

"I need a drink," he proclaimed at last.

He started toward the phone, with every intention of accepting a bar-hopping invitation from Eli, when his foot struck the tip of a ball point pen. He winced with the sting and bent to grab for the pen and the paper that lay beside it. Reading the scrawled words, he dropped into the recliner again, as his eyes grew wide in astonishment. What he was sure had been a dream took on a new reality. The paper contained the list of names that he thought had echoed from the voice of an illusion. At the bottom of the page there was an illegible title, the last to be spoken, smeared in the stain of a tear. The only symbol preserved in the name was the letter "J."

Anxiety churned his gut. Although he kept a dream journal that he wrote in most mornings, Andrew was always awake when jotting down his thoughts. Never before had he experienced a complete loss of time, a blackout resulting in automatic writing. This was too strange for him, too surreal, as he sat dumfounded, heart palpitating in his tightening chest.

CHAPTER 8

The sun disappeared into the misty hills of Nuwara Eliya.

On the distant horizon, hazy in orange light and nearly imperceptible to the untrained eye, was the faint outline of Sri Pada's humped form. At the top of the mountain known more commonly as *Adam's Peak* was a geological anomaly that had earned itself a spot among the most sacred places on earth. There, pressed into the rock, was the impression of a human footprint, over five feet long and almost three feet wide. Sri Pada, or "Holy Footprint," had come to represent the melding thoughts of the four great religions. Hinduism preached the footprint to be that of Shiva as she performed her creative dance at the dawn of time, while Buddhists believed it to be but merely the marker for Buddha's real footprint, cast in sapphire and buried in the heart of the mountain. Conversely, Muslim and Christian tradition held that Adam himself had made the impression when he stood on one foot for a thousand years as penance for his sin.

Mara had come here from Wales only eight months earlier, moved from the constant drizzle of southwestern Britain to the cool mountain wilderness of central Sri Lanka. Her stepfather had made a fortune directing one of England's largest tea companies, so when asked to pack up the estate and journey to Nuwara Eliya, Lord Bullard graciously obliged.

Now, in her bedroom, she pressed a handkerchief to her nose with one hand and rested her head in the other.

Bloody nose.

Alone and shivering at the edge of her bed, Mara whimpered as the sweat of her brow drew glistening lines down her temples, mixing their design with salty tears. She'd been working on a paper for her economics class, and the research she'd done into the coincidental collapses of many of the world's largest companies over the last decade lay spread all around her like a newspaper quilt. Her head slumped forward and she pressed an open hand against the newspaper clippings, crushing them into the soft mattress. Her head felt heavy, and the sound of the wind in the tea fields outside her bedroom window hissed annoyingly in her ears. Pain in her lower back brought her into a fetal position, the handkerchief, stained crimson, fell from her hand onto the floor. The swelling in her brain, the pressure in her skull, promised a vision—another story, another piece of who she was, another...

From the chaotic, elbow-bruising marketplace he had followed her out of the dusty village and into the open countryside. She seemed unaware of his presence, though she had peered back at him once, over the heads of sheep crossing the stony road, only to survey the safety of her journey in the fading heat of early evening. But then, as her mind wandered over the mundane tasks and circumstances of her life, she had forgotten the young man behind her, and walked quickly on through lengthening shadows of sycamore trees, with two loaves of bread pressed against her chest and protected by a woven shawl that was draped over her square shoulders.

The peasant woman's beauty stunned him as he had brushed by her in the noisy street hours ago. He had studied her from a distance, between the soiled bodies of her kind, until finally he saw the light within her glow warmly in her tired eyes and in the complexion of her tarnished cheeks. Suddenly, he had fallen in love with her, and wondered if in the First Time a piece of God had fluttered from the dewy wings of the eternal Butterfly and found itself in the bloodstream of this singular goddess. He had to know her. Yet the impulse of his emotions would someday cause him pain. This he understood; for he had been instructed in the Sacred Ways from the instant of his being.

The fire had spread quickly in him, nullifying all ancient codes and wisdom, all laws and restrictions, and even the Covenant. Then again, though his rags betrayed the image and his humble nature sought the opposite, he was one of the highest among them, and he was suddenly arrogant in his feelings of entitlement to this desirous pursuit.

Two old men greeted him kindly as he approached and sat with them under the transparent protection of a barren tree, stripped of its foliage from disease and age. In silence, he watched the young woman enter the crumbling stone house across the road. When she disappeared behind a tattered wool blanket hanging in the doorway, he smiled, feeling her home again, relieved and weary. Rising, he crossed the road and stood before the house.

"The darkness settles fast," an old man remarked. "I thought it early evening not so long ago."

"It is not the setting sun that has darkened the place," the other uttered. "It is the shade of this tree."

"This old thing? Why, it has hardly got enough..."

The stranger made his way around the house as the old men gazed up in gaping wonder at the branches of the tree now pregnant with leaves.

Outside the back window—the perfectly square opening carved out of the rock—he watched her as she stoked the cooking fire. The incandescent glow of the flames in the dim room formed an orange aura along her profile that only intensified her physical beauty. Slowly, she lifted her head and turned toward the opening. She saw him there, suddenly, and became stiff with fear, but as she continued to stare at him, her body began to sway slightly, and she felt as if the stranger was absorbing her, one drop of spirit at a time. She became lost in the blue of his shimmering eyes, in the sharp and smooth angles of the virgin face framed in locks of flowing brown hair. His form was that of a man, but softer, somehow, as if within him was some element of her own soul—a female soul— also occupying the russet clothes of a common man. His essence, it appeared, ran as the fluid nature of the universal soul.

He stepped nearer to the window and extended a hand toward her. The tips of his long pale fingers broke through the invisible barrier of stale air stretched over the open hole, and touched the dampness within the house.

"Mary," he said as he breathed easily, himself as entranced in her beauty as she was in his image. He was so close to her now that he saw how pure she was, how unblemished was her skin. The glow in her eyes grew brighter.

"Mary," he repeated, and she gently slid a hand into his.

A heat crept through her body as if a fire had been lit at her bare feet and its flames had begun to lap at her sides. The intensity of his eyes, a liquid blue, penetrated her heart, and the stimulated muscle beat hotly. At once her pulse quickened, and she began to sweat.

Sliding her hand from his, she staggered backward, cupping a trembling hand over her mouth. She could not look away from him, and he held the gaze long and hard to her pounding heart. Perspiration streaked down her temples, leaking into the whites of her eyes, and she squinted with the salty burn. She pulled the shawl from her shoulders in an effort to lessen the heat which was still building beneath the silk of her supple skin. Yet he had to burn her, to raise her spirit to a level far more unstable than those of the bottom-dwellers she crawled among each and every grueling day. She would have to be elevated, now, for the union to occur—for the blood of God to survive within her.

Back against the wall, she could no longer fight the urge to be with him as the vibration in her soul quivered through her fingertips. Slowly, she moved her hands down the curves of her slender body as she bent her head to one side and closed her stinging eyes. Her mouth split open in a wanting sigh as the hands, pressed prayer-like together, slid between her legs.

A rush of pulse climaxed in the drums of her ears, and opening her eyes to the lightheadedness, she found herself not in the sweat of an erotic trance, but remaining still beside the window, her hand safely in that of the blue-eyed stranger.

"Come out," he said, not harshly, not commandingly, but suggestively. "Come out to me." He released her hand and pulled back into the night that had fallen as fast as torrential rain in the haunted desert.

And Mary, longing to feel him again inside of her, passed through the curtained portal and searched for him in the stagnate darkness.

She found him not far from the crumbling abode she called her home—only yards away, at the edge of a steep embankment that fell in rocky barbs to the river's flesh. He stood as a peasant—russet-clad, but young and noble—beneath an ancient tree from which hung the phantom of a betraying man yet to hang himself.

His blue eyes burned in the suffocating night. Without a word, she came to him, and he took her into his arms. Bringing her face to his, he lost himself in eyes that echoed true the depths of her heart. Leaning to kiss the virgin, he erupted into a quasar of white light. The vibration holding, her back arched and her arms spread to the heavens as a million shards of purity sliced through her body and raced into the obscurity of the black horizon. She swelled with light, bled with heat. From every orifice of her body the light freely, violently flowed.

Then it was gone.

Absorbed into itself and lost to the air.

Morning settled rudely on her dusty face. Awakened by the bleating of sheep, she found herself lying on her side at the edge of the embankment. Leafy shadows from the nearby gallows danced in her hair, and the sun through the thick branches exposed the rippled breath of a waking world, whetting the illusion.

A man's voice called in the distance, then his shadow was over her, and she was cradled in his arms.

"Joseph," she choked, as he carried her toward the house, but the name seemed lost in her throat—foreign to her now—while in her breast still burned some fragment of the passion, some golden seed of seduction...

"My god, girl!" The farmhand yanked off his cap as he knelt in the wheat and scooped her into his soiled arms. "What are you doin' out here?"

She didn't respond. Her body remained limp in his arms.

"We've been searchin' all night for you," he continued. "Lord knows how cold it gets in these fields at night. It's not right that you..."

The words fell short, as he suddenly realized that he was standing in a clearing of crushed and matted wheat. As he turned slowly in each direction, following the outline of the bent stems around him, he knew that he'd stumbled into a piece of the area's latest phenomenon. They had begun to appear all over the mid-western countryside weeks ago, and now this farm, too, had been victimized. Though admittedly some of the designs were fascinating, farmers were not pleased with the amount of crop lost to the creation of the circles. Local superstition claimed the crop circles to be the work of aliens, while others believed them to be the product of careless human genius.

Either way, the farmhand was standing in one, cradling an unconscious Mara, his employer's adopted daughter. A shadow crept over him, and he turned, startled to see the girl's grandfather watching him.

"I found her," he uttered.

"Take her to the house," the silver-eyed man said. "Her mother will take care of her."

Nodding, the farmhand hurried away with the girl while the old man grinned at the sight of the crop circle. "Always one step behind," he muttered, "and this is not your finest work."

CHAPTER 9

Eli didn't know exactly why he made the suggestion. In the process of collecting his few remaining possessions still left in the apartment he used to share with Andrew, it struck him that Andrew now officially lived *alone*. He thought a little companionship would be good for his reclusive best friend.

"I think you should get a dog."

"A dog?" Andrew questioned.

"Yes, a dog," Eli replied. "You need companionship. Now that I'm gone, who are you going to talk to? Who's going to watch you gobble your meals? Who's going to be at your side when you're working into the wee hours of the night doing research?"

"Myself," Andrew said flatly. "As usual."

Eli stared at him.

"I suppose the correct answer is a *dog*," he conceded.

"Now you've got it. I knew you'd see the logic of it all," Eli said with a satisfied grin, thinking the idea made perfect sense.

"Are you out of your mind?" Andrew retorted. "I don't have time for a dog. I don't know anything about dogs. I've never had a dog. How could you possibly think that I would want a dog?"

"Get your coat," Eli said, ignoring the ravings of his friend. "We're going to Salem."

"Why the hell are we going to Salem?" Andrew asked.

Eli ignored the question. He threw a coat at Andrew, grabbed his arm and pulled the protesting man with him out to the car.. Eli couldn't explain why he chose to go to Salem, save for the fact that the shelters in their area were usually empty and boarded some of nature's more sickly animals. Regardless, he had only a vague notion that there was a shelter in Salem. But somehow, instinctively, he knew where it was, and his compulsion guided him.

Oddly enough, although Andrew complained during the entire trip, he didn't demand that Eli turn around.

When they entered the shelter, the lingering odor of urine and feces assaulted them. It was not overwhelming, since the place was very well-kept, but years of excrement had taken its toll, no matter how often the place had been cleaned. Eli approached the attendant to explain why they were there, while Andrew walked past the section of cats and wandered toward the dogs.

***

All shapes, sizes and colors were present, contained behind chain link fencing, whining with pleading eyes, hungry for rescue. While Andrew understood the necessity of the confining cages, the sight of these mini-prisons was heartbreaking. Andrew wished he had a huge estate where he could house all of these homeless creatures.

He saw Eli in the corner of his eye keeping his distance so Andrew could look at the dogs without interference.

Andrew's eyes suddenly fell on a brown and white dog off to one side, sleeping. While obviously young, it was very thin and seemingly malnourished. He bent to pet the dog through the small openings of the fence, and sensing the human touch, the puppy lifted its long snout and turned its large almond eyes toward him. It was love at first sight, no matter what he tried to tell himself, as the puppy licked at his hand.

He stood and motioned for the attendant. When she came over, Andrew asked why the puppy was so skinny and learned that the dog was a wolfhound—part Saluki and part Borzoi. The breed was notably a thin, but large dog. She explained that the pup would reach eighty to ninety pounds, but that it would always look ribby like a greyhound, a relative to the breed. They liked to eat a lot of small meals rather than one or two large ones, and they had a rather fast metabolism. Also, the breed was a very fast runner, one of the fastest on the planet.

"I don't think I understand what a *wolfhound* is," Andrew said.

"This is one of the oldest domesticated breeds," she answered, "and their statues were found among the pharaohs of Egypt. They were bred, actually, to protect against wolves, and were used for hunting on the plains. The Russian version of the dog has long hair and those of the desert regions have short hair. This pup was a cross and could go either way in terms of hair length. Unfortunately, the cross was not planned and the pup was brought here."

"Are they barkers?"

"No," she said, smiling at him. "At least not this one. He does howl sometimes, but he doesn't spend his days barking for nothing. He'll need regular exercise, so if you plan on confining the dog for most of the day, this is not the breed you want."

Andrew looked at Eli and then at the dog, who'd sat up and was now wagging his tail furiously. He considered the small creature for a moment longer, gazing into his glassy eyes.

"I suppose I'll take him."

"In that case," the attendant replied, "I have some paperwork for you to fill out and I'll give you some instructions on feeding and housebreaking."

Andrew hadn't really thought about the issue of housebreaking or the need to exercise the dog. After looking into the puppy's eyes, he had no choice. The dog owned him.

On the way to the car, Eli chided Andrew for being such a softy. "What are you going to name him?" he asked.

"Nevyn," Andrew said assuredly.

"Nevyn? How'd you come up with that name?"

"It's from a book about reincarnation. The name actually means "no one." I like it. How about you, little Nevyn? Do you like it?" The puppy licked Andrew's petting hand.

A few moments later, as they made their way onto the highway, Nevyn got car sick and threw up all over Eli's back seat. Andrew laughed.

***

For most of the evening, Andrew chased the puppy around the house with sections of newspaper in an attempt to keep the small creature from pissing on everything he owned. Now the furry little dog lay sleeping on the kitchen tile, and Andrew took the opportunity to sit in the recliner and put up his feet.

Beside him, on the end table, were a legal pad and an unopened package of *Bic* pens. He considered them for a moment, telling himself that he should try to write something now that the semester was over and he was in danger of allowing his academic focus to dull over the summer term. Instead, he glanced at the clock on the far wall—7:22 pm— and laid his head back, closing his eyes.

For just a minute, he thought, *then I'll do some work. Then I'll…*

He sat up, heart racing, hair and shirt soaked in sweat. The puppy lay at his feet, whining. He looked down to see the pens scattered all over the living room carpet and the legal pad turned face down, under Nevyn. Reaching down for the pad, he realized he was trembling. He looked at the clock again, the time—10:12 pm.

"Three hours?" he muttered. "How did I sleep for three hours?" He gazed down at the dog. "Should have woken me, little buddy," he said. "Who knows what you've done while I was sleeping." He pulled the legal pad out from under the dog. "I must've had a nightmare."

Flipping the pad over, he pressed his back into the chair as he stared at the scrawled writing across the yellow pages. "What the hell?" he stammered. It was undeniably his handwriting, scribbled over three pages. He breathed slowly, trying to pace the pounding of his heart as he carefully read the words—

What have you done, Blue Eyes?
My desire!
What have you done? Seduced a virgin girl ... and now, a child?
A boy, yes. My child of light!
The punishment will be severe!
Punishment? How could you—
Take your wings? From the Dawn we have agreed. From the First Time we have honored the Covenant! Now, there is a child.
Yes, my child!
They'll call him Son of God! And his reign will be only momentary.
But you cannot!
But we will. I am the Strength of the world. I am the finger of God.
And you would destroy so noble a being?
It cannot be! We cannot be with the child alive! And you have only helped him now. You must spend a moment out of the Light.
Do not take from me my very being!
For a time you shall live on earth, as earthlings do. You shall follow the path of the Other, and be denied of the Light. In the darkness of the physical illusion you will grovel...denied of the Light...

Andrew blinked to wet his burning eyes before he continued reading. *What is this?* he wondered in disbelief. *What have I written?*

Adam...
Yes, Mantrella.
It has begun again.
What has begun, Mantrella?
Their attempt of ten millennia ago.
Will they never cease?
I am afraid not. They have lost control once again. This time they will pursue the Awakening to the end. They fear that the cusp of this Age will spell their doom.
And will it, Mantrella?
If I have my way, it will.
Is there hope this time? Can the dream really reach fruition?
This has been our Magnus Opus. But they are aware of Her.
Earth and Sun!
The Unnamable. They are searching for Her now. We, too, must find Her. I had hoped there was time to bring Her along gradually, but we no longer have the luxury of a courtship. Adam...
Yes, Mantrella?
She is the Vessel. It is time for the Chalice to fulfill its destiny, my son. If we fail, it is over. Truly, this will be the End of Days...

Andrew…prepare for Rome!

And his writing abruptly ended.

Andrew closed his eyes and allowed himself to swirl into the glittering darkness behind his eyelids. Exhaustion pressed him evenly into the recliner, and soon he no longer felt the movement of air around him or the palpitations in his chest.

CHAPTER 10

Mara ran through the house from the backyard as soon as she heard the rumble of his rusted burgundy pickup circle into the gravel driveway. The warm Nebraska wind streamed through the window screens, pushing at the curtains as she glided through the farmhouse.

"Papa!" she cried in joy, arms outstretched to the old man with the pretty red box. Today was her eighteenth birthday.

"My girl!" the old man exclaimed, setting the box on an end table and wrapping his arms around her. Embracing her, his white hair clashed with the shiny copper of her own, and at a glance it was ironic that they were in any way related. He had an air of ancient nobility that shone in his shimmering silver eyes, though his hands wore the calluses of a farmer, and his clothing the stains of one working with the soil of his craft.

Conversely, she was the old man's pride and joy—the beautifully dark and mysterious granddaughter—and it had become a custom among family members to limit any conversation of her ethnicity. She was theirs, no matter who had given birth to her, and her adoption or biological heritage had never, and would never, become an issue. Besides, today she would turn eighteen-years-old, and he couldn't have been happier.

She pushed herself away from him playfully, the green of her eyes sparkling in excitement. "What did you bring me, Papa?" she asked, reaching for the red box.

"Not so fast," the old man said, snatching the box from the table. He shook it, and its hidden contents scratched against the cardboard. "You'll have to wait," he teased. "When all's said and done, you can open it." He was tall, and looked down at her easily, as she smiled widely at him. "C'mon," he said at last, "I hear there's a party in the backyard."

The birthday girl enjoyed nothing more than family gatherings. She had come to view them as times well-spent with the closest people in her life: Her mother, hardworking and patient, devoted herself to the role of country hostess, donning her apron and oven mitts and preparing an edible spread that might embarrass the Queen herself; and dad, tall and silver-eyed like her grandfather, always maintained his silence unless the need arose for his commentary. His only true vice was his daughter, whom he doted on and protected with every ounce of spirit in his hardened body.

Relatives often came by the dozens three or four times a summer to take part in the barbecued food and freshly made salads. She was always among them, too, her dark skin in definite opposition to their white bodies, but they never seemed to notice. She was one of them, plainly and simply. And she loved them all.

Today marked a very special day, however, for it was not only her birthday, but her eighteenth at that. Nothing, of course, could have dwarfed the bizarre events of her sweet sixteenth. She would always remember how the morning of her sixteenth birthday had begun, and she still wondered from time to time what exactly it was that had happened. When the farmhand discovered her unconscious in the wheat field he had uncovered a phenomenon that would haunt the county for months to come. Reporters and crop circle enthusiasts had to be chased from the farm on many occasions, and that summer the air went garbled with the beating of helicopter blades and the whining of single-engine airplanes. On her father's order, no one in the family had been permitted to be interviewed or to appear in any newspaper article or on any television program. He had this dread in his eyes, she recalled, a darkness swirling behind the silver, and made frequent phone calls to "people he knew" in order to ensure the safety of his family, especially his daughter. They lived like prisoners that summer, only venturing from the house for their daily chores. From her bedroom window she often looked down into the silent and empty backyard. No barbecues, no parties. Anniversaries, birthdays, reunions passed untold, uncelebrated.

Later that fall she came to realize that her beauty was her saving grace. Popular in school, she was reserved, well-mannered, at the top of her class, and relying on her academic and personal character, she hoped someday to be accepted to Harvard University. When Shyamalan's movie *Signs,* starring Mel Gibson, was released in August of the year of her sixteenth birthday, her world seemed to erupt again. Upon returning to school, talk among her classmates began the rumor that the movie was about her father's farm and the mysterious crop circle found in his wheat field. Though she denied it, the rumor spread out into the community, taxing the family's patience with the general public once again. At one point, her father, in desperation, suggested that they move—that they *must* move—or graver things would happen. But time passed, the rumors died away, and she won prom queen in the spring. It was too difficult, it seemed, to overcome her beauty with absurd rumors, or even the threat of alien invasion. And much to her own joy, Harvard did open its doors to her shortly after the start of her senior year in high school.

The negative happenings were all family history now, and some even joked about it. She pulled her grandfather by his hand off the back porch steps as her Uncle Roger called out to them, "Did you two land alone, or are there others coming?" The relatives laughed and the old man waved it off with a smile.

Hamburgers and hotdogs passed around, salads dug into and pleasantly consumed, and the sun rode low on the horizon when the last of the partygoers kissed her forehead, wished her a happy birthday, and headed home again. The backyard became still as she and her grandfather sat together on the porch swing and gazed at the pink twilight which appeared to be a million miles away. His arm was laid easily across her shoulders, and on his lap rested the pretty red box.

Grandfather cleared his throat. "What about boys, my girl?" he asked, grinning.

She glanced up at him, then nestled her body into his. "Boys?" she answered. "I don't have time for boys, Papa. I have to get ready for college."

He squeezed her shoulder. "I suppose there'll be time for that," he breathed easily. "Someday you'll meet that perfect man, the one who will change your whole existence. You'll have a child, rediscover the world…"

"Sounds like you already have it planned," she interrupted, looking up at him.

"I'm only hoping," he said. "It's only the hope I have for my beautiful granddaughter."

Suddenly, she sat up. "So, what's in the box?"

"This box?" he asked playfully, grabbing its sides and shaking it again.

"Papa!"

He set the box on her lap. "Take it upstairs," he said. "I want you to open it in the privacy of your own bedroom."

"Why?"

"Because it has to be that way," he answered, running a finger through her black hair. "Now, go."

She hesitated, staring at him, then smiled and hugged him. With the box in her arms, she ran into the house and through the kitchen. Her mother yelled at her to slow down as she passed, but she was too excited to hear the words. Up the stairs she flew, nearly pinning her father against the wall in the stairwell. She exploded into her bedroom, slamming the door behind her.

Jumping onto her bed, she held the box for a moment, daring to guess what might be inside. Her grandfather was always thoughtful and unpredictable. Slowly, she began to unwrap the box, pulling the tape from the corners, careful not to tear the paper. Then a pain pierced her temple and she winced. Bringing both hands to the sides of her head, she pressed them against her skull, her eyes tightly closed and her mouth twisting in agony. Yet no sound escaped from her lungs because her throat had constricted, driving the pain deeply into her stomach. Without warning, without any control of her movement, she fell over, thumping against the floorboards. Forcing her eyes open, the world spinning and fading, she held a bloody hand in front of her eyes—her nose was bleeding and her inner ears grew crimson with blood. The pain came again, one more savage time, and she fell into convulsions.

Then there was blackness.

And a butterfly lighted softly on her window sill.

CHAPTER 11

Andrew's early months with his new roommate were simply hell. The puppy, like most, had one major flaw—he loved to chew. Nevyn's first target was Andrew's slippers. When Andrew awoke each morning he automatically slid his feet into the slippers beside the bed. His current set was a moccasin-style made of leather and lined with wool. On day two of "puppydom," Andrew slid his feet into dog-slimed slippers. On day three his second pair of slippers was discovered in a half-mangled state in the kitchen. Andrew decided that his slippers would have to spend the night on the nightstand rather than on the floor.

He knew that the dog needed to be housebroken. The problem was that he worked at the college and was gone most of the day. He hired a stay-at-home mom who lived several units away to take Nevyn for walks in the morning, midday, and late afternoon. He figured that the cost was a small price to pay to protect several rather expensive Persian rugs. Samantha, the woman who walked the dog, told him that Nevyn was doing very well and had few accidents. Nights were a different story. Andrew was advised by his dog-owning colleagues that a regular schedule was important to house-training, and that praise was also a key component.

Every night at eight Andrew took Nev for a stroll. The first week was a disaster. Almost every evening the pup didn't do his duty during their walks, but the moment they entered the apartment, Nev let loose. Thinking it was a timing issue, Andrew took Nev on longer and longer walks and stayed out for extended periods. Every time, the pee came when they returned to the apartment. Consulting with another friend, he discovered that praise was a definite "no-no." While it was good for other kinds of training, it was not good for housebreaking. The dog began to think that it was good to pee because he kept being praised for doing so. Looking for Andrew's praise, Nev came in and proudly did his duty. Fortunately, this problem soon disappeared.

Next, Nevyn developed a liking for plastic. If it was petroleum based, it was chewed. The favorite was electrical outlets. Nev managed to remove fifteen out of twenty electrical covers without being fried. Andrew was forced to either replace anything plastic below the four foot mark or discard the item altogether. Out of sight, out of mind—the plastic issue was soon replaced by wood. Corners of end tables, chair legs, the mahogany dinner table, and any other item of a wooden nature became fair game for the jaws of the wolfhound. Andrew discovered that none of the products advertised to prevent chewing worked. As a matter of fact, Nevyn acquired a taste for hot sauce, which was an anti-chewing remedy suggested by another friend who loved to give advice about natural cures for everything.

Then suddenly the bad habits stopped.

Within an incredibly short period of time Nevyn had become a dog— a rather large dog. He could put his paws on Andrew's shoulders, five feet ten inches high, and look him square in the eye. His shoulders were even with the dining room table, and if he didn't behave, dinner would never stand a chance. While Nev went a good hundred pounds, the nature of the breed was such that they always looked underfed. When he and Nev went for walks, he got looks of admiration, but also the occasional, *Hey, why don't you feed the dog?*

Whenever possible, Andrew spent time with his "puppy." Nev slept beside Andrew, but was always willing to give up his side of the bed if there was a sleepover guest, though the situation was rare. When Andrew was at his desk, Nev was always at his feet. Andrew felt a kind of Zen comfort in Nev's presence. If he was stuck on a word or phrase for one of his lectures or speeches he would stop, give the pup a pat, and the fog would clear, bringing words of inspiration.

Nevyn didn't take to many people. He loved Eli, tolerated his new wife, Jen, but hated the mailman. Those he liked got a tail wag and a half-hearted lick. Those he didn't trust got a low growl if they got too close to Andrew, he always positioned himself between his master and the "intruder."

Later, Andrew noticed a rather odd behavior. When he began to receive his mysterious dream thoughts or messages, Nevyn acted most peculiar. Just prior to a dream, Nev would herd Andrew to his recliner. At times he got rather pushy, and on one occasion he growled at Andrew because his urgings were being ignored. Andrew thought Nev was just hoping to take a rest and wanted to be close to his master when he did so.

He soon realized that Nev somehow knew what was going to happen, and he wanted to be sure that Andrew was ready to receive his dreams.

CHAPTER 12

EARTHWIRE NEWS—Tensions skyrocketed behind Vatican walls today, according to inside sources. The debate continues over the recently announced intentions of Pope Peter II, whom conservative Catholics are now calling "Peter the Last," suggesting a widespread fear that the Church is in danger of total collapse.

The College of Cardinals met this morning to persuade the pope to reconsider his plan to open parts of the inner Vatican Archives to the public and reveal "secrets" of the papacy.

The pope's closest advisors still maintain that the pontiff's Reconstruction of Faith mission requires a "solid foundation, based on many doctrines and ideas that have been either lost or withheld from the faithful."

There has been no word yet as to what exactly Pope Peter II intends to release from the Archives. What has been made very public, however, is the outrage of the College, which insists that the pope's intentions border on heresy and sacrilege…

***

He was so goddamn sick of reading this bullshit.

He'd claimed it privately at least a dozen times, far out of earshot of those who believed him to be a different person altogether, and after the lady with the three kids nearly knocked him over at the baggage claim he'd lividly tossed the newspaper into the nearest receptacle, and with clenched hands, marched toward the exits. Still, the thought echoed in his head that made it all worth it, that kept him focused: *Ironclad kingdom…it will all be mine.*

"The world has sought a leader, and that leader has emerged as Pope Peter," the female BBC newscaster was saying in an alluring British accent. Annoyed, he tried to ignore it, but a rush to the exit locked him into the crowd—and her voice.

"Prophesied to be the last pope," she continued, "Petrus Romanus entered the scene after the short reign of his predecessor."

Drawn to the green of her round eyes, he forced his way to the large television screen which hung suspended above the travelers' heads with cables and steel strapping, and stood transfixed.

"Urged by the entire College of Cardinals not to use the name, Peter argued that the time was right for a new vision of the Church and that the times demanded a 'new rock' upon which not only to build the church, but human society as a whole. To many this was truly the 'End Times'—the fulfillment of the Revelations and the Apocalypse."

He looked away and scowled at those who were moving like ants around him. A mother yanked her small daughter away from the perimeter of his personal space with disgust.

"Fuck you!" he breathed, watching her through narrowed eyes as she disappeared with her child into the crowd.

"With brother seemingly against brother, nation against nation, and the list of world calamities growing at an unprecedented rate over the past year," green-eyes went on, "most think that evil stalks the world unabated and that the Church must rise to the occasion, prophecy be damned, according to the latest surveys…"

The picture flickered to an older man being interviewed on an anonymous street in an anonymous city. "Peter has inside information," the man jabbered in a thick French accent. "He knows that the world is on the cusp of unsurpassed change and that it is his destiny to usher in that change…"

Ironclad kingdom…

"Fuck you, too," he spit, shaking his head and turning abruptly into the crowd.

CHAPTER 13

Party hat cocked to one side of her head, Wanda raised a beer mug high above the crowd from her perch on the barroom table. She had threatened her friend with this only an hour earlier.

"Ladies and gentlemen," she yelled, swaying a bit to the fumes in her blood, "I have an announcement to make."

The bar went silent as all eyes turned up to her but two—and those were buried in the slender hands of an embarrassed young woman, turning on her stool.

"Today is my good friend's birthday," Wanda continued boisterously, "and for those of you who don't know her, she's the really pretty one over there trying to hide."

The crowd erupted into clapping and hooting, and the embarrassed girl had no choice but to drop her hands and acknowledge timidly the congratulations of the strangers swarming around her with a nod and red cheeks.

"Not only is it her birthday," Wanda went on relentlessly, "but she's *twenty-one* today." The crowd roared and she had to scream over the noise: "We've got a new *legal* member of Hooligan's, so let's hear it!"

In relative unity, the patrons broke into discordant song, bellowing out "Happy Birthday." On the bar, mugs of beer had been lined up, and the bartender waited for the song to end before sliding the first glass toward the birthday girl. The crowd, leaning over her, chanted, "Chug, chug, chug..."

Thirty minutes later, Wanda and the birthday girl stepped out of Hooligan's and onto Beacon Street, their breath rising like phantoms into the crisp air.

"I can't believe you embarrassed me like that."

"C'mon, Mara, it's your birthday," Wanda said, wrapping an arm around the girl's shoulders.

"You're drunk," Mara answered.

Wanda shook her head. "No, not me. Besides, you've been in town what, almost three years? It's about time you saw the *other* side of Boston."

"Other side?"

"Yeah." They crossed the street hand-in-hand. "You know, the one outside your cubicle."

Mara didn't answer. After three years of living in Boston, she'd accomplished nothing, socially. It wasn't that she had no interest, but that she found herself uncommonly devoted to the mundane routines of her working life. As a low-level clerk for an insurance company, she was infatuated with paperwork. Her grandfather, a retired lawyer, had insisted that she come to work at his firm, but she wanted to do something on her own that she had earned through hard work and dedication. Sandra, her little sister, was in her second year at Cornell University, and continued to pressure Mara to go to school, but two years at a local community college had gained the young woman an Associates in Business Management, and she hoped someday to run the department of the very company in which she worked.

It wasn't that the thought of boys made her anxious. If anything, she could have had her pick of any man in the city. She was, in a word, beautiful, and her Middle Eastern appearance, accented in long, flowing black hair and green eyes, turned heads all the time, but she always imagined herself saving what soul she had to give away for the right guy, whoever he may be. So evenings alone in her apartment with cartons of Chinese food, paperwork, and classic movies had become the private side of her existence. Until she met Wanda.

Tall, thin, with raging red hair, Wanda's personality fit her appearance. She was "cute, rather than pretty," as she liked to think of herself, with an insatiable appetite for the occult and impulsive ideas. Her cubicle was nine divisions away from Mara's, the fabric walls decorated in sun and moon images, and a single copy of Sir Arthur Waite's *Guide to the Tarot* beside her computer, which she mostly used as a coaster for her "Bite Me!" coffee mug.

Six months earlier, she accidentally slammed into Mara in the mailroom, sending the young girl onto a sorting table. Embarrassed, she apologized and offered to buy her victim a drink after work. Mara, sore and somewhat reluctant, agreed anyway, and the two soon became friends.

Yet no matter how hard Wanda tried, she could never completely separate Mara from her reclusive existence, but an evening here and there with the latest thriller or romantic comedy fragmented at least some of the tedious routine.

"Now we're going to a meeting," Wanda announced.

Stopping on the corner, Mara crossed her arms and refused to move. "Meeting? What are you talking about?"

"It's Friday night, babe," Wanda declared. "Meeting night. It's all part of my evil plan. First, I let all of Boston know it's your birthday at the most popular pub in the city, now I'll completely mystify you. Believe me, you won't forget your twenty-first for the rest of your life." She continued down the street, pulling Mara with her.

"Where are you taking me?" Mara insisted.

Wanda halted and faced her squarely. "We're going to a meeting, you know—with a *psychic*."

"What a minute." She stepped away from her. "You're kidding me, right?"

"Hey, talk around the office says I'm crazy, remember?" Wanda teased.

Mara smiled. "I don't think so. I think you're just—different."

Wanda put her arm around Mara's shoulders again and led her slowly down the street. "Different, whatever," she said. "We're going to have fun, Mara. Trust me. Don't you want to know anything about your destiny or past lives?"

"No."

"Three years ago a friend of mine brought me to one of these meetings, and it totally changed my life. I'm serious. Just give it a try."

Mara sighed and relaxed under the weight of her friend's arm. "I'll try it," she conceded, "but if these people are a bunch of weirdoes or something, I'm leaving."

Wanda, excited that her friend was willing to try something new, hurried her along. "We need to catch a cab."

***

"The NYSE opened today under the cloud of International Oil's announcement of bankruptcy last Friday," the newscaster was saying. Andrew stared at the silver diagonal lines of the gray-haired anchorman's tie, absently absorbing the headline.

"With its stock having been slowly on the decline since last quarter, few traders were surprised that IO was experiencing what were rumored to be *non-crucial* financial problems. The shock to the world community came, however, with the sudden announcement that IO was bankrupt.

"The NYSE took a heavy hit Friday afternoon, dropping fifteen percent by the closing bell. The NASDAQ experienced a twelve-percent drop, with the Amex losing almost as much. This blow to the economy comes at a pivotal point in current affairs and hard on the heels of United Agriculture's collapse only eleven months ago. Speculation of federal investigation into IO's bankruptcy is already circulating, and with the pressure on, IO CEOs have made themselves unavailable for comment. Sources claim…"

Click.

Pressing the power button on the remote, he killed the television.

He sat rigidly on the center cushion of the couch, Nevyn's head on his lap, and stared at the cold television, its screen now broadcasting only the darkness behind its glass, and the reflection of a light from a lamp in the corner of the room.

Andrew was under considerable self-imposed pressure, and he could feel the weight of it at the base of his neck and deep in his shoulders. He was musing over a theory that he wanted to present in just the right way to his graduate class in the fall, and he'd already spent many sleepless nights at his computer doing research, writing, re-writing. Now, a sense of uneasiness and anxiety was clouding his thoughts. Not about his theory, but about what seemed to be spilling from his unconscious mind and onto the sterile lines of a legal pad.

He was known by his colleagues and students alike as a solid academian and a superb speaker, so these were things that had never given him pause. There was just something not right in the known universe—a kind of "disturbance in the force" — and proof of it was now coming to him in the darkness of sleep. At times he was filled with expectation and excitement. Something was going to happen that would be life-changing. Then his feeling of wonder would dive deeply into the abyss of dread and he sensed his life-changing event become life-threatening. Andrew had even started buying cigarettes. He never really smoked them, but rather lit them and transfixed his thoughts on the whirling eddies of smoke. It became his way to "zone out" and to balance his thoughts between what he felt was an impending conflict between light and dark, pleasure and pain, hope and despair, and all the rest of the dualities—the foundations of all existence.

He blinked at the sound of the front door opening.

Nevyn raised his head from Andrew's lap, woofed once, and jumped off the couch. Andrew watched curiously as the dog wandered into the bedroom and disappeared.

Eli entered with Jen and marched into the living room. "All right *Mr. Britannica,* you obviously need a break from your eternal acquisition of useless knowledge," he announced.

Andrew glanced at him, then smiled slightly at Jen. "I hate that name," he grumbled. "What do you want?"

"C'mon out with us," Eli insisted.

Closing his eyes, he drew in a deep breath and held it in his lungs. "I just want to relax tonight."

Jen sat beside him and touched his knee. "I don't think I've ever seen you relax," she said. "Besides, we're up to something really exciting."

"Like what?" Andrew asked, fixing his eyes on her.

"Come with us," Eli said. "You need this."

Andrew never considered himself one to embark on any experience impulsively, and as a true skeptic, he was not easily talked into things. However, in his exhaustion he bent to their will and decided to go, with the understanding that, "If you're wasting my time, I'm coming home."

"Be good, Nev," he called into the empty living room as he pulled his coat off the arm of the couch and followed Eli and Jen into the foyer. "Be back soon," he added, "so don't get into anything."

In Eli's Ford Explorer, the three meandered through narrow streets and entered the on-ramp for the Southeast Expressway. Andrew sat in the back seat, gazing through the newly formed droplets on the window. The wind had suddenly picked up, and the driving rain seemed in keeping with the melancholy and sense of foreboding that weighed on his heart and mind. He caught a glimpse of a road sign, announcing mileage to Cape Cod. He didn't know anyone south of Boston, and didn't think Eli did either. About to ask their destination, the twin blinkers flashed, illuminating the increasingly dense fog. The exit sign read "Gingham."

"Where the hell are we going?" Andrew muttered.

"We're going to a group," Jen responded.

"What's a *group*?" Andrew asked suspiciously.

"A bunch of people that get together," she said.

Given the circumspect answer, Andrew knew that further inquiry would be futile. While it was difficult to see out the window, he concluded that they were in a rather wealthy town on the coast. The smell of the ocean permeated the fog, and the streets were lined with large old colonial homes whose ornate front doors were lit by spotlights, as if to declare, "Look at my new, beautiful home."

Eli finally pulled off the road when Jen commanded, "Park there."

"Not many cars for a party," Andrew said, as they stepped carefully into the mouth of the slick driveway.

"It's not a party," Jen replied. "It's a channeling session."

"Jesus Christ," Andrew breathed. "Eli, what the hell are we doing here?"

Eli led them quickly up the driveway toward a deceivingly large house that, for a suburban home, was surrounded by an unusual bit of well-manicured, landscaped yard. The front walk was lined with colonial carriage lights that marked the entrance to the home. The milky fog and driving rain limited close observation of construction detail, but enough could be noted to understand that the owners maintained the house in keeping with the standards of a rather plush neighborhood. Once under the protection of the porch, Eli pushed the doorbell, then allowed himself into the house.

"It's routine," he said back to Andrew as they passed through the entranceway, "just to let them know we're here."

Passing through the doorway, Andrew glanced out onto the porch again. He was startled to find that a silent group of strangers had appeared, but they remained on the porch until the door closed behind him.

"They have to ring the bell, too," Jen whispered at Andrew's shoulder.

Andrew considered the idea for a moment, then shook his head at the absurdity.

They entered a spacious foyer that blocked an immediate view to the inside of the dimly lit house. Andrew's first impression was the scent of roses. He took a few steps forward in search of Eli, who had disappeared around a corner. Jen gave him a slight nudge to move him on as the strangers entered and crowded behind them.

Once in the living room, Andrew felt like he had run into an electric fence. The hairs stood up on the nape of his neck, and a tingle of electric current rippled up his spine, exploding outwardly from the crown of his head. His wavering motion prompted Jen to grab his arm to keep him from falling.

"Are you all right?" she whispered.

The energy subsided, and he quickly recovered his composure with a slight shiver. "I think I'm all right. Ask me again later."

He moved farther into the large living room, passing quietly through soft light and an atmosphere filled with stratified layers of rose-scented smoke. At one end of the room he noticed a circle of chairs. Candles were lit at four corners—the cardinal points—creating a square around the circle. At the center of the circle was a triangular shaped table that supported the tallest and fifth candle in the room. On the easternmost wall was a painting of an eye. In hidden passages of memory, Andrew felt a familiarity with this setting, though his conscious mind could remember no such place.

He saw Eli talking to a man in the corner of the room, and he realized that Jen had joined the pair. The man sported a scruffy beard and wisps of gray hair on the top of his head. He was stocky, although not fat, and as Andrew imagined it, built like a compact refrigerator.

All three pairs of eyes turned toward him, and Eli gestured for Andrew to join them. Hesitantly, he moved slowly across the room.

As he approached the trinity, Eli said, "Andrew, I want you to meet our host, Doug Blackman."

Mr. Blackman extended a hand that showcased a very heavy gold ring with an equal-armed cross in the center. The man had extended his hand in such a way as to keep the palm pointed mostly down, making the ring very noticeable. It was almost as if Mr. Blackman was attempting an odd handshake that perhaps would invite the receiver of the gesture to kiss the strange symbol in bishopric reverence, but he had to make a mid-course correction when Andrew stiffly offered his hand in the conventional manner, refusing submission to such suggested arrogance.

"Nice to meet you, Andrew."

"Likewise," Andrew responded.

"Were you expecting to have to kiss my ring?" Blackman asked with a smile.

"The thought had crossed my mind."

"I'm not the pope," he said easily. "Perhaps someday you'll come to understand the workings of the universe." He studied Andrew for a moment. "I understand from Eli that you have never been to a group like this," he said.

"No, I wouldn't normally attend such ..." Andrew's voice trailed off as he subtly refrained from making an offensive remark. "I mean," he added, "this is definitely an area that hasn't attracted my attention. What I've heard of such groups never seemed a promising avenue of investigation."

Mr. Blackman grinned. "A non-believer," he said. "Unfortunately, I tend to agree. However, I'm confident that you'll be in for an enlightening evening."

Strangely enough, something inside himself believed Mr. Blackman, and dual feelings of excitement and dread rattled in his solar plexus.

"This way," Doug said abruptly, inviting Andrew and his friends to enter the circle of chairs.

When Andrew turned to take a seat, he froze, just as the victims of ancient Pompeii had under the paralyzing ash of Vesuvius.

Already seated in the circle was a young woman with long black hair. She wore a medium-length red skirt that left everything to the imagination except her legs. Her white blouse had a neckline just low enough to create speculation, as well as a sharp contrast to her dark skin, and a string of pearls graced her slender neck.

Initially, it was the legs that had drawn his eye, but then her head lifted as if sensing she was being scrutinized. The thunder in his head nearly burst within his eardrums, and as if iced in the moment, he stood mesmerized by the woman's beautiful green eyes.

I've known you through all of eternity, he thought.

Guests were moving all around him, taking their seats. Soon, the only empty chair left was beside her. Andrew looked at the chair, and then at her. An invitingly shy smile and a barely perceptible nod gave approval, and he slowly moved to take his seat.

Definitely a precipitating event. As he sat down, her soul-piercing eyes never left his, as if the recognition appeared somehow divinely mutual.

While inklings of conversation coursed through Andrew's mind, Doug took a seat and interrupted the fantasy, asking everyone to close their eyes for a moment of silence. On cue, music drifted into the room. Andrew could not identify the piece, but he had heard something similar to it on one of public radio's New Age music presentations.

Eyes closed, Andrew began to drift. His thoughts couldn't focus. He could hear Doug's voice, but it was incoherent. The host introduced someone, but he didn't catch the name. He heard a woman's voice. Then it was a man's voice. Confusion filled his mind like the swirling incense infiltrating the room. *Channeling. Maybe she was…* A discharge of what felt like static electricity slammed through his retinas and chose a pathway directly to his brain. He heard a voice talking to the woman at his side.

"*Mara.*"

He knew the name and all that came with it. He tried to turn, but was paralyzed. A woman's hand took hold of his as his mind became a collage of images of ancient places and times. The images began to sort themselves at blurring speeds, before suddenly colliding together into one…

He is standing on a cliff, looking over a magnificent city of multi-colored marble. In the center of a round concourse stands a crystal obelisk, stretching nine hundred feet into the liquid sky. A bearded man, dressed in a black robe with its cowl raised to frame his face, holds in his right hand a ruby-capped staff, encircled by an engraved serpent, its tail at the base, and fanged jaws embracing the precious gemstone. A blast of cold air rushes over him, as the winds gust to monsoon proportions, and he stands mesmerized that he can feel the swiftly moving air. Then the staff is in his hand and he realizes that the observed and the observer are one. He raises the staff in anger and shouts chants in a language long since lost to the human tongue. Suddenly the torrent pours into the valley below. Black, rubble-filled waters, thirsty for death, slam into the city below. For the inhabitants, there is no mercy. Finally, a giant tidal wave withdraws the killing flood for just a moment, then, in all its savagery, it strikes the obelisk. Withstanding for only a moment, the monument must topple to this overwhelming tool of nature, and so it crumbles into the depths of a fable, the fragments crashing into the water. He feels the spray of ocean and sees that his beloved city—his beloved country—is gone. Salty tears blend with the sea, and he raises his gaze. Across the disappearing valley, on another precipice, stands a final image of beauty and grace. She is wearing a white robe and holds a diamond-crowned staff. The gem is wrapped in the tail of a serpent, and the jaws form its base. The staff is held high in her left hand. Her hood has blown back and her long black hair flies horizontally in the growing fury of wind and water. They lock eyes and he screams the woman's name in agony and longing: "MARA!" There is a brief echo of her name, and then the image bursts, as if made of glass and hit by a bullet…

Andrew shivered and opened his eyes on an empty circle of seats. The woman was no longer beside him; no one was in the room at all. He heard voices coming from an outside patio, along with the clank of coffee cups and the subtle drone of polite conversation. The rain had stopped, and he sat wide-eyed, bewildered.

Eli's sudden appearance finally broke his daze. "Hey, buddy, are you going to sit in here all night? Come out for some coffee."

"Where's Mara?" he asked automatically.

"Who?"

"The woman who was sitting beside me."

Eli frowned. "I was sitting beside you," he said frankly, but Andrew didn't hear him. Instead, he rushed toward the front door, knowing he was too late.

At the porch railing, he let out a silver breath into the night. She was gone, but he felt he would see her again, soon. Somehow, he was certain of this. In fact, it was now one of the only certainties in his life. He stared out into the hazy darkness, trying desperately to make sense of the night. He had met the most beautiful woman in the world, whom he'd never seen before, but whose every gesture, movement, crease and pose were intimately familiar. The touch of her hand, the tone of her voice, the very smell of her breath had somehow been preprogrammed into his memory. He intuitively knew that life as he lived it and understood it would soon change forever. For that matter, life for everyone would soon change. *It was perhaps a major precipitating event*, he mused, *maybe one with worldwide consequences.*

***

The agonizing pain in her skull had forced her out of the meeting and into the icy night. Three doors down the dark street, Mara didn't realize she was being erased again. Suddenly, she fell to the damp pavement.

Streetlights exploded and showers of broken glass beat down on her. Then she was gone.

CHAPTER 14

The gates remained open well into the night. Even as the guards continued their frequent patrols of the grounds, the gates were still open, as if no one had noticed the gaping security breach. Vatican City, in its midnight silence, seemed to be waiting for something, welcomingly.

He moved through the shadows of the wide corridors, undetected. After all, he was the hunter, and as such, he was appointed to carry out the deeds of those much higher than himself. He wore no face mask, no gloves. Dressed only in black pants and shirt, he strolled into the foyer of the papal living estate, holding in one hand an olive branch—a special gift for a special god.

"*In nomine dominus,*" he whispered lightly into the ear of a Swiss guard.

The soldier and his partner drew their staffs toward their bodies, allowing for the stranger's passage through the vaulting doorway and into the main hall. He could see another pair of Swiss guards at the far end, standing at attention, near the apartment door. Approaching the guards, he spoke out the secret phrase again, and their eyes respectfully averted his as they, too, pulled in their staffs. Then, turning the corner, he was startled at the sudden appearance of a cardinal, stepping out of a side chamber unaware.

"*Santo cielo!*" the cardinal coughed, stumbling against the wall. Fear welled in the black eyes wildly begging for the guards to take action. But the soldiers didn't move.

Smiling, the stranger withdrew the weapon tucked snuggly against his lower back by his leather belt.

The cardinal pressed his hands toward the ceiling, whimpering, "*Ciò che stai facendo?*"

"I'm killin' you," he answered wryly, voice barbed in an American southern accent, "that's what I'm doin'." Squeezing the trigger, the slug ticked out of the silencer and into the holy man's forehead. "Now I'm done," the assassin quipped, dropping the pistol to his side. He blew on the olive branch, for a moment gazing proudly at it, then stepped away from the cardinal's corpse as a thin stream of blood leaked out of the hole in the man's head.

Before proceeding to the door of the papal apartment, the stranger took a second to nod at the guards in quiet gratitude for allowing him to do his job, no matter what distractions might make the mess a little harder to clean or a bit more difficult to disguise. Then he walked confidently to the apartment door, grasped the ornate brass knob, and threw it open.

"Pardon me, Your Excellency," he called emphatically as he entered the room to find the pope kneeling in prayer before a small, candlelit altar.

"*Che?*" the old man uttered, rising painfully from his supplication.

The assassin spread his arms, olive branch in one hand, 9mm pistol in the other. "What?" he answered, smiling wildly. "You weren't expecting me?"

The Pope stumbled backwards against a bookcase, his hand knocking over a porcelain water pitcher from a small mahogany end table.

"I offer you this," the assassin continued, tossing the olive branch at the pontiff's feet as the pitcher crashed onto the floor, shattering. "Of course, you probably recognize the gesture. Thought I'd return the favor with a 'no thanks.' I've other plans for my vocation."

The Pope glanced down at the olive branch, terror pounding through his chest, then looked up again, directly into the tiny hole of the pistol's silencer.

"And this," the assassin said, planting a lead seed in the Garden of Eden.

CHAPTER 15

Andrew shoved the door to his apartment open, a copy of the *Boston Globe* tucked under his arm. As he entered the foyer, Nevyn bounded over the couch, reared up, and laid his paws on his master's shoulders. He didn't lick Andrew on the face—the wolfhound was not a licker. Andrew had come to assume that licking was beneath the dog's dignity. Instead, Nev's long nose touched Andrew's, and he gave a sniff of recognition, before sitting obediently. Andrew still couldn't believe how long his puppy had gotten. On his hind legs, Nevyn could easily look a six-foot-six person in the eye. Setting his laptop case on the coffee table, he dropped onto the couch and unfolded the *Globe*. Nev followed him, lying at his feet, with his head raised as he studied the man.

The headline simply read, "POPE ASSASSINATED."

All the way home, every radio station carried the shocking story of the pope's murder. With a foreboding pit in his stomach, Andrew began to think about the implications of the death and how he might possibly present the assassination in a lecture. What would be the implications for the Church? For what was *this* a precipitating event? Was Peter really going to be the last pope, as prophesied? If the Church collapsed, what would take its place?

As the thoughts compounded in his mind, Nevyn's barking suddenly brought Andrew back from his momentary contemplation.

Nevyn now sat in front of his master, eyes locked steadfastly on Andrew.

"What?"

The dog held a cardboard FedEx mailing envelope in his mouth.

"What's this?" Andrew asked, reaching for the envelope.

Nevyn released the mail from his mouth, allowing Andrew to take it. *The carrier must have slid it under the door*, he thought. *Wonder why I didn't have to sign for it?*

"If you hadn't attacked me on the way in," Andrew said lightly, "I would have noticed this." He scratched Nevyn behind the ear with one hand, while he turned the envelope over in the other and read the return address. It simply read, "Rome, Italy."

"Who'd be sending me a letter from Rome?" he asked rhetorically, though his eyes met the dog's.

Nevyn yelped.

"You've always had such a wonderful command of the English language, Nev. Are you sure you're really a dog?"

The dog whined softly and lay at Andrew's feet again, as if offended by the man's easy sarcasm. After an apologetic pat on Nevyn's head, Andrew opened the FedEx package.

Inside the cardboard mailing envelope was a second one of parchment, bearing the words "THE VATICAN" in gold at the top left-hand corner. His name had been handwritten across the middle.

"Who could have sent this?" he asked aloud.

Nevyn peered up at Andrew, his tail wagging.

Andrew slowly broke the wax seal on the envelope and removed a letter written on heavy cotton bond paper. Opening the tri-fold, he saw that the top of the letter was headed with "THE VATICAN" in gold-embossed letters. The only other letterhead he had ever seen presented in the same way had been from "THE WHITE HOUSE." A friend of his was an acquaintance with a White House staffer, and he occasionally received personal notes on White House stationary.

The correspondence was handwritten in beautiful script, and he found himself admiring the exquisite formation of the letters. Pulling his thoughts from the letter's appearance, he read the message:

Your presence is urgently requested at the Vatican. Given the current circumstances, I am sure that this request will be honored. Enclosed is a ticket for a direct flight from Boston to Rome. Leave immediately.

Sincerely,

Monsignor Giovanni

Andrew stared at the text for several minutes, his eyes continually shifting from the heading, "THE VATICAN," to the Monsignor's signature.

Finally, he set the letter on the coffee table and considered the dog. "Who the hell is Monsignor Giovanni?"

Nevyn stared at him.

Then it suddenly struck him — "How the Christ did it get here today? The Pope was killed late last night."

He grabbed the FedEx envelope and noted that it had been time-stamped for noon of the day before, and that it had been mailed *next day delivery*. The letter itself bore no date. He pulled the airline ticket out of the parchment envelope. It had been purchased only yesterday from a ticket agent in Rome.

"Strange," he said, gazing at the dog. Though Nevyn appeared to have fallen fast asleep, he still talked to him. "Do you think the pope was killed yesterday and they kept it a secret for a day? But why would they do that? Something like the pope's murder couldn't be kept quiet."

When Andrew looked down at his feet for the dog's acknowledgement, he realized that Nevyn was gone. Standing, he looked around the living room but still saw no dog. He searched the kitchen — not there either. He checked his watch. 11 p.m. Walking to the bedroom, he found Nevyn stretched over the full length of the bed, snoring as only a wolfhound could, as if the creature had already discovered the mystery and had grown bored with watching his master wrestle with the unknown.

"All right, my furry friend," he whispered, "we'll work on solving this in the morning while I pack my bags."

Andrew lay awake for some time, trying to sort out the letter, its timing, and why he had been summoned to the Vatican. At last, admitting that he could make no real sense of the matter, he fell asleep — he and Nev subconsciously existing in heavy slumber as the night moved quietly on without them.

CHAPTER 16

Sitting bolt upright, Mara looked wildly around the room.

Lace curtains, draped over open balcony doors, flailed against the casings as warm ocean air rushed into the chamber. Above him, a vaulting canopy, detailed in representations of cherubs accented in gold-leaf, seemed to press down on her, and the four thick bedposts surrounding her appeared as heavy bars. She was in a white satin nightgown, and covered with thick, soft bedding, its warmth and weight infusing her with a sudden sense of claustrophobia. Like a mad woman, she threw herself out of the bed and onto the cold tile floor.

All around her, unfamiliar objects of another time and place reeled in and out of focus: a gaping marble fireplace, alabaster urns and pitchers, gold-framed portraits of people she didn't know, elaborate carvings in the plaster trim of the domed ceiling high above.

Pushing herself off the floor, Mara ran through the open doors, driving away the curtains with clenched hands, and stumbled onto the balcony. Her body thrust against the smooth railing and thick stone balusters, she gazed at the surf as it crashed against the rocks far below, the ocean wind slapping at her and the blazing sun wetting her cheeks and forehead.

She almost collapsed in disbelief, falling to her knees and sobbing. Flashing over her brain were images of what she'd last known—of Hooligan's and of Wanda on the bar table, party hats and beer, candles, circles, the stranger beside her...staff and serpent. She lowered her head between her knees and trembled. The blackness, she remembered, explosions and then—nothing.

Here.

Waking up in the strange bedroom, a chamber of white and marble.

Feeling the presence of someone near her, she lifted her head and saw the outline of a figure standing in the doorway. Hurrying to her feet, she clenched the stone railing.

"Who are you?" she gasped.

"You must be calm," the figure said, with a subtle Italian accent, stepping onto the balcony. It was an older woman, portly, with silver hair tied into a bun on the top of her head. She wore a gray maid's dress and an apron. Hands open and extended in front of her, she tried to appear non-threatening.

"Now, dear, you've had quite a startle." She smiled warmly at Mara. "Let's get you dressed and downstairs. There's someone waiting who'd like to explain all of this to you."

She hesitated. Then reluctantly, Mara stepped away from the railing and allowed the woman to slip a thick arm around her waist, easing her back into the bedroom.

"I want to know how I got here," Mara insisted. She hadn't realized how weak she was; her legs were shaking and her muscles twitching. She was exhausted.

"Now, now, miss," the woman replied, leading Mara to the bedside and helping her to sit. "In time, all things will be revealed."

"Where am I?"

The woman considered her for a moment, a slight grin hinting at the corners of her mouth. "Safe," she answered simply.

Mara's eyes opened widely. "Safe?" she choked. "How did I get here?" She pressed her open hands to her temples. "I must be going crazy. How did I get from…from Boston to here? My god…" She began to cry, and the chambermaid gently patted Mara's knee.

"You must not be so upset," she said. "I'm sure this will all make sense just as soon as the master has seen you."

"The master?" She wiped the wet strands of black hair from her glassy green eyes.

"The master of the house, of course." The chambermaid had already slid clean stockings over Mara's bare feet, and now she helped the distraught young lady to her feet and pulled the nightgown over her head. Though the warm ocean air brushed over her slender body, Mara showed no reaction to being naked in front of the old woman. Instead, she stood lifelessly entranced, her face stained with tears and sweat, hair disheveled, as the maid carefully dressed her upper body in a bra and a silk blouse, then sat her down and worked a pair of panties up the woman's legs, followed by a pair of light slacks.

"You'll have to stand one more time, sweetheart," the chambermaid said. "I have to get these pants buttoned and adjusted."

Fully dressed, Mara was placed in front of a mirror while the old woman gently brushed her raven hair.

"Slip on those leather shoes by the door," the old woman suggested, "and you'll be all ready to meet the man of the house."

Mara gazed up at the chambermaid. "And he'll tell me why I'm here?" she uttered.

The old woman smiled warmly again. "I'm sure he'll tell you everything."

CHAPTER 17

Andrew boarded flight 180, which would take him from Boston's Logan Airport to Rome. How he managed to get a seat was anyone's guess. The turmoil caused by the pope's assassination resulted in every flight from every airport being overbooked by all major airline carriers. In the confusion, seats were being given away on a first-come, first-serve basis, regardless of reserved seating. For every person trying to get to Rome, there was a person trying to flee the place. Persistent riots in and around the Vatican sent tourists flocking to any destination, as long as it was out of Italy. Conversely, diehard Catholics, as well as clergy from each level of the hierarchy down to parish priest, caught any available flight to the Holy City. Never before had so many been called to attend a pope's funeral, a right usually reserved for the upper echelons of the church and high ranking diplomats. Now, however, the Vatican had sent a message to all dioceses requiring a show of numbers and solidarity for their Mother Church. The hope was that the presence of tens of thousands of the faithful would help stunt the growing tide of violence sweeping not only Rome, but also other global religious centers.

For Andrew, his own situation proved even more unsettling than the brooding chaos. He had received a journal entry from his "imaginary" friend that he should prepare for a trip to Rome. And then, after the assassination, he had received a special delivery from a Monsignor Giovanni, requesting his immediate presence in Rome—a letter that had been mailed *before* the pope's murder. What he didn't understand was why the ticket included with the letter offered no return trip.

When he finally made his way through the mass of humanity to the ticket counter, he was confronted by a very agitated clerk. The ticket clerk could not have cared less that Andrew had a personal invitation and a ticket. She curtly explained that he and the growing line of the hundreds behind him also had invitations and tickets, but that all flights were overbooked.

Andrew's frustration began to peak. It had already taken him three hours to find a parking space. When he finally entered the terminal he discovered, like the thousands around him, that the airport air conditioning was unable to keep up with the sudden rush of people and the 95-degree temperatures. The terminal felt like a Finnish sauna and tempers were running high. If parishioners could have heard the curses uttered by their sweat-soaked priests, collection plates would have risked the fate of running on empty. Furthermore, airport security proved to be excruciating. Crucifixes wreaked havoc with the metal detectors, and the incessant noise of ringing bells raised the level of irritation. Yet to his surprise he was able to move easily and quickly through the throngs.

Having spent all day unjustifiably denying seats to ticketed priests, she was ready to argue, and the job be damned. Since Andrew was not a man of the cloth, she took this as a golden opportunity to erupt. He was seen as her personal crusade for frustration release. As she was readying her tirade a man from the back office handed the clerk a note. She almost broke his hand when she grabbed the scrap of paper, and the man made a very quick exit. She read the note, and in an exasperated tone and a smile that bordered on a snarl, she told him to proceed to gate 24, reluctantly pointing to her left.

While Andrew believed in neither fate nor coincidence, he knew nothing was going to keep him from boarding a plane to Rome. As he left the counter, he felt sorry for the priest next in line because the clerk, apparently not Catholic, was now unleashing a firestorm that would have brought a blush to the cheeks of the Whore of Babylon.

As his flight began to arch upward, slipping through the heat and humidity to higher altitudes, he gazed out the window at the shrinking city below. He could not help but wonder if his one-way ticket meant that this would be his last glimpse of Boston Harbor.

***

When Andrew emerged from his self-induced fugue state, he glimpsed the last of the New England coastline as the aircraft cruised eastward. He'd had to leave a message on Eli's answering machine, informing him that he was taking a much-needed, albeit sudden vacation to Italy. Unfortunately, Eli was somewhere in Martha's Vineyard with his wife, due to return that evening, and Andrew hadn't been able to toss the mystery of the letter and the airline ticket around with his best friend. He'd thought it safer not to divulge any more than the basic details in his recorded message to Eli, along with a plea for his friend to care for Nevyn.

In the first class cabin, Andrew thought it odd no one was sitting next to him. With the entire clamor of overbooked flights, why was there a vacant seat? Standing, he surveyed his surroundings and immediately noticed the second oddity—the plane was filled with men in black. The door to the coach class was open, since the stewardesses were preparing their snack carts, and as far as he could see, the fuselage was packed window-to-window with priests. He smiled thinking that at any moment these men would pull out laser guns and tell him to sit, as they escorted him to their home world. He enjoyed the *Men In Black* movies, but he never thought he'd find himself in one.

"Sir, are you okay?"

The stewardess's words snapped him out of his humorous fantasy.

"Yes," he answered, "I'm fine. I was just noticing all the…"

"It is kind of funny," she whispered. "Not too many bottom pinchers on this flight."

"Well, you never know." He smiled at her. "I would guess the call for liquor will be fairly minimal, too, although white wine might be in high demand."

Her agreeing smile was pretty, and her tall figure and neatly cropped red hair didn't go unnoticed either. Her dark blue and gold jacket and knee-length skirt fit perfectly, accentuating her slender curves. Two small dimples accompanied her smile, and her greenish-blue eyes were a tribute to Irish descent. In all, she was a welcome change from the other stewardesses, who appeared to be Italian.

"This week has been so hectic," she offered. "Everyone has been called in. Normally this flight has only Italian staff, but somehow I got suckered onto the shift. I certainly stand out, don't I?"

Her grinning eyes drew him in. "An emerald amidst rubies," he commented.

"So, what will you be having this evening, Mister…"

"Andrew," he said.

"And what can I get for you, Andrew?"

"Scotch, rocks, a twist, and a little visit next time you have a chance," Andrew said. He was unusually forward, and lightly entertained the idea that maybe the presence of all the priests was bringing out the devil in him.

"Coming right up," she said, stepping down the aisle, then she paused and glanced back at him. "And I will *certainly* find some time."

Andrew watched the gentle sway of her hips as she headed for the galley. As if knowing he was looking, she added an exaggerated movement to her walk. He smiled, before realizing that several of the priests were glaring at him disapprovingly.

"If I remember correctly," he said easily, "watching a good-looking woman is not a mortal sin." He chuckled as he lowered himself into his seat, remarking, "Beam me up!"

Kathleen, the stewardess, was gone for some time, but gradually made her way back to Andrew with his scotch.

"So much for juice and soda," she confided. "I'm not sure we have enough liquor on the plane. Father Mahoney, now he liked his ale, but these priests are tipping the hard stuff like it's holy water." She leaned closer so as not to be overheard.

Andrew liked the sensations caused by her closeness to him, and the subtle scent of her perfume.

"They don't say anything," she whispered. "It's like a funeral back there."

He could only hear the dull hum of the jet's engines. There were no undertones of conversation, no crying babies, and no children purposely trying to irritate each other and the strangers around them. Surrounded by clergy, Andrew felt a little mischievous. He asked if she would have any free time when they landed in Italy. She said that she wished she did, but with the mayhem at the airports, all personnel had to work triple shifts. She wrote her telephone number on a napkin and gave it to Andrew. He studied the numbers for a moment, finding them strangely familiar, before folding the napkin and tucking it neatly into his wallet, knowing well enough that he would never have the opportunity to call her.

They continued to flirt when moments allowed, but the clergy were very demanding and kept her occupied. He could tell that she was beginning to feel a little guilty as the priests watched the flirtations with scowls, and wondered why Catholics were always so hung up on guilt trips. Priests didn't seem to mind if the flock made plenty of little Catholics, but God forbid that they enjoyed doing it.

With three more hours of flight time ahead of him, he put on the earphones stored in the pouch on the back of the seat in front of him and flipped down the LCD screen. Kathleen walked by once more, tossing him a sheepish grin, and he noticed that her blouse, partially opened earlier, was now buttoned to her neck.

The anchorwoman delivered the news in Italian, and somewhat irritated that he couldn't close his eyes and listen, he read the streaming banner of the news in the translation which appeared at the bottom of the screen:

WELCOME TO MUNDI ITALIANA'S WORLD NEWS UPDATE IN WHAT HAS BECOME ANOTHER BLOW TO THE CATHOLIC CHURCH'S RECENT ECUMENICAL MOVEMENT. THE ASSASSINATION OF POPE PETER HAS PRECIPITATED RELIGIOUS RIOTS IN SEVERAL MAJOR EUROPEAN AND MIDDLE EASTERN CITIES. RECENT INFORMATION REVEALS THAT AMERICAN CONSERVATIVE BAPTIST MINISTER VICTOR M. WOOLGRABB WAS NOT ACTING ALONE WHEN HE ENDED THE POPE'S LIFE. FROM UNCONFIRMED SOURCES WE'VE LEARNED TWO MORE ACCOMPLICES HAVE BEEN IMPLICATED. A SUFI CLERIC FROM SRI LANKA WHO GOES BY THE NAME OF HAMEED NAZ AND JOSEPH SCHNEIDER, A GERMAN- BORN JEW REPORTED TO HAVE TIES WITH A GROUP KNOWN AS "THE ELDERS OF ZION." BOTH WERE AT THE VATICAN AT THE TIME OF THE ASSASSINATION AND

ARE BEING SOUGHT BY INTERPOL FOR QUESTIONING. FOR MORE INFORMATION WE GO NOW TO SERGIO BALTA, MUNDI ITALIANA'S CORRESPONDENT AT THE VATICAN. SERGIO, ARE YOU THERE?

YES, I'M HERE. REPORTERS HAVE BEEN REMOVED FROM THE GROUNDS OF THE VATICAN. AN EVER-GROWING NUMBER OF CLERGY HAVE DESCENDED ON ROME AND ALL AROUND THE CITY CAN BE HEARD THE BLARE OF SIRENS. RIOTING HAS BROKEN OUT BETWEEN TOURISTS OF DIFFERING RELIGIOUS BACKGROUNDS AS ACCUSATIONS FLY REGARDING THE IDENTITIES OF THE POPE'S ASSAILANTS.

SERGIO, WHAT CAN YOU TELL US ABOUT THE TWO MEN WHO ARE ALLEGEDLY CONNECTED TO REVEREND WOOLGRABB?

WELL, ROSA, INFORMATION IS VERY SKETCHY AT THIS POINT AND IT IS NOT AT ALL CERTAIN THAT THESE MEN WERE ACTUAL ACCOMPLICES IN THIS HORRENDOUS CRIME. WE DO KNOW THAT THESE MEN ARE BEING SOUGHT FOR QUESTIONING BY ITALIAN AUTHORITIES. NAZ IS A POPULAR, THOUGH RECLUSIVE SUFI LEADER WHO ALLEGEDLY HAS TIES TO EXTREME SUNI FACTIONS OPERATING OUT OF IRAN AND SYRIA. SCHNEIDER LIVES BOTH IN GERMANY AND ISRAEL AND HAS REPUTED TIES TO A GROUP OF ZIONISTS KNOWN AS "THE ELDERS." IT IS THIS GROUP THAT HAD PUT FORWARD THE HISTORICAL AND CONTROVERSIAL PROTOCOLS WHICH ARE REFUTED BY JEWISH MODERATES AND LABELED AS FORGERIES...

Andrew shifted in his seat, leaning toward the miniature television screen in interest. He knew some of the basic elements of the pope's assassination, but he hoped to gain a clue as to why he'd been summoned to Rome. Surely the invitation must have had to do with more than just the young professor's academic acclaim or controversial notions of the universe. There must have been some other reason, and he might discover it in the roots of the most shocking murder in human history...

ROSA, THIS HAS JUST COME IN. IT APPEARS THAT MR. NAZ IS ALSO SAID TO BE THE HEAD OF A GROUP CALLED "AL-BANNA," A SECRET SUFI SOCIETY WITH TIES TO MASONIC ORGANIZATIONS. SCHNEIDER APPARENTLY ALSO BELONGS TO A GROUP CALLED "EVEN HA SHETTIYA," WHICH CLAIMS ABSOLUTE ISRAELI CONTROL OVER THE CITY OF JERUSALEM. WHILE LITTLE IS KNOWN OF THESE ORGANIZATIONS, WE HAVE LEARNED THAT THE REVEREND WOOLGRABB WAS SAID TO BE WEARING A RING WITH AN EIGHT-POINTED CROSS. THIS SAME

RING WAS PURPORTEDLY WORN BY HIS ALLEGED CO-CONSPIRATORS.

THANK YOU, SERGIO, FOR THAT UPDATE AND WE WILL CONTINUE TO KEEP YOU INFORMED AS EVENTS UNFOLD IN ROME AND ELSEWHERE AROUND THE WORLD. FOR MORE ON THESE BREAKING EVENTS WE NOW GO TO WILLIAM BAKERSFIELD, LEADER OF A GROUP CALLED "CONSPIRACY WATCH." WILLIAM, WHAT IS YOUR TAKE ON THESE RECENT TRAGIC EVENTS?

Of course this guy was speaking Italian also, though he looked as Anglo-Saxon as any English bureaucrat Andrew had ever seen. He focused on the banner again, shaking his head…

THERE IS NO QUESTION THAT WORLD TURMOIL WILL BE ON THE RISE IF IT IS TRULY FOUND THAT THE POPE'S DEATH WAS THE RESULT OF ACTIONS ON THE PART OF RELIGIOUS ZEALOTS. THE QUESTION WE MUST NOW ASK IS WHETHER THERE IS ALSO SOME SECRET CONSPIRACY ON THE PART OF ARCANE SOCIETIES. HAVE, IN FACT, THE MASONS GONE TOO FAR IN MEDDLING WITH WORLD HISTORY? WHAT IS THE SIGNIFICANCE OF THIS EIGHT-POINTED CROSS, AND WHY, WHEN THE WORLD IS ON THE VERGE OF A NEW ERA OF RELIGIOUS TOLERANCE, DID SOMEONE OR SOME GROUP STRIKE DOWN A POPE WHO IS NO DOUBT BOUND TO BE NAMED A SAINT?

Andrew grasped the armrests of his seat as the airplane hit a pocket of turbulence and all the LCD screens onboard went black. He slapped the screen once, in a futile attempt to regain the picture. The captain's metallic voice came over the speakers, assuring passengers that the drop and rattle of the plane was a result of a high pressure system, and that soon they would regain reception of satellite programming. "For safety reasons," he continued, "please fasten your seatbelts until further notice."

***

Whispered rantings hissed in the cell block.

The guard's rounds were over; Reverend Woolgrab knew that he wouldn't see the fat, greasy man's inflated shadow pass the bars of his cell for hours, slapping his night stick against the palm of his hand in order to keep his courage awake. Silence reigned all around him, in perfect intercourse with the darkness.

"And his kingdom shall be mine," he murmured, sitting on the edge of the mattress, rocking back and forth in deranged excitement. He sat naked, a bedspring that he'd worked off its metal frame hours before, clenched in his hands. "And I shall have his kingdom...Promises," he gasped, wild-eyed.

Suddenly rising, he pressed his face between the bars of the cell, round, glazed eyes flitting in their sockets. "No one," he whispered. "No one left to witness the crucifixion." The sound of his own voice startled him, and he stumbled backwards, the bedspring held tightly to his chest as if he possessed a golden ankh of immortality.

"And he told me I would rule in heaven!" Stretching his arms out, he threw his head back and whimpered before falling to his knees, "The archangel promised me salvation...Yes, of course—an *ironclad* kingdom!"

Grasping his sides, he began to laugh quietly as tears leaked down his wrinkled face. "Yet," he chuckled, "I will have my redemption!"

Clenching the bedspring, he lifted it high above his head, then drove it down through the darkness and into the open palm of his hand. Wincing in pain, a scream escaped from his lungs and he fell against the wall. Instantly, warm blood flowing from the wound, he covered his mouth with his free hand, hoping the cry had not disturbed the stillness. Moments passed as he lay silently checking the sound of his breathing— of his pounding heart.

Satisfied that his error would not challenge the completion of his act of redemption, he pushed himself to his knees again.

"They put their fingers into his holes," he mumbled. Bracing himself for the pain, he yanked the bedspring from his hand. "Oh, poor Thomas...Will you never believe?"

The sting was almost unbearable as he made a fist and felt the hot blood run down his forearm. Arms shaking, body trembling, he weakly held the weapon in his wounded hand and raised it. "Nails to both his hands," he muttered as he stabbed the other palm, again yelping. But he didn't fall this time. Instead, he bit his tongue as hard as he could, his body hunched over in absolute pain.

Abruptly, with little thought, he pulled the bedspring from his hand, holding it in front of his face. "Redemption, my people," he said, his voice cracking in a low sob, "is for the weak of heart..." Then, "Blessed are the weak, for the kingdom of God is theirs!"

The last of his screams drew the guard from his post, far at the end of block, as he plunged the bedspring into his side, twisted it up underneath his ribcage and into his own heart.

CHAPTER 18

WEEKLY WORLD MAGAZINE—*The recent assassination of Pope Peter has resurrected interest in a series of prophesies refuted by the Vatican.*

In 1909, Pope Pius X was said to have had a vision and afterwards cried out, "What I have seen is terrifying! What is certain is that a pope will leave Rome, and in leaving the Vatican, he will pass over the dead bodies of his priests."

Just prior to his death he had another vision and said, "I have seen one of my successors, of the same name, who was fleeing over the bodies of his brethren. He will take refuge in some hiding place, but after a brief respite, he will die a cruel death. This perversity is nothing less than the beginning of the last days of the world."

What does not escape notice is that after the death of Pope John Paul II, the newly elected pontiff, Benedict XVI, sought refuge against the turmoil that engulfed Rome after his election, and later died of cancer. Further, when Pope Peter's casket left Rome, it was carried over the bodies of priests that had died during the recent religious turmoil plaguing the Holy City since his murder.

Today, the black smoke still rises over the Vatican.

Are the supposed forged prophecies of Saint Malachy coming true, or will his predictions be proven wrong? Saint Malachy was said to have gone to Rome in 1139 and disclosed a series of prophecies that listed all future popes down to the very last, Petrus Romanus, or Peter the Roman.

He went on to say, "In extreme persecution, the seat of the Holy Roman Church will be occupied by Peter the Roman, who will feed the sheep through many tribulations, at the term of which the city of seven hills will be destroyed..."

Today in Rome it seems that at the very least the city of seven hills is being spiritually and physically destroyed. UN forces have entered Rome in an effort to quell the latest violence that is shocking the faithful of all religions.

***

"Ladies and gentlemen, welcome to the Skip Whalen show," the fat man with the red cheeks announced, exposing large white teeth to the television audience.

Skip Whalen's show was both popular and controversial, all features that brought in the ratings to the delight of the network. After all, with more controversy came more viewers. Despite the many lawsuits filed by disgruntled guests, the network continued to back the program because any publicity was good for ratings.

"Tonight my guest is the most Reverend Jay J. Dooley," he continued, a suggestion of sarcasm threading his speech, "a close friend and associate of the late Reverend Woolgrabb, who shot and killed Pope Peter II before taking his own life in his cell. But before we bring out the reverend, I would like to bring you up to date on some current news.

"As you all know, the College of Cardinals at the Vatican has been unable to choose a successor to the late pope. Black smoke is now a common sight above the Sistine Chapel. The Church and the world are in turmoil. Religious strife is everywhere. Economies are on the brink of collapse. Throughout the tropics, loggers have refused to enter the rain forests for lumber because of rumors of strange apparitions and deaths in the forests. Wherever you turn, there is violence and chaos. "And so, against this backdrop, I would now like to introduce tonight's guest, the Reverend Jay J. Dooley."

The Reverend Dooley strode onto the stage to both applause and jeers, waving his hands in the air as he walked to his chair beside the host's desk. The minister was a short, rotund man, with well-clipped sandy hair. A gaping smile traversed his ruddy complexion, and his blue eyes twinkled.

The host stood when his guest came out, and extended a large hand, which Dooley shook with great vigor. Since Skip tended to lean far to the right in many of his talk show executions, Dooley surely figured that he was shaking the hand of a true believer.

"Call me J.J., Skip. That's how I'm known to the flock," he said beaming.

Skip gestured for the reverend to sit, before taking his own seat behind the interview desk.

"Now, folks, as I've said," Skip began, "J.J. was a close personal friend of the late Reverend Victor M. Woolgrabb. As a matter of fact, J.J. will probably replace Woolgrabb as head of *New Life Evangelical Ministries*. He is here tonight as an apologist for the actions of the deceased Reverend Woolgrabb, and will try to explain how a God-fearing man like the late reverend could possibly commit such a heinous act as murdering a pope in cold blood."

J.J.'s face turned an even brighter shade of red, his broad grin mutating toward a snarl. "Now hold it one minute!" J.J. insisted, a hint of rising anger vibrating in his voice. "I am *not* here to apologize for the actions of anyone."

"So you think it was okay for Reverend Woolgrabb to murder the pope? Pope Peter sent him, and all religious leaders, the famous olive branch, and Woolgrabb used that offering of peace as a tool to commit murder."

"I know what you're trying to do," J.J. said, his eyes narrowing. "My good friend was no murderer. At worst, he was kidnapped by Moslem terrorists and brainwashed. But you must remember that God works in mysterious ways."

"Are you saying that it might have been God's will that Woolgrabb shot the pope?"

"What I am saying is that who knows the will of God? Maybe God felt that this pope had gone astray. After all, he *was* cavorting with those heathen Moslems, Hindus, and anyone else who failed to recognize Jesus as their Savior. For all we know, Pope Peter was doing the work of Satan."

Skip smiled in disbelief. "That's the problem with you holy rollers. If someone disagrees with your self-serving point of view, you accuse them of being in league with the devil."

"The devil has many legions and plays many tricks on people, including you," he said as he pointed his finger at the host.

"So in your mind, God or *Jeeesus* made Woolgrabb commit murder. What kind of god is that? A god that puts out a hit on a pope? You've got to be kidding."

The audience conceded with approving nods and murmurs. Some even clapped.

"See? See? The devil is using you now to speak his blasphemous words," J.J. stammered, struggling for the upper hand.

"So you think some heathen Arabs brainwashed Woolgrabb?"

"Well, the good reverend went missing for a few days, and then he ended up in Rome. We know that those *Satan-worshipping-turban-heads* will do anything to cause problems."

The people booed him.

"Now, wait," J.J. insisted, raising his hands. "Those Catholics have really gone astray. They helped Adolph kill the Jews; they did nothing for those poor African Tutsi in Rowanda, and let's face it, they are way too rich to be doing God's work. By their deeds you shall know them, praise Jesus!"

"I don't think there was any great *evangelical* movement to stop the slaughter of the Jews," Skip countered, "and what have you done for the poor Africans?"

"We give the Africans the Word of Jesus. We feed their souls so that maybe God will forgive their sins and won't send them to the fiery pits of Satan. And we always pay proper respect to our Jewish friends, misguided though they are." The minister had begun to squirm a little in his hot seat.

"Okay, what about the gruesome way Woolgrabb committed suicide?" Skip asked pointedly.

"Who says it was suicide? I think that they crucified the late great reverend. And if he had to go, then that is how he would've wanted it. He walked a mile in our Savior's shoes and like our Great Redeemer, he suffered the wounds of the wicked."

"How can you possibly compare this lowlife to Jesus? That man, under a flag of truce, cold-bloodily put a bullet in the pope's head. I think you're all a bunch of nuts. You rob from the widow's purse to line your own pockets. If anyone disagrees with you, you simply say that they're the tool of the devil. I noticed you came to this show in a chauffeured limo. Was that paid for with God's money?"

"Wait!"

"You're nothing but a hypocrite," Skip declared. "What do you think, audience?"

In unison the audience began to shout, "*Hypocrite, hypocrite, hypocrite…*"

J.J. jumped to his feet in outrage, yelling over the fading chorus of the audience, "Jesus is watching you! He knows the evil in your hearts. On the day of judgment you will *not* be among the fortunate!" He turned to Skip and whispered forcefully, "You will hear from my lawyers," then he stormed off the stage.

"There you have it, folks," the host called after him. "I think J.J. was cut from the same cloth as the late *not-so-great* Reverend Victor M. Woolgrabb. We may never know why Woolgrabb did what he did, but I think that we can all rest assured that he was not following the will of God.

"After the commercial break, we'll be back with members of a Satanic cult to get their views on the current problems confronting the world."

And with that, the controversial television program gave way to a paper towel commercial.

CHAPTER 19

Andrew had heard enough, anyway—at least for the moment—so even after the airplane gained satellite programming again, he didn't watch the news. Besides, his eyes ached in their sockets.

Yet the irony of this situation didn't escape him. His mind recalled those avatars in history that came with messages of peace and tolerance only to be rejected by the very people they fought to help. He wondered how one could go from the teachings of Jesus to the Inquisition or the Crusades. What would Muhammad think of the perverted use of Jihad? How many teachers brought humanity to the verge of a life worth living only to be cut down, their teachings twisted beyond all recognition? What force prevented the fulfillment of the dream? What was it that humanity just didn't get?

And we finally had a pope that may have been the first that truly deserved the title, he thought, *and they cut him down.*

With his famous rose and olive branch, Pope Peter had sought out every major and minor religious leader to bring peace and reconciliation among all religious thought. Like Andrew himself, the pope also sought the unified theory of religion that would end millennia of wars and atrocities. "We can work together" was his motto.

The man was gutsy, Andrew thought.

To each leader the pontiff sent an olive branch, and invited all those truly devoted to the amalgamation of faith to return the offering to the Vatican in order to receive the rose as a symbol of mutual commitment. The olive branch, in effect, served as a personal invitation to meet with him at the time of their choosing; it was a guaranteed entrance into the inner sanctum of the Holy City. Throughout the world, religious tensions had been abating. Unfortunately, zealots and extremists around the globe were now at each others' throats with a vengeance that promised to write the bloodiest chapter in man's history.

Andrew's mind drifted to the mention of the eight-pointed cross. He knew this symbol well and made frequent references to it in his writings and lectures. It was a number of importance to the Moslems, Persians, and Mesopotamians, and later, to the Templars. The two circles forming the number eight represented the union of heaven and earth and the alchemic path to enlightenment. He remembered the eight-sided dome of the Rock of Jerusalem and the octagonal design of the al-Aqsa mosque. The Templars were notorious for eight-sided churches and fortifications. He wondered how the hell some right-wing preacher from the Deep South came to be wearing an eight-pointed cross.

Andrew speculated that his summons to Rome was to take advantage of his expertise in symbolism, and yet he was not endeared to church authorities since part of his mission in life had been to expose church dogma as being not only out of touch, but also blatantly false. But the intimation that he would go to Rome came before the pope's death and…

"Please put your seats in the upright position and fasten your seatbelts," a flight attendant announced. "We will be landing in just a few moments."

Andrew came out of his mental meanderings as he recognized Kathleen's voice over the speaker. He glanced out the window, expecting to see the beautiful Roman skyline. Instead, he saw an atmosphere darkened by city-wide fires. He saw Kathleen helping several elderly priests retrieve their items from the overhead storage compartments. He winked at her, and she returned the gesture before the throng of passengers forced him to move to the exit.

When he stepped off the plane and onto the platform a thought struck him. Digging the wallet out of his back pocket, he pulled out the folded napkin that Kathleen had given him. Unfolding the napkin, he stared at the numbers again.

"What the…" he breathed. "This is *Eli's* phone number. No wonder I thought I'd seen it somewhere." He scanned the area around him. "How in the hell…"

Before he could finish the thought, his jaw nearly hit the floor. What he suddenly saw in every direction, like a swarm of millions of ants, were men in black.

"This can't be real," he muttered to himself.

CHAPTER 20

From the second level of the airport, Andrew stared down in awe at the colony of priests hurrying back and forth over the glossy floor, their unintelligible voices echoing into the humidity. Never before had he seen so many holy men in one spot, nor had he ever expected to see such a divine mob in an airport. It was all so surreal to him, and he blinked a few times to remind himself that he wasn't dreaming.

Dragging his wheeled suitcase by its flimsy plastic handle, Andrew shoved it through the automatic glass doors leading to the pick-up area. He would flag down a taxi and have it take him to a nearby hotel. Later he'd try to contact Giovanni and make arrangements for the meeting.

Once on the concrete, he stood at the curb and attempted to hail a taxi. He had little knowledge of Italian, so he made no vain motion to ask anyone how he might secure a ride to a hotel. Instead, he continued to yell "Taxi!" and wave his hand in the air, until a long black limousine rolled slowly past him, its trunk stopping directly in front of him.

Irritated, Andrew slapped the back fender of the limousine, half hoping for someone to emerge from the vehicle ready for a confrontation. His buttons had certainly been pushed enough since he'd gotten off the airplane and had been thrown through customs. Then he spent sixty-eight minutes looking for his one suitcase on a turning conveyor belt before being tossed through the sacred mosh pit as he struggled to escape the mass of priests and get a ride out of there. Now this idiot had the audacity to park in front of him while he was trying to hail a...

"*Tassì?*" she asked, stepping out of the front passenger side of the limo. The woman was hauntingly beautiful, tall and slender, and packed neatly into a red leather ensemble. Her hair, so blond it shimmered almost white, hung straight and lifelessly over her shoulders. "*State cercando un tassì?*" she continued in Italian, walking suggestively toward him.

Andrew's ire quickly drained out of his eyes. "Yes," he answered tentatively. "I need a ride—to a hotel."

As if floating on the soles of her feet, she slid dangerously close to him and reached slowly down his body, moving deliberately with an open hand toward his crotch. Andrew's body went rigid and he released the handle of his suitcase, letting the luggage thud to the concrete. Holding his breath, he felt as if he'd just submerged himself in icy water, and he waited for the touch, for the beautiful woman's hand to...

She grabbed the handle and pulled open the back door of the limo in one quick movement. "Get in," she commanded in perfect English.

Andrew released his breath, his pulse crashing, and stumbled away from her. "Get in?" he said. He pulled his wheeled suitcase from the sidewalk. "I don't even know who you are."

From the driver's side, a hulking black man in a silver suit emerged. He was bald, and his black glassy eyes reflected a hatred—a violence more cruel than Andrew could imagine.

"Giovanni." The black man spoke clearly and forcefully, staring at Andrew.

The woman smiled at Andrew. "We'll take you there."

***

The chambermaid led Mara through a spacious hallway, richly carpeted and lit by elaborate gold sconces. The walls were bare. Sterile. As she walked, Mara slowly came to realize that she was in some kind of mansion. *Somewhere tropical*, she thought, remembering the warm air, the balcony over the crashing waves. Maybe Mediterranean. A humid place, a high place. Instantly, her brain began frantically to work out a scenario for escape, for running from this strange place. If anything was certain in her life at this point it was that she was no longer in Boston.

At the end of the hallway they turned left, entering another corridor, much darker and more decorated than the first. The walls were lined with framed images of people, animals, plants, and geological formations, combined in such a way as to create pictures she had never before seen.

Mara stopped suddenly at the mouth of the corridor, resisting the chambermaid's slight tug at her elbow. "What are these?" she insisted, her eyes hastily scanning the rows of gold-framed art.

"Paintings, my dear," the old woman answered. "Just common paintings."

"Common? I've never seen art like this," Mara said. She stepped into the corridor slowly, the chambermaid still guiding her lightly by the wrist. All around her, the images in the gilded frames seemed to stare at her, to dance at the tip of her nose, and something in each spoke to her until the echoes in her mind made her dizzy with noise.

One of the paintings showed a woman in white, shoulders draped with a blue cape, sitting on a throne flanked by two pillars—one black and one white. On each of the columns was a symbol that she didn't recognize, nor did either captivate her. Instead, Mara was drawn to the stoic expression on the woman's beautiful face. Her eyes quickly took in the bursts of red and green surrounding the throned woman, before settling on the equal-armed cross on the woman's chest, then at the parchment scroll the image held. Mara moved closer to the painting in an attempt to read the letters on the scroll, but her eyes blurred, and suddenly the entire corridor spun. Darkness spilled in and out of her mind as she closed her eyes and braced herself against the wall, fighting to remain conscious. She could hear the old woman—the chambermaid—calling to her; she could feel the fat woman's hands on her body.

Nausea stabbed at her and she opened her eyes to see the figures of a man and woman, both naked. The two spread their hands toward an angel, emerging from a cloud just above their heads. In the background, rising between the nude pair, was a perfectly symmetrical mountain that Mara reached out and touched. Strobing images drove her to the other side of the corridor—*Mountain...In a bedroom, on the floor. Blood. Blood on her face, on the newspaper clippings...crimson handkerchief...*

Then the racing images were gone, lost to a picture of a woman in green who was sitting near a heart with a female symbol on it. In her hand was a scepter; on her head a crown of stars. The wheat in the foreground stung Mara—*Wind rushing over her, the old man's hands under her back and legs...the circle...wheat...farm and the man with the pretty red box.* A man with a crown of stars, knightly and noble, stood in a chariot guarded by a black sphinx, and a white one. In the background on both sides, the tops of castles—*her favorite spot, looking out over the cold sea...glistening stone...mist in the hills and the man with the silver eyes—Father...shattered glass and blood on the head rest...explosions in her ears...*There was a picture of a naked woman, with flowing blond hair, pouring water from decorated pitchers into a pool. Overhead burned a brilliant star in the night sky, surrounded by seven white stars—*taste of beer in her mouth...party hats and singing...circle of people...candles...stranger beside her...so familiar...*

She pressed her opens hands against the sides of her face as the pressure built in her skull. She could see nothing now but the framed paintings and the vicious pounding of the visions. Where were they coming from? She didn't understand; she didn't recognize most of the visions flashing like disjointed memories. Memories? They weren't hers, she thought. They couldn't be. She would have remembered them. Yet, despite her confusion and rejection, she could not deny the mysterious familiarity she had with the visions. Though she didn't believe they were her memories, there was still something about them that she recognized, if only vaguely...

Another image rushed on her—a naked woman, wrapped in a purple cloth, holding a double helix in each hand, suspended in a green wreath. Then two children, a boy and a girl, naked and holding hands while the happy-faced sun looked down on them—*howl of wolves...a woman screaming...gunshots...*Rising from a tomb, a child raised its hands toward a trumpeting angel. On either side of him, a woman and a man also rose up from what must have been death—*wailing baby and gunshots…explosions of light…smell of antiseptic leaks into her nose…*

Mara fell to her knees, trembling. The sweat on her brow ran down her face, mingling with her tears. At once the chambermaid reached for her, grabbing the young woman firmly by the arms and pulling at her. In a rise of anger, Mara glared up at the old woman, only to see the final image in her view—that of the devil sitting with the talons of a large bird, high above the chained images of a disrobed woman and man. Both wore horns, as well as loose chains, around their necks. Nestled in the long horns of the beast was a pentagram—*faster now…the silver…the old man…young man…dead in the car…pretty red box…silver eyes…silver eyes…*

Mara raised herself from the floor, shoving the chambermaid against the wall, and sprinted down the corridor back toward the bedroom. She didn't know where she was going. She only ran as fast she could. Instinct commanded her now, and she was all too willing to let it guide her through the unknown hallways and rooms.

A flight of stairs, far in the back of the building, led her to the first floor, to an unmarked exit. She exploded through the door and into the blindness of the brilliant sunlight. Falling forward, she rolled across the sand, her body coming to rest in a thicket of sea grass.

The ocean.

She could hear the ocean, crashing against the shriek of the alarm sounding in the stairwell behind her. Her eyes barely accustomed to the bright light, she struggled to her feet, knowing where the water was, tasting the salty ocean in her throat. Once she was on the beach, only yards from where she'd fallen, she ran through the wet sand, racing away from the house—from the villa. Glancing over her shoulder, the sun outlined the structure in clear, sharp lines, beautifully built of white stone with balconied windows, a terrace, and a clay tile roof.

Fading in and out of the ocean spray, Mara continued on. She still had no idea where she was going—no idea where her feet would take her. Other buildings—villas and cottages—rose on the ridgeline above her. She would have to make it over the ridge. She would have to disappear beyond the houses and somehow find a way back home.

Her heart pounded against her ribcage at the sound of thunder behind her. From the direction of the villa, a helicopter swept into view, flying lowly over the ocean. It was coming for her; she knew it. In a desperate effort, she clawed at the sea grass as she struggled up a hill toward the houses beyond. Stumbling to the top, Mara ran for the first buildings she saw, frantically slapping at windows and doors as the helicopter beat overhead. The wind from its blades drove down on her and blasted sand and gravel into her face. No answer, no movement came from the houses, so she darted down the alley and toward the daylight at the end. She could see cars passing by, people talking in the streets.

Emerging into the bustle of the town, she drew in deep breaths in an attempt to slow the beating of her heart and restore her exhausted body. The helicopter was gone. She hadn't seen it fly away, and she wasn't naïve enough to let down her guard. Instead, trying to appear as normal as possible, she brushed the hair out of her eyes, straightened her blouse, and crossed the street to a café. She found an empty table near the walk and pulled out the wrought iron chair, wanting to sit for a moment and gather her senses. But before she could do so, the sound of screeching tires startled her. A black car jolted to a stop at the curb on the other side of the street. Two men in suits quickly exited the vehicle and jogged threateningly toward her.

In a moment she was gone again, running through the crowds, through the streets. She turned a corner and stopped, panic-stricken, confused. She stepped forward, her mind screaming for her to change directions again, to stop turning in the street. She felt trapped, like a wild animal, her head spinning from one strange face to another, her heart charging at each noise, every sound.

"*Mara!*"

A heavy hand came down on her shoulder, and with savagery in her eyes, she flung herself into the arms of the man in a cotton suit. His narrow eyes, crystal blue, suddenly calmed her, and putting an arm around her, he ushered her back onto the street.

"I'll protect you," he said, moving them lithely through the crowd.

"Who are you?"

"A friend," he answered. "I know why you're here, and the identity of the man who kidnapped you."

Mara pushed herself out of the man's arms and slapped him away from her. "Who are you?" she yelled.

Heads turned as he came at her, but no one moved to rescue her.

"I'm not responsible for you being here," he insisted, "but if we don't go now, those who are will catch you." He took her by the arm, drawing her into him again. "This may seem absurd, but I'm asking you to trust me." They continued down the street. "I know your family. I've been tracking you for a long time, and I knew this day would come. Someone wants to harm you, and it isn't me. Let me get you to safety, and then we'll talk. But you have to cooperate. I have a car on the next block. I'll take you…"

A gunshot echoed behind them. Pedestrians screamed and scattered for cover.

"They're coming," the stranger breathed. "Quickly, we have to go."

He pulled her into the street and led her to the opposite corner while the two men pursued them, firing at will. As their feet hit the cobblestone sidewalk, another car—a limousine—came to a screeching halt at the corner and they ducked for cover.

CHAPTER 21

As the limousine sped through the small winding roads, Andrew began to doze. The sway of each turn was like being rocked in a cradle as his tired body sunk deeper into the luxurious leather seats. Far too exhausted from the long flight and mentally drained from a mind in overdrive, he succumbed to the temptation of sleep.

Andrew.

He knew the voice of the companion and teacher. His journal was filled with enigmatic lectures and symbols that seemed to be leading him to—he had no idea where it was leading.

"Yes, Mantrella," he answered in the silence of his sleeping mind.

Open your eyes.

Mantrella's voice was always so mesmerizing, his requests impossible to deny. Andrew knew that when he opened his eyes, he would still be asleep. He had become accustomed to dreams within dreams.

His eyelids slowly opened in hesitant anticipation of this latest revelation. Even in sleep, the image that was before him caused a sharp inhalation of surprise and awe—a person, perhaps male or maybe female, of such intense beauty that he almost felt ashamed to turn his human eyes to it.

The translucent creature appeared to sleep. It lay beneath a tree of such proportion that it defied imagination. Strange and mythical beings abounded—unicorns, centaurs, dragons, the phoenix, griffins and other unknown, but wonderful life forms all around it.

Every feature of this being was in exact proportion, and the use of the word "perfection," he thought, was as mediocre as calling the sun "warm." Its skin was ephemeral, a wisp of cosmic fabric that provided form to something almost formless. What appeared to be human organs each had its own color following the spectrum of the rainbow. An unbelievably beautiful ruby red in the groin led to the purest white above the head. Each center of color pulsed in harmony with, and in tones of the musical scale. What would have been blood was a flow of ether, nous, life force, and each breath was in keeping with the tide of time, birth, death, and rebirth.

These things he simply knew.

The cortex sparkled like billions of electric impulses, and within those flashes Andrew caught momentary glimpses of the forces of creation. All life—past, present, and future—rose and fell as it evolved into the next tidal wave of creation, each idea improving on the former as it melded into an ever-changing tapestry. Every end was a beginning, and every beginning an end that vibrated along a continuous line of existence.

The eyes were hypnotic. Swirling galaxies erupted like supernovas sucked into black holes on one end, then reforming at the other, the process synchronized with every beat of a double helix heart containing the blueprint of all that there was to be. Yet in the totality of this perfection, there was something missing. In the helix was an empty space, a hole as dark as the deepest abyss.

A black hole.

"Andrew."

Deep from his sense of rapture the voice emerged, dragging him away from the godlike image.

"Who was that?" Andrew asked drowsily.

"Adam," the voice responded sorrowfully. "The Anthropos."

Andrew's mind whirred like a computer on a data search as he sifted through his internal files. This, too, he knew, somewhere in his mind.

Anthropos—the archetype or spiritual essence of humanity. The Gnostic Valentinius believed that when God revealed Itself, It was in the form of Anthropos, meaning humanity or the primal father or beginning. They maintained that Jesus was the Son of Anthropos, Son of Man...

A sudden veering of the limo and a rapid acceleration jolted him back to reality. Another sharp turn sent him skittering across the seat as the sliding tires threatened a rollover. Abruptly the vehicle came to a halt, tires screaming across the surface of the poorly paved road.

Andrew's head slammed against the window, and his body twisted, sending him into the privacy divider that separated him from the drivers. Aching, vision slightly blurred, he steadied himself in the cabin and moved to the back window to see what was happening.

Then he saw her. She was tucked under the arm of a stranger, being shot at by the very two who had taken him away from the airport. He pounded on the glass, trying to get her attention. *It has to be her*, he thought. He knew the long black hair. The slender form. The movement of her body. And when she glanced, for only a fraction of a second, in the direction of the limousine, he saw the flash of her green eyes. He pounded harder on the window, but it was useless; the force of his fists merely absorbed into the protective glass in dull thuds.

Then she was gone—a ghost dissipating with the stranger into the streets, while two men with weapons drawn pursued them.

The limousine lurched forward and was moving again, rapidly, away from the corner. Andrew slid down into the seat, chest aching, mind racing. He felt scared, uncertain, and anxious. Deep in his gut bubbled an unsettling feeling, one of absolute dread for the well-being of a woman he didn't even know.

Nothing made sense. He bent his head into the ice bucket and vomited.

CHAPTER 22

Andrew began to sweat shortly after the dramatic incident in the town. He could still smell the faint scent of vomit in the limousine, but he couldn't exactly open a window and air out the space. Instead, he squirmed in the sticky warmth of the cabin, unbuttoning his shirt and wiping his face with the palms of his hands.

The limo moved quickly as he stared blankly at the wall of trees rushing across the tinted windows. It was all he saw for many minutes—trees. Then they disappeared, giving way to a rocky landscape, scattered with patches of brown grass and bushes. The ocean churned silently in the hazy distance. Soon he felt the vehicle slow, coming almost to a complete stop, then half of a wrought iron gate, hinged to a large stone column, crept by the window.

Were on the grounds of an estate, he thought.

A beautifully manicured lawn with colorful beds of flowers and fruit trees passed beside the car. His windows buzzed, dropping open two inches, both startling and refreshing him as cool air hurried into the cabin, carrying with it the distinct odor of the ocean.

A bend in the drive brought into view a white stone villa. From the spread of its clay tile roof to its corner towers, the building was majestic. Large square windows, crowned with half-round glass, looked down on him like a many-eyed structure carefully watching the limo approach. The vehicle finally came to rest beneath a vaulting carport whose canopy was supported by a dozen smooth, round columns. Directly in Andrew's line of sight was the front door made of thick timbers and steel strapping, set at the top of a sweeping stone staircase.

The car door swung open. The woman stood in the doorway, her long bleached hair now pulled away from her face and tied into a ponytail. She grinned at him, and his eyes moved slowly from her pretty face to the pistol holstered under her arm.

"We're here," she said.

Pushing his legs out the door, he slid forward, forcing himself to stand. His muscles ached and he still felt like he was in motion, rumbling over the road, yet the cool breeze, moving comfortingly over his body and through his hair, was a gift he chose not to return in exchange for another ride through hell in the cabin of the limousine.

"He's waiting inside," the large black man said deeply. He appeared from behind the vehicle, his engulfing shadow sliding over Andrew. Reached a large hand behind Andrew, he shoved the door closed in one powerful break of his wrist. Then he stepped away, returning to the driver's side and disappearing into the car. The woman moved to the front passenger door. She smiled at him again, her glance inching over his body, before she, too, disappeared into the limousine.

As the vehicle rolled away, Andrew was left alone on the walk, gazing up at the large front door. He looked behind him—at the lawn, the flowers and trees. He had to admit that it was beautiful, and that it somehow comforted him, leveling his pulse and stomach. The scent of salt water stung his nostrils, and he could hear the sound of the crashing surf somewhere beyond the massive stone structure before him.

The slow, steady groan of the front door drew his attention back to the villa. A short, aged man in a white suit, peered down at him. Very thin, the white suit only accentuated the deep tan in his face and hands.

"Hello," Andrew called tentatively.

The old man nodded once, then gestured for Andrew to enter the house. Though his mind raced with a thousand reasons why he shouldn't enter the house, his will pushed him on, and he heeded the desires of the strange little man, making his way up the steps and into the villa.

Andrew stepped into a spacious foyer, laid in marble tile and decorated in intricate plaster reliefs, displaying what appeared to be scenes of Roman life. To either side and continuing down the hallway were sets of oak doors, leading, he suspected, to large dens and parlors, and beyond, he could see that the hallway opened into a large room with a curved staircase and a marble fountain.

The door closed behind him, and the old man moved quickly to a set of oak doors on Andrew's left. Sliding the panels open, he leaned his head toward the revealed den, as if to invite the newly-arrived guest into the room.

"I'm looking for Giovanni," Andrew said, more loudly than he meant to, his voice resounding into the domed ceiling. "Monsignor Giovanni," he continued more softly. "I was told I would be taken to him."

Raising a hand to his mouth, every movement deliberate, the old man coughed once before smiling at Andrew. "I'm Giovanni," he answered, in accented English.

"You're Giovanni?"

The old man nodded again. "Yes," he said, "but I am no minister of God. I'm only the butler."

"Then who…"

"Come," the little man said. "Sit in here and wait. The one who wants you will arrive shortly."

Andrew hesitated. "Wait a minute. Why am I here?"

"Please, sir," the man insisted, "Come, sit. Soon enough you'll know exactly why you're here."

He studied Giovanni's face for a moment, before reluctantly entering the den. The old man slid the doors closed and disappeared with the view of the foyer. While waiting Andrew examined the room. It reminded him of a typical English library, with its tall bookcases lined with hundreds of leather-bound volumes accented in gold leaf. The high, timber-strapped ceiling created an effect that mimicked the inside hull of a wooden ship, and a heavy desk and coffee table were perfectly complimentary. Weary, he sat in one of the two chairs facing the desk and the large window behind it. The sky had grown subtly darker since he'd arrived some minutes before, and he noticed the tops of the trees swaying rhythmically in the wind. Drawn to the movement of the natural world outside the window, Andrew's mind began to wander, to drift through the countless thoughts he'd had over the past few days. Then, like a sting in the arm, he remembered the face of the woman in the town. He heard the gunshots all around him again. And he knew it. It must have been her...he remembered...

The den doors opened and Giovanni entered.

"Sir," he said, "I present to you *Don Mantrella*."

Mantrella?

He rose slowly from his chair, pulse quickening, heart thumping. It couldn't be real.

He knew the name. And it knew him.

From the dreams...

From the...

It was as if Andrew's blood froze as the man, tall, slender, and silver-eyed, stepped through the doorway and extended a hand and a smile to his honored guest.

CHAPTER 23

The closer Mantrella came to him, the farther back Andrew stepped, until at last his back was against a bookcase and Mantrella was standing directly before him.

"Andrew," the man said, smiling, his silver eyes glistening. He reached out and clapped his hands to Andrew's shoulders, squeezing them. "Finally, we meet in person."

Andrew shuddered from the pressure of Mantrella's hands, his own eyes drawn to the man's angular face and slick, shining eyes. Mantrella was tall, much taller than Andrew, and donned in the gray silk suit, his shoulders were broad and square. He was both austere and intimidating.

"You," Andrew uttered. "From my dreams."

Giovanni, standing in the doorway, shuffled backwards into the foyer, and pulled the den doors closed behind him.

Mantrella's smile broadened as he released Andrew's shoulders. Going to the desk, he thumbed nonchalantly through some scattered papers, as if he were routinely checking his mail before settling into the high-backed leather office chair, and crossing his legs. The grin on his lips and the glow in his eyes suggested that he was savoring the moment, the deliberately dramatic pause.

"Please," he said softly, "sit. We have much to talk about, you and me. Would you like a drink?"

"Why am I here?" Andrew asked. He moved cautiously toward a chair to the right of Mantrella's constant gaze.

"I am Don Mantrella," he answered.

Andrew held his breath as frustration and anger built inside of him.

"What is in your heart, Andrew?"

Exhaling, Andrew looked away from Mantrella, trying to sort the emotions within. He could feel, every time he made eye contact with Mantrella, something pulling at him, drawing the life from his body. Against his will, he was moved to answer this man, to acknowledge and accept this unnatural conversation.

"There's something wrong," Andrew said, meeting Mantrella's eyes.

"You are very right." Mantrella tapped the ends of his long, manicured fingers together. "I know what you want to believe about your gods and religion, Andrew. We've talked so many times, felt so many things..."

"In my dreams," Andrew interrupted. He leaned toward the desk adamantly. "I know you from inside my goddamn head! Tell me *how!*"

Mantrella thought a moment, sighing. "Not in your dreams, but in your subconscious," he said. "Let me enlighten such a learned man as you." As he spoke, he wore that signature grin, as if what he said was personally satisfying. "It is not about saving humanity; it has never been," he began frankly.

Easing himself into the chair, Andrew frowned. "What hasn't?" He was warm now, and the heat in his clothes made him uncomfortable.

"*Israel*—or humanity," Mantrella continued eloquently, "is the sum total of a collection of *individuals*. It has no independent existence. You cannot save something that doesn't exist. The whole concept of salvation is nonsensical."

"Salvation from *what*?" Andrew was not following the man's speech, not understanding in it any relevance to his present situation.

"Is this not what troubles us?" Mantrella asked. "You want to be saved right now, don't you? You want to be rescued and returned to where you believe you belong. But tell me, from what would you be saved? The concept of sin or evil is a myth perpetuated by those who would keep you enslaved and prevent the course of human evolution from fulfilling its divine destiny."

"What does this all mean?" Andrew was growing tired, and Mantrella's words only added to the mounting confusion in his brain.

"You must understand that when many individuals choose to be on the same road at the same time, a traffic jam occurs. The traffic jam, like humanity, has no independent existence. The same is true of a nation, or even a religion; each has no independent existence other than what is given by a collection of individuals who have made similar decisions and are willing to share like consequences. You cannot *save* humanity, because it really does not exist."

Andrew rubbed his forehead. "So?"

"Such notions are doomed from their very inception," Mantrella said patiently, "because they are based upon a false premise. The only thing one can be saved from is ignorance, and that is the root of all of your problems. But truth is a personal revelation. When enough people know and understand the truth, then there will be a perception that *humanity* as a whole has changed, or been saved. And while you all have the same destination, you do not travel the same road to get there."

Peering at his host through cloudy eyes, Andrew said, "That's a long way around to a simple point, isn't it?"

"It may be," Mantrella answered. He had not lost his composure, nor the glow in his eyes.

"Religious movements," Andrew said, "have always tried to convince people that their teachings are the truth. They say that their way is the only way to achieve salvation. Usually, through the use of force and some form of physical or mental coercion, they make people follow their dictum and dogma. There's nothing *individual* about it."

"Exactly."

"So," Andrew continued, "based on what you're preaching, their efforts have been in vain."

"You are getting it, Andrew," Mantrella replied. "I've said nothing by accident. You're getting closer to understanding why you are here."

"Tell me why."

"None of the great holy men had any intention of starting a religion or creating a church," Mantrella answered instead. "On the contrary, they insisted that each must find truth and revelation individually. The experience of one cannot be transferred to, or forced upon another. Each experience is individual and perceived individually. An individual that does not experience the embrace of the universe will never know the embrace of himself."

Suddenly, Andrew could hear the pounding surf whispering in his ears. He loved the ocean—its smell and its ceaseless rhythm. Any time he ever sat by the shore he felt at peace and a part of the womb of life. He remembered the great elements of existence merging there. The great pentacle brought to life. There was no question in his own mind that churchianity was inherently wrong, that it enslaved free thinking and was merely a tool to control the masses. His thoughts were beginning to clarify. Perhaps there was no universal teaching, but rather a universal approach to self-discovery. *To save the world it must be done one person at a time*, he thought.

"Correct," Mantrella said.

Andrew stared at him, wide-eyed. "You can hear me thinking, can't you?"

"I can hear many things," the man answered. He grasped the armrests of his chair and stiffened his back. "Now," he said abruptly, "we must go."

"Go?" Andrew responded. "Go where?"

"Away, to find someone that I'm missing."

"But we've only just begun here," Andrew said forcefully. "You trick me into coming here, throw some philosophically irrelevant point at me, then tell me I have to go to God knows where…"

"*He* doesn't."

"To look for someone that you're *missing*. What does that mean, anyway?"

Mantrella crossed his legs again, still grinning. "Relax, Andrew. You seem misled."

"Misled?" he answered emphatically. "You could say that."

"Much is missing, I know," Mantrella said calmly. "Let me pose this question: How does one of your degree and intellect account for all the cloak and dagger that surrounds religious history? The Templars,

Cathars, Masons, the Priory, Knights of Malta, Teutonic Knights, the Rosae Crucis—they didn't suffer the trials and tribulations of the Church, nor remain shrouded in a cloak of secrecy just to protect some notion of personal salvation that you can now find in many bookstores."

Andrew centered his thoughts. Mantrella was now entering into an area that he knew all too well, that he had always suspected was far more important than anything he had ever read. His brain awoke, its neurons firing, and all of his years of study came flowing back to his conscious memory.

"What you're offering me is dime-store theology," Andrew said. He was indignant and angry, mainly at himself for letting Mantrella believe that he could lull Andrew's brain to sleep. Endless worrying over strange dreams, automatic writing, flying all the way to Italy...And what had been accomplished?

He stood and squarely faced Mantrella, his thoughts defiant and confrontational. His host stood, suggesting that both sides were prepared to duel.

What Andrew saw in a sudden flash of light caused his heart to skip. His body became paralyzed with fear. His mouth went dry and his throat painfully constricted. It was only by sheer force of a dwindling will that he didn't piss his pants.

***

General Rami Abdul had little tolerance for two things: chaos and religion. The two, he felt, were inextricably intertwined. Now, as Supreme Commander of UN peacekeeping forces, he had to confront his two demons on a worldwide scale. Since the assassination of the pope gave the appearance of conspiracy, growing tensions and violence were spreading among sects on a global basis. General Abdul was now faced with using his multi-national and multi-religious forces to try to prevent a pandemic of religious upheaval. He couldn't help but wonder if his troops would be willing to use force against their own brethren when they themselves were becoming caught up in the rapidly growing calls for *jihad* and the crusade. If this were not enough, he also had to contend with the growing reports of strange phenomena that were being attributed to everything from the Apocalypse and Second Coming to the wrath of God.

Three days before, when he had questioned how things could possibly get worse, his aide handed him a communiqué from the Secretary General. It simply read, "Dow Jones collapsing—Tokyo, London, German exchanges follow New York—Send 5000 troops to Vatican to restore order and protect civilians." At that moment, the general's nightmare had grown to biblical proportions as he was forced to come face to face with both economic *and* religious chaos.

"Fan them out through the square," he commanded his lieutenant. "Rubber bullets and tear gas." From a rooftop he surveyed the turmoil in St. Peter's Square, while UN tanks and supply wagons groaned through the streets below.

"Yes, sir," the young lieutenant answered, raising a radio to his mouth.

"And Jacques," the general added, his eyes meeting the lieutenant's, "there are to be no casualties. For God's sake, not here."

"Understood, General."

The order was given for one hundred troops in full riot gear to enter the square and to control the crowd. Another two hundred men took positions around the perimeter. The Italian government had petitioned the United Nations to send military support to them, fearing that an overwhelming presence of national troops would foster more outrage among the population. Jews, Moslems, and Christians alike wailed in the square while members of countless countries raged in the streets, burning automobiles and breaking storefront windows. The Vatican had been flooded by protestors, the faithful, and those who deemed the pope's murder a justifiable action.

Either way, General Rami Abdul didn't care.

He was doing his job, and today he would carry out a mission that he'd completed many times before—ensuring human protection and safety. As he examined the crowd through a pair of high-powered binoculars, he was satisfied knowing that the otherwise confrontational crowd seemed to be receiving his soldiers with relative indifference. And just in case the militant civilians hadn't, 4,700 more troops waited just outside the Holy City for orders to mobilize.

"It is going well," he muttered.

"The men have successfully infiltrated the crowd," the lieutenant said. "Delta group is preparing to surround them."

"They are only to observe," the general reminded him. "Only if threatened is force to be used."

"Understood, sir."

An explosion rocked the square, and a twisting band of flame shot up into the humid afternoon.

"What was that?" he demanded.

"Bomb detonated," the lieutenant called frantically to him. "Three men down, sir!"

General Abdul glared through the binoculars again, watching the seizing crowd scatter away from the smoke and flames, a shower of granite raining down on the square. The soldiers had become entangled in the mass hysteria, struggling to keep their hold in the screaming wave of bodies. Then the people turned on the troops, shoving them to the stony ground, throwing rocks, stampeding them.

"Tear gas!" he commanded.

The lieutenant radioed down the order, and canisters of tear gas were released into the crowd. They screamed and covered their heads. Some tore off their shirts and wrapped them around their mouths, but their advance toward the UN soldiers wasn't hindered. Still, they rushed on the soldiers, savagely overpowering them.

"Is the perimeter secure?"

"Yes, sir."

"Delta group subdue the civilians."

The order given, the two hundred men surrounding the square raised their weapons to the crowd and readied for their commander's signal to engage the target. Seconds later, the first of a series of gunshots crackled into the air. Civilians fell, writhing in pain. Screams grew in pitch and intensity. Another rip of gunfire spit over the crowd. And another.

"Target engaged," the lieutenant informed him.

"Keep on them. Put the medical unit on standby."

Shot after shot rang through the Holy City. People continued to go down, clutching at their stomachs, their legs and arms. Others ran, fighting their way through the bodies and darting for the street. Still others fell heavily to the stone, seemingly unconscious. The troops took careful aim, ensuring that their rubber bullets didn't strike vital areas, but only stung each target.

"No," the lieutenant gasped into his radio. He pressed a finger against the receiver in his left ear. "Please repeat."

The general noticed that some of the soldiers had lowered their weapons and were yanking the magazines from them. One had dropped his magazine and was running down the line of soldiers, swatting at his fellow soldiers' M-16s.

"General, sir," the lieutenant choked, stepping toward his superior officer.

The general lowered the binoculars in time to receive the whitened face of the perspiring lieutenant.

"They're real, sir," Lieutenant Jacques sputtered.

"Real?"

"Live rounds, sir."

The general's heart thumped against his ribcage, and he felt his blood run hotly through his temples. Cheeks flushed, he held his breath for a moment as he stared at the young lieutenant's wild eyes.

"I specifically ordered rubber bullets and tear gas *only*," he breathed through clenched teeth.

"They locked and loaded with rubber rounds, sir," Jacques insisted. "Their weapons were checked before deployment."

Rami could hear the hectic voices of his men chirping metallically from the lieutenant's earpiece, horribly mingled with the screams of civilians in the street below.

"Pull them out!" he yelled. "Get them the hell out of there!"

CHAPTER 24

Standing before Andrew, from floor to ceiling, was *Baphomet*. How his mind grasped the name he didn't know, but there stood a creature with cloven feet, the body and arms of a man, and the head of a horned goat. On its brow was a pulsing five-pointed star—the pentagram formed of interlacing triangles—and on its finger, an emerald stone whose luminescent green filled the room. Its breasts were that of a female, though the magnificent beast possessed an obvious male organ.

Frozen in fear, Andrew could not move, nor could he scream anywhere but in his own mind. Then the image softened—the horns retracted, the feet became normal, the chest returned to that of a male, and in its place the specter of the Messiah formed.

A silent, loving command penetrated Andrew's disjointed thoughts. "Sit."

Andrew collapsed into his chair. He blinked to wet his stinging eyes, and in an instant the same man he met in person a short time ago returned, and the illusion was gone. He closed his eyes for a moment, welcoming the flickering darkness, then hesitantly, he opened them, fearing the apparitions would appear again.

Mantrella spoke softly. "If you had not questioned or challenged me, I would never have revealed such an image. The trait within you must not be recessive if we are to continue. All indications were that dominance had finally been achieved, but one can never be too certain."

The young professor heard the words, but he didn't understand their intended meaning. Recessive trait? Dominance? "I still don't understand. I can't...." Recovering from cold sweats, moisture was gradually returned to his constricted throat, and, while still pounding, his heart began to beat more evenly.

"It is time for the truth to be known," Mantrella replied. He walked to the window and glanced up at the darkening sky. "You have been driven all of your life by the pursuit of personal revelation. Your quest nears its end." He paused, choosing carefully the thoughts to be spoken.

"Because of the pressures of time," he continued, "this will have to be the short version, but it should be sufficient for your immediate needs. Clear your mind and follow this story closely."

Andrew settled into the cushions of the chair. His body drained, he felt strangely relaxed, almost sleepy. As Mantrella sat and placed his elbows on the desk, his words fell on Andrew in a cascade of soothing tones that removed all extraneous thought. Without realizing it, the only point of focus in Andrew's world at this moment became Mantrella.

"Man has been led to believe that all creation was for him," Mantrella explained. "Not even knowing his own true history, he was convinced that the cosmos was created for him and revolves around him. Know this—there are levels of godhood. That which is behind all that there is is unknowable, even to the gods. The universes, seen and unseen, are thoughts made manifest. When, where, and why the thought of a physical universe first came to be is not knowable."

He pulled open a desk drawer and withdrew a heavy volume of the Bible. Opening the book, he read, "In the beginning, God…" Pausing, he met Andrew's gaze, then slapped the Bible shut. "These words in the Christian Bible refer to a god in time. The Unknowable All is beyond time. The god in question—the one *in the beginning*—is not *the* god. Nonetheless, being a god, Its thoughts create a reality. You see, the purpose of the gods is to express the creative power inherent in all things. The Unknowable has no desire, no wants, likes or dislikes. It is totally impersonal, and anything I can say about It is inaccurate, because any words used place limits upon It, and It has no limits.

"What you call 'God' created man in Its mind, in Its *own image* or imagination. If your Bible had been read and understood as allegorical, much pain and suffering could have been avoided. The gods speak in pictures and sounds. They do not have a propensity to write or give dictation. Know also that much preceded what you call *Genesis*, and that *Genesis* is not specific to our earth.

"Man, being both male and female, as is the imagination of his creator, is a *godseed*. In him is the potential for the manifestation of all of the laws of the universe. Man is a god in the making. As the Word that cannot be spoken vibrated the universe into existence as if on the wings of the eternal butterfly, the physical began to manifest itself, requiring for its survival polarity—positive and negative. To the bane of man's history, you have been deceived into believing that this polarity means good and bad. This could not be further from the truth. God did the job and created spiritual man, being both male and female, and gave him all of the spiritual things that were needful. It was done. Because that which is infinite cannot enter the finite, God cannot enter time or physical space which is finite and limiting—your perceived *reality*. Then the Lord God, a being of a slightly lower vibration, continued God's creative process, making the stage for all the world to play its part."

"'All the world's a stage,'" Andrew mumbled, "'and all the men and women merely players.'"

Mantrella's eyes sparkled. "'They have their exits and entrances,'" he added, "'and one man in his time plays many parts, his acts being seven ages.'"

"William Shakespeare," Andrew said.

"Yes, Francis Bacon," Mantrella countered, "but that's a different subject entirely. You see, the Lord God created a garden, a place of life. In this garden was born the possibility of the physical world, duality. The Tree of Life and the Tree of Knowledge, the Yin and Yang, positive and negative, were the potentials created at this level of creation. In a manner of speaking, this was my birthplace."

"Did you say *your* birthplace?"

Raising an open hand, Mantrella silenced Andrew. "Please, let me explain. The thoughts of the gods and the godlike are real. What is imagined takes on eternal life and it, too, becomes a creator. As above, so below, the macro and the microcosm are one. Are you following this?"

"Go on," Andrew answered flatly. "I'm anxious to hear what you think you know."

Mantrella grinned at the challenge. "We are now in a plane of existence called the Garden of Eden. In this place is the Lord God, and at an even lower vibration, the Lords. Here lies the Anthropos, Adam Kadman, both male and female. The Lords are the upper hierarchy of the angelic realm, me included."

Andrew leaned forward in his chair. "Are you trying to tell me that you're…"

"Something very different from what you are used to," Mantrella replied. "And if you look within yourself, Andrew, you will come to see that what I say is real. The Lords were given the opportunity to partake of free will, which is inherent in all created things, since it is the nature of the creator. Some saw no need for free will and chose to simply be of service to the Lord God. They would not cross the *Veil*, for they feared the idea of feeling separated from the Source of their creator."

"And this is the Veil?" Andrew questioned, raising his arms to all that surrounded them in the den.

"Not exactly. The Veil is that space between reality and actuality, your world and ours. Even though the Lords knew that the feeling of separation was illusory, they simply could not break conscious contact with the Light. Remember, the manifestation of the physical requires duality — positive and negative. However, the negative has no actuality. In effect, the negative does not really exist as anything more than a concept. If there is only light, it is impossible to know that light exists unless the idea of no light, or darkness, is introduced. But darkness is a *non-thing* and has no *real* existence."

"There can be no concept of good unless you introduce the notion of something less than good," Andrew said. "Hot means nothing without cold, up without down, right without left. There could not be a chair unless there was no chair."

"Perfect," Mantrella commended, proud of his new student, "but there is no such thing as *no chair*," he clarified. "You cannot possess such a thought. The physical is made manifest, or is defined by, what it is *not* — its opposite. Since the opposite is something that is not, its existence is an illusion; it has *reality*, but not *actuality*. In the so-called *spiritual* realm, all things potentially exist and can only be made manifest when a place opens within which a single potential — a thing — can be made to appear. Consequently, man had two options: remain as potential, a seed; or partake of life and flower to achieve a level of godhood, based upon the experience of the manifest world.

"When Adam was formed, the angels — the Lords — bowed to the perfection of his potential. I did not. I will only bow when the potential is made manifest. There was no fall, no sin, and no banishment. When presented with the choice, Adam — humanity — chose the Tree of Knowledge. Man chose to undertake the journey into the physical world, to cross the Veil and to enter an evolutionary path that began in a state of forgetfulness. The Prodigal embarked upon his path of wisdom, and the rest stayed home, fearful of such a journey. Man was to experience separation, isolation, individuality, the positive and the negative. Adam went to sleep and to this day has still not awakened. I placed the seed of knowledge into the Vessel, Eve, and she told Adam to open his eyes, and she gave him Knowledge. Man would go where gods could not, and where the angels dared not."

"Wait a minute. Are you telling me that you're the devil?" Andrew asked solemnly.

"I expected more from someone who is so much more," Mantrella replied. "Man's devils are as ridiculous as his whims. The seed was placed within man, and he was given a living garment, flesh and blood, to hold the seed of *humanity-to-be*. We did not fall; we volunteered to accompany man on his journey through the trials and tribulations of this drama in which the universe would experience the glory of its nature in a physical world and through the conscience of man."

Wiping his forehead, Andrew felt like he was melting into the chair. "This is a lot of information," he said at last.

Mantrella nodded. "Yes, but you have always known these things, Andrew. You also know that I was appointed as Prince of the World and as the Bringer of Light, the Morning Star."

"How have I known?" Andrew asked tentatively. He knew that no matter what the answer might be, either way it would change his life forever.

"We share a birthright of *the* common seed," Mantrella said.

"We're related?" Andrew questioned, his voice slightly cracking in the revelation.

Mantrella sat back in his chair and considered the Boston College professor in front of him. "Let's just say," he answered, "that our blood has touched."

Andrew was anxious, uncomfortable, and believed only half of what was being said to him.

"I would light man's way through the very darkness that I had to create," Mantrella went on. "My seed, the seed of light, was placed within humanity through Eve, also called Isis. The genetic code is the hermit on the mount. And so *Baphomet*, the Father of Wisdom and the Temple of Peace, was placed in humanity until the end of time. And Eve got a man-child with the help of the Lord. It is this code that is the subject of intense genetic research."

"This is only a new twist on an old story," Andrew remarked. "How many different ways can someone reinvent Genesis?"

Mantrella ignored him. Instead, he said, "Michael fought for me to stay."

"The Archangel Michael?" There was a numbness working its way into his head, and he found himself consciously keeping himself focused. He hadn't been able to identify the feeling, the muddiness, but he wondered if there was something in the air that Mantrella might be using to drug him, to draw him away from his senses. The course and tone of the conversation was changing. He could hear it in the way Mantrella's speech had become quietly solemn. No longer did the noble with the silver eyes grin like when he was at first revealing the foundation of his explanation. No, this was serious now, and Andrew could feel the gravity of the situation sitting heavily in his chest, yet something in Mantrella's voice, in his expression, worried Andrew, because slowly he was beginning to realize that what the man was saying just might be true. He was willing, at least, to hear him out.

"Yes," Mantrella said. "Michael saw the completion of the dream and man's ascension to godhood as an end. Man was the pinnacle of creation as he embodied the heavenly archetype. His greatness would surpass that of the Lords. Michael lived to serve his creator, not the creation that would surpass him in glory. We argued and parted company as adversaries. I entered the *Magnum Opus* with man to complete the work of the Grand Architect. Thus began the great illusion. I, and those with me who became known as Watchers, planted more seeds in the daughters of man so that as the scenes of the great play progressed, that which was hidden would one day be revealed; the recessive would become the dominant when evolution was ready for its quantum leap."

"Angels and demons," Andrew uttered. "But how do I know which is which?"

"The early days were a time of wonder," Mantrella continued. "A great race was in the making, but it contained only half of the code. Their lives were filled with trials, tribulations, and temptations of the physical world. We tempted them not away from the light, but forced them to discover it, choose it, and spread it of their own free will. They made choices and took responsibility for those choices. There was no good and evil, simply positive and negative. It was a time of giants. Not large creatures, but giants of the heart, courage and daring. They became the inhabitants of your myth and folklore. Civilization grew and flourished in Lemuria and Atlantis. Even more primitive spirits and creatures thrived. Some returned to the Source when their lessons and growth were complete. Some continue to evolve even to the present. The dream world, this land of illusion, came close to completing the cycle in which the tide of existence could gradually begin to return to its beginning and prepare for its next journey on the Great Spiral."

"I still don't completely understand."

"Adam is sleeping, Andrew. We are his dream, existing in it and of it. When he comes to realize his own existence, then we will move onto the next spiritual plane. But, and I dread the thought, if he is awakened before the dream has run its course, then we are doomed, all of us."

Andrew stiffened his back and moved to the edge of his seat. What he had feared, was happening—he was being drawn in, one image at a time—and he welcomed it.

"How are we doomed?" he questioned.

Mantrella finally grinned again, but there was no self-satisfaction in it. "A dream unfinished," he said, "is a creation unfulfilled."

"The dream," Andrew mused, "is in all of us. I can dream, so…"

"And so you create," Mantrella interrupted the thought. "Is it not written in your law, I said, Ye are gods?"

It was Andrew's turn to grin. "Words of Jesus in the *Gospel of John*."

"Of course," Mantrella said, "he was simply echoing a notion already centuries old."

"And you?" Andrew asked. "You are an angel, so to speak. In our literature and lore, you present yourself as the engine of evil. You are, by very definition, the representation of all that is bad."

"And hence we delve into the great fallacy that there is such a thing as evil," Mantrella warned. "Polarity, Andrew. Remember polarity." He took a deep breath. "So deep and corrupting are the dogmas of man's so-called *religions*." He shook his head, obviously irritated. Narrowing his eyes, he stared at Andrew. "I have done nothing but sacrifice for mankind, no matter what image has been perpetuated about me."

"So where did you get the bad rap? It wasn't you, it was the other guy. Right?"

Mantrella gazed at him for a moment, his eyes blank. Grinning, he said, "How awful it must be to feel like a human, Andrew."

Andrew smiled self-consciously. "What do you mean?"

"So limited. So base and self-absorbed." Mantrella rose from his seat and circled the desk, a long finger tracing the edge of its top. He stood over Andrew, and his shadow, as if having life itself, slithered over the awed man's body. "You have no idea the realm you are about to enter, the play in which you will be forced to star."

He eased himself into the chair beside Andrew and crossed his legs again, relaxing his body. "Understand that when my kind descends into matter, much is sacrificed," he said. "The descent dampens our abilities immensely, and while we can still extend our perception beyond the Veil, it is but a wisp of sight. It is this Veil that gives man his sense of isolation, but for the Prodigal to succeed, it must be. The Hosts did not descend out of fear. They can now stay only briefly on the physical plane. They can, however, manipulate the unseen forces of nature quite readily. This they did with a vengeance, and they are doing it again."

"Who?" Andrew replied abruptly.

Mantrella stiffened, and he seized Andrew's wrist, gripping it with such force that Andrew winced in pain. "The Others, the Lords who would not make the sacrifice to guide mankind," he breathed, "they are the enemy, Andrew. Hear me!"

He released Andrew's wrist, throwing the man's arm over his lap. Automatically, Andrew rubbed the tender joint as Mantrella left his seat and went to the window.

"I will not go into detail," he said, gazing out into the evening haze, "but to preserve their own status, and out of what they felt was in God's best interest, we fought. But this was not until they had destroyed two continents, flooded vast areas of others, and shifted what was once a great civilization to a frozen wasteland. It happened so fast and without warning that we barely prevented the destruction of all of humanity. The epic *Mahabharata* is perhaps the most accurate account of events in those days. All have heard of the Great Flood, or Deluge, as it appears in the *myths* of all great cultures. Free will has its good and bad, or should I say positive and negative points. God would not, could not interfere. It does not violate Its own laws. All of what happened was and is part of the *Magnum Opus*."

"The Great Work," Andrew said, flexing his wrist to restore the circulation.

Mantrella went on. "Remnants survived and were hidden, but much was lost to this angelic-induced destruction. Look to sacred texts and you will find that almost all destruction and plagues are the result of angelic action. Even in the much misunderstood book of *Revelation,* the seals are opened and the destruction caused by angels. It is they who are the great deceivers. With so much lost in these early disasters, new mating had to occur with non-evolved creatures, and man began again on a much slower and more difficult path of remembrance. The great ark was symbolic of the preserving of the seed and the genetic code. The helix, the pairs, the chromosomes buried in a primitive substance did not really know how to emerge. Being on the alert, the Lords had to choose a new course of action: control the mind and you control the dream. In a way, this became easier for them. Once the descent into matter occurred, we were no longer able to instill our seed directly into the genetic pool. Our interaction with Adam was confined to the physical plane. Adam had to create, in his dream reality, man in *his* own image. Thus the line of Seth emerged. My line—the line of Cain—was greatly decimated. Those of the godseed scattered far and wide and founded the later civilizations of the Egyptians, the Aztecs, Incas, Mayans, the Hopi and Anasasi, and on and on."

He paused, breathing deeply, as if the story demanded more energy than his body possessed. "The effort has been the interbreeding of those two lines so that one day the ripening would occur."

As thick night bloomed over the ocean and lamplight shined in the panes of the large den window, Mantrella continued his story, dedicated to the turning of Andrew's beliefs. As he recounted his version of *Genesis*, Andrew's mind swarmed with images.

He had not moved from his seat, had not so much as shifted, and now, his eyes growing heavy, Andrew saw the beauty of the ancient lost civilizations. He saw no churches, but rather gardens and temples of meditation—a world of gnosis where each performed a priestly function to those who might still be struggling with understanding. There was no dogma, only an ever-evolving sense of enlightenment.

Then the earth shook and the Gardens of Hesperides sank to the ocean depths. Part of a great continent broke off and slid to the bottom of the earth, to be encased in thousands of feet of ice. When the seas quieted, the Ark that contained the future seed of the world emerged, and life began once again to embark on its sacred journey.

As new civilizations arose under the tutelage of the remaining Watchers and those that survived the flood, the Lords were able to twist and corrupt the truth. He saw them forcing the hands of scribes, creating and revealing false premonitions, dictating canon lies through the mouths of traitors. Their aim was to keep man in a constant state of darkness and ignorance, and to prevent the Awakening in which the place of the Lords in the universe would be questionable. The Veil pulsed and sweat in the Lords' fear of extinction.

Andrew understood that it was They who created the strict commandments, the rituals and practices required to appease a vengeful god which They created, but which did not exist. By instilling fear, They manipulated the flock. Their priests were the only path to so-called salvation, and as long as the people fed the church and did its bidding, the sheep were guaranteed a place in some non-existent heaven. Testaments of truth brought forward were burned, prophets were slain, and teachings perverted. Inquisitions arose, and crusades were waged.

Wisdom went underground, hidden in secret texts and in pictures passed down through the generations. The initiated formed hidden groups to preserve the truth and light, lest they be persecuted and slain. Those who did the bidding of the Lords built great temples to appease their god of hate, and a great shadow was cast on the mind of man. Avatars appeared to lead the weary back to knowledge, but as quickly as they arose, there were those ready to pervert their teachings.

Andrew could feel the darkness in his heart, and his blood ran hot with anger. He shook his head, trying to throw off the dread, the irons of suppression. His mind swam in chaos, only to become slowly ordered as he heard the words of Mantrella.

"One of them made a major error," he was saying. "Mary was of the line of Cain, my line. Mary had a child with the help of the Lord. In this case, the Lord was Gabriel. I incarnated with the DNA of both lines. My DNA was diluted in Mary from generations of intermarriage. It would take a thousand years to rebuild the code in humanity.

"As Jeshua, I came to reveal the truth, to dispel the myth of the vengeful god and to provide the map for humanity's ascension to its rightful place in the universe—*Did I not say ye are gods*? Only my closest followers understood my message, and even they were hard to convince. Michael set out to destroy me, turning Pilate against me. He worked on those in the temple to have me silenced. Pilate saw the truth in the end. It was not I that drank the gall and suffered the nails. My public teaching had to come to an end, so I returned to the Essene community, and there we laid the plans that may now come to fruition.

"But Michael was to have his way. He labeled me a martyr and a savior and built a church that would control human destiny. The worship of human suffering was his creed, and my teachings were twisted to keep all in a state of ignorance, and now, when there was a pope who was to reveal the truth, they had him killed."

Andrew's back stiffened. "Peter," he breathed.

Mantrella nodded and faced him squarely. "On the advent of the pontiff's murder, I realized that now more than ever mankind's ascension is threatened. I needed you, Andrew, so I had you summoned under false pretenses.

"My purpose is so immediate because something else happened that the Lords did not discover until it was too late," Mantrella added. "Mary gave birth to Sara, and the combined seed survived well after I shed my earthly skin. To that end, my line has continued to the present, guarded by those who would keep the temple as pure as possible. Throughout the generations, careful breeding has been instrumental in purifying the strain in order to bring the recessive genes into dominance."

Andrew rose and began to wander the room as he sought a distraction to calm his firing neurons. *Ignorance is indeed bliss,* he thought, *and those who never question things might go through life suffering the slings and arrows of outrageous fortune, but they somehow seem happier than those who dare to take arms against them.*

"This is too much," he whispered.

Mantrella looked at his hands. "Forgive me," he said. "I am nearly at the end of what you must know." He closed his eyes and breathed deeply, sorting his thoughts, then he said, "The Church tried to end the line in their attempt to destroy the Knights Templar, the Cathars, the Militia Crucifera, and others. Their silence during the Second World War was also an attempt to end a line they thought contained the code of light. Even now, their scientists have almost completely decoded the human genome in search of the godseed. If they find it, they will destroy it."

Halting before multiple leather-bound volumes of Augustine's writings, Andrew slowly turned toward Mantrella. "And then?"

"Destroy the seed, preserve the illusion forever."

"And the Lords remain powerful."

"You and Mara are God-bloods," Mantrella explained.

"Mara?" Andrew asked in disbelief as fleeting images of the young woman's beautiful face, her long black hair and brilliant green eyes, flickered through his mind.

Mantrella stood, meeting Andrew's gaze. He felt the connection now, saw in the man's face the survival of the code of light, of the God-bloods, and he could feel the understanding and acceptance. "The two of you can activate the seed."

"Activate the seed?" he questioned. "How?"

"The pope was murdered because he was of the line. If he was able to proclaim your union and explain the true history of humanity, we would all have been on our way home by now."

"Union?" Andrew stepped closer to Mantrella.

"We must find Mara," Mantrella said. "You have sought your precipitating event, and I believe you now have it."

"But, you're telling me that you are..." Andrew paused, searching for the words.

"Yes," Mantrella answered frankly.

"So that beast thing a while ago was not my imagination?"

"No, it was my imagination," Mantrella said. "That is the image They like to give me—an evil monster ready to devour all. This is how They scare the children." He smiled, moving toward the desk. "I am negative, not evil," he reminded Andrew. "Evil has no inherent existence. If it did, then the universe would be just the battleground of opposing gods. I am the Bringer of Light, a messiah."

"And I am part of you." Andrew waited for an answer, and when none came, he pursued Mantrella.

"I met her. Did you arrange that?" he asked.

Mantrella grinned, glancing away from Andrew. "No," he said. "Somehow we lose track of her periodically. How Michael does this I do not know. If we had known she was there, we would have been on the verge of completing our quest. We have been her protector since birth, awaiting the ripening of her age and seed. Even as a child, she had a knack for vanishing unexpectedly." He studied Andrew's face. "Somehow we always found her again; she always found her way back."

"Good versus evil, the greatest conspiracy of all time," Andrew said contemplatively. He dropped into his chair again.

"Michael's minions created the churches and mosques to do their bidding, to keep humanity in darkness when it was their destiny to rise out of it."

"The mosques?"

"This is not just a Christian conspiracy. As Mohammed, I gave the truth to the east. As Buddha, to Asia. I have been the Serpent of truth and wisdom in every major culture. Sadly, only the native peoples and some of the followers of Zen have managed to keep any semblance of the true teachings. For most, the truth had to be kept secret."

Andrew stared at the window and wrapped his mind into its darkness. He did, after all, believe that some form of intelligence guided all things. Mantrella's *All* let loose the cannon of creative thought, and all things came into being. These things would also have the genetic code for creative thought, and the evolution would continue infinitely. *The creation becomes the creator, ad infinitum*, he thought. He believed in right and wrong, not good versus evil. He felt that some people did get *it*, whatever *it* may be. He also felt that organized religions had crushed the human spirit, and that they had degraded themselves into an endless stream of meaningless litanies. They had undeniably been the cause of the bloodiest wars and massacres in human history.

"And what of the mindless flocks?" he asked finally.

Mantrella leaned against the desk. "Their intentions are…"

"The road to hell," Andrew interrupted.

"As They would have you believe. Hell," he mused, running a finger along the grain of the desktop. "Its creation was an ingenious way for Michael to control the masses."

Andrew looked into his lap. "What about UFOs?"

Mantrella's eyes widened, and he burst into laughter.

"Seriously," Andrew continued, staring at him, "if you're going to shatter all my illusions, I need some answers."

Visibly amused, Mantrella replied, "Man is not the only being in the universe. On this lovely planet, two of the most powerful creative forces are vying for dominance. The outcome will affect all reality, so the struggle has certainly drawn attention from elsewhere. This is the happening place for galactic events."

"And the angels—the Lords—are the bad guys," Andrew conceded.

"Break away from such a literal understanding of things, Andrew. Suffice it to say, the Lords do not have humanity's best interests at heart."

Momentary silence spread between them. The silver-eyed man straightened his back and regarded his guest with quiet contemplation, while Andrew returned his gaze to the dark window.

Then, turning his eyes on his host once again, he asked, "Why do you call yourself Mantrella?"

The man's grin returned, his eyes shimmering. "I am not sure that using my real name in public would be very wise," he responded. "Nonetheless, it is a veiled name—Estrella de la Mañana, most easily translated as *Morning Star*."

Andrew grinned now and looked away. "Of course," he mumbled. He paused, taking in the books beside him. Data scrolled through his head in a continuous stream and he silently struggled to grasp a fraction of it.

"You mentioned that all of what you said was passed down in images," he said at last. "What were you referring to?"

"Numerous images and methods have been used," Mantrella said, going to a desk drawer, "but I will mention only one." From the drawer he took a thin deck of oversized cards and offered them to Andrew. "The Tarot has been the purloined letter for centuries. It contains the true teachings and exposes religious myths and their opiate effects on humanity."

Andrew shuffled through the cards slowly, taking in bits and pieces of the different scenes depicted on each.

"There are twenty-two cards in your hands, and they contain man's history and reveal his destiny," Mantrella said. "The mastery of its symbols, colors, images, and alphabet can lead one to master reality. Take the card the church attributes to me — *The Devil*."

Locating the card labeled as such, Andrew withdrew it from the deck and studied it. On its face was an image of the devil, a creature with great horns and a pentacle between them. Below the beast stood a woman and a man, both naked and bearing loose chains around their necks.

"Cabalistically, I am TEMOHPAB, Temple Omnium Hominum Pacis ABBAS," Mantrella explained. "Meaning 'Father of the Temple of Peace of all men.' It is an image that only a short while ago filled you with such dread. Both male and female are chained, yet the chains are so loose that a child could remove them. The restriction is an illusion. The blackness reflects all color. The pentacle, the symbol of Venus, the position of the hands, the flame and the fruit, the cloven feet of the people, the all-seeing Ayin — all of these symbols combine to give the true picture of what has been called evil. I am the Prince of Darkness, but I am also the King of Light. My nature is not divided, the appearance of illusion." He rounded the desk and supported himself against its front, his shadow falling over Andrew.

"The Judgment card," he went on, "shows the seed called forth by our unsuspecting ally, Gabriel. The figures form the word 'Lux,' who emerge from their four square prisons of illusion. Light emerges from the subconscious depths, and the future is sealed under the sign of the Red Cross. These are but some of the codes that have been used to preserve the truth and to prevent persecution."

He paused, as if he had lost the thought, then he said abruptly, "We must leave and find Mara."

Andrew looked up at him.

"More information will be given as needed," Mantrella assured him.

"And now?"

"Now we go," Mantrella said.

"Just like that?" Andrew asked. "Suddenly the lesson's over?"

Giovanni shoved open the den doors and appeared in a flood of light from the foyer. "He's ready?" the old man asked.

Mantrella nodded, and Andrew stood.

"Ready?" he replied. "Ready for what? Where are you taking me? We're in the middle of something here."

"Don't let me lose you now," Mantrella said. He approached Andrew and laid a hand on the man's shoulder. "It must begin," he continued. "We must go."

CHAPTER 25

Andrew was en route to somewhere. Where, exactly, he didn't know. When he left Mantrella's, the Mercedes headed north toward the Alps. He was accompanied by a driver and a female bodyguard—the same pair that had arrived at the airport to take him to the fictitious *Monsignor Giovanni*. He shook his head, wondering how he could have been so stupid as to be sucked into some underhanded ploy to get him to Italy. His attendants, he'd been informed, were "Watchers." The driver scared him the most—dark ebony-skinned with the blackest of eyes mirroring only hatred and anger. The woman, in stark contrast, was very pale, though strangely alluring. Her green eyes were the most riveting part of her appearance, and a notable relief from the milky white skin and bleached hair.

From the comfort of the thick leather backseat Andrew asked through the open privacy glass, "Where we are going?"

"North," the driver responded, his voice deep and unwelcoming.

"I know we're heading north," Andrew continued tentatively, "but that could take us anywhere from Switzerland to Norway."

The woman's cellular phone rang. She flipped it open and pressed it to her ear. "I understand," she said, then slapped the phone shut. She turned to Andrew. "Poland."

"Poland," Andrew repeated flatly.

"Yes." She offered no further details but continued to stare at Andrew.

Lost in her emerald green eyes, he began to swoon.

She gave a slow blink and the spell was broken. "I am sorry. Force of habit," she said softly.

Andrew jerked awake from the strange woman's mesmerizing eyes. "What did you do?" He rubbed his forehead, amazed that he could be so easily hypnotized.

She didn't respond.

He was silent for a moment as he gathered his thoughts and composure. Then he asked, "Would it be too much of an imposition to ask your names, since we'll be spending the next how many hours together? It's not like Poland's only a few miles away."

"He is Moloc and I am Nilaihah," she replied.

"Interesting," he commented. "Those aren't names you hear every day." He glanced out the window at the permanent mural of rushing trees. "I noticed at Mantrella's villa that you two are always paired—like partners. Please take no offense, but are there always a pair of light and dark-skinned people together?"

Nilaihah peered at Andrew through the privacy glass, and he quickly averted his eyes from hers.

"Do not worry," she assured him, "what happened before will not happen again."

Cautiously, Andrew met her green eyes.

"Mantrella did not tell you about us?"

"There wasn't time," he answered. "I was only told that you're Watchers, and that I would be under your protection."

Moloc chuckled in a low growl, but he didn't speak.

"Our existence has been greatly demonized to frighten people into the arms of those who claim that we are the stealers of souls," Nilaihah said. "Almost all of what is portrayed is a lie."

"Then what exactly are you?" Andrew asked.

"I am a Watcher, but some call us the 'Vie-pyre.' The term means 'life-fire' or 'altar'."

"You mean you're a *vampire*—a B-movie bloodsucker?" He became immediately aware of how bold and offensive his statement was, and stiffened his back in fear of retribution.

Smiling, she said, "That is what *they* would have you believe." Though she spoke softly, there was contempt in her voice. "We do not suck blood. The Church invented this myth to frighten the young. And since they claimed to have the weapons to defeat these *bloodsuckers*, those who scare easily went running into their folds. We are great healers. The blood contains the *life-fire,* and we can both give and take that fire. There is life-fire in the air; it permeates all. We can use that force to heal a wound or disease, or to extract defective fire. It is the extraction that gave rise to the blood legends."

Andrew wasn't sure how to pursue this line of discussion, or whether it was even wise to do so.

"And Moloc?" he asked.

"Moloc is a 'Dog of Isis.' In the beginning time, words had meanings that differ from the words of today," she explained. "The term means 'those devoted to Eve or Isis.' Before Paradise was lost we were as one being. When the Veil formed and duality permitted the physical, our nature was separated as we entered the illusion. Consciousness separated into the higher and the lower. Moloc is the lower, and he, too, is a healer on the gross physical level. He and those like him take the form of the wolf, for it is closest in meaning to those who practice undying devotion and loyalty to the Goddess. Those of the *collar* took to hunting the Molocs of the world because of their ties to the female, rather than the male creative force. It is the *Moon* that guides Moloc's path, but he is not controlled by it. I am fire and air; Moloc is water and earth."

His moments by the sea as a child came rushing back to him. Perhaps it was for this reason that he ultimately grasped the elements, yet Andrew felt a sense of great sorrow in Nilaihah's tone. He couldn't imagine having his nature divided and his alter ego ripped from his being only to be made manifest as a separate being. He understood the reference to the Tarot. The Moon card—number eighteen, he remembered—portrayed a wolf and a dog howling at a combined image of the sun and moon. As he recalled, these creatures were poised between two towers that he thought represented duality.

Before Andrew could explore these beings in greater depth, Moloc slammed on the brakes, catapulting him through the privacy glass, against the dashboard, and into oblivion.

He woke to the deafening sounds of helicopter blades. As the blurred vision and dizziness began to fade, he slowly realized that the helicopter was filled with armed men, dressed in military fatigues.

"What the hell happened?" he asked wearily, feeling his weight slumping against a stranger's body, "and who the hell are you?"

CHAPTER 26

A pain had worked its way deeply into the center of Mara's brain, causing her eyes to water and her mouth to turn dry. She loathed the headaches, but for as long as she could remember she'd been a victim of them. "Frequent migraines," her doctor in Boston had diagnosed, scratching her out a prescription for *Zomig*. But she didn't have any medication with her now. The unexpected shift of events in her life— from the psychic meeting, to the collapse, to the waking in the strange villa, to this moment—had hardly lent itself to the proper preparation for traveling abroad. The low lighting and solid placidity of the room offered some relief from the throbbing in her head, as did the cool dampness of the stone chamber.

Embers of a fire smoldered orange in the hearth at the far end of the room. The chandelier hanging over the long mahogany table she sat at softly lit the surrounding walls and their framed art, the large square gray and white floor tiles, and the heavy burgundy curtains no doubt hiding a grand window. A man stood at a door in the wall opposite the fireplace. She hadn't decided whether he was some kind of servant or somebody left there to guard her. His posture mimicked a soldier at ease. He stared straight ahead, as if unaware of her presence. As if he'd been turned into stone and condemned to an eternity of staring at the cold walls of this medieval dining room. He was dressed like a butler or a common manservant. A short black, double-breasted coat, fully buttoned, rode just above his waistline hugging his thin body, allowing only the white shirt beneath it to show around the base of his pallid neck.

Somehow, though, his presence in the room comforted her. Mara awoke to a nightmare and was just now coming down from the pulse-pounding episode, the headache dampening her senses to the point of exhaustion. She knew that if she collapsed again, if she became incapacitated, he would probably help her. Something in the soft gray of his transfixed eyes told her so. The lines in his face didn't seem to be the creases of frowns or scowls. He reminded her of the man in the street who had promised to rescue her.

So much was flashing through her brain in stabs of recollection and pangs of memory—the hallway of pictures, framed in gold and haunting her. What did it all mean? Why was it so frightening, yet so familiar? Like the man in the limousine. She had dreamt of his face before. She had recognized it as soon as she'd seen him. Who was he? What was all this around her? Questions were frothing at her temples, the roots boiling in the center of her mind. She stared at the even grain of the tabletop, trying to grasp some small comprehension of her life and the turmoil that seemed to be raging in her soul. If only she could understand her destiny.

The doorknob turned, and she looked up to see the man who had saved her enter the room, a smile vibrating at the corners of his mouth. He nodded to the guard, who bowed his head and left the room, closing the door behind him.

"You must be exhausted," her savior said gently. He approached her and laid his hands on her shoulders. "I'm sure there's so much you need to know."

Mara gazed up at him, her large, dark eyes wet with tears. "What's happening to me?" she asked, her voice trembling.

The man kneaded the muscles in her shoulders and neck for a moment, then slowly walked away from her, taking a seat in a high-backed chair at the head of the table. Crossing his legs, he cupped his hands on his knees and studied the haggard young woman, the smile still echoing warmly on his lips.

For an instant, her eyes met his, but she looked away and stared at the tabletop again, suddenly sheepish and uncertain. The nobility on the man's brow, the careful grooming of his hair and the pale complexion of his skin made her feel as though she was in the company of a prince or of some individual of high social status. She felt inadequate, like a peasant in the shadow of a pharaoh.

"If only someone could make sense of who you are and what this is all about," he said at last, "then you could rest peacefully."

"Everything is so strange," she whispered.

"You are a perfect beauty," he commented. "Your appearance reminds me of the absolute loveliness of the fabled Scheherazade."

She felt the blood rush warmly into her cheeks. Mara loved the story of *Scheherazade*, admiring for as long as she could remember the strength and resolution of the beautiful woman who had saved herself from certain execution by telling stories.

"But beauty aside," he continued, "there is much to be said about the restlessness of your soul."

Mara closed her eyes, feeling them burn in their sockets. "I'm so confused. So lost," she uttered. "Why am I here?" She turned her head toward him, careful not to look into his eyes.

"You are here," the man answered, "because I ran into a scared girl in the streets and wanted to help you."

"But they were *shooting* at us—and you knew my name."

He nodded. "I know who took you, Mara," he said frankly. "I know why he wants you and how it is that you came to be who you are. Of course," he added, "many of the details are only assumptions on my part, but logical ones, nonetheless."

Wide-eyed, she found herself staring at him, concentrating on a spot of his neck just below the chin. "Tell me…please."

"Where do I start?" he sighed.

"At the beginning," she said. "Tell me as much as you know."

"You were stolen at birth," he said abruptly. "They entered your mother's room in the maternity ward, shot her in the head, and killed your father. From that moment on your life has been a series of different experiences in all parts of the world, all of which have ended in the same manner."

An icy ridge ran up her spine. "My mother? I've never known her," she said. "How do you know this?"

"I've been following the man who kidnapped you," he answered dryly. Raising a hand to his chin, his face relaxed and his disposition became contemplative. "Throughout the years, collecting information about him has become somewhat of an obsession of mine. I have studied him, detailing his every move. I must admit, though, that I have lost track of him from time to time, and hence, I've lost track of you."

She met his eyes, though she'd told herself she wouldn't do it. His stony orbs pierced her. "Lost track of me? Why would someone want me? Why would they kill my mother?"

"Your mother died simply because she was your mother," he answered. "Mara, you have migraines, don't you?"

Nodding, her eyes strayed around the room until they found a Monet on the wall across from her. Focusing on the *Jardin De Giverny*, she absorbed the muted lines of purple and green. "I have terrible headaches," she conceded. "Sometimes my nose bleeds and I black out."

He waited a moment, considering her words. "I told you that after you were stolen at birth you experienced a series of events that helped to define who you are now," he began. "Each of these episodes ended with the migraines shutting off your conscious mind and plunging you into darkness. Each time you awoke you were in a different place, with a different family. You took on all their memories, though you were always somehow different. You don't remember, do you, Mara?"

Closing her eyes, she felt the world move beneath her. "I don't know what you're talking about?" she muttered. "I remember my family and who I am."

He smiled. "You remember who you are *now*, Mara," he said, "but you have been many different people for many years. There have been, however, some constants in your life. You have always been Mara. That is your name, and it will continue to be until the end of time. It was planted in your mother's dreams, and she made it real. Even God cannot take it away from you. In each instance you were told the same story — you were given up for adoption at birth, and whoever happened to be standing as your parents at any given point had adopted you and had sworn to protect and love you, so on and so forth." He waved a hand in the air. "The most interesting facet of your different lives, however, has been the fact that in each of them a single male has stood out as a dominating force, guiding your life."

She wiped the tears from her eyes again as she thought about her family back in Massachusetts. What he said was true, at least in the life she was now living. She had been adopted and had never known her mother, but the parents whom she thought had raised her were no less her mother and father. She had a sister, two years younger than she, whom she loved more than anything in the world—almost as much as her grandfather. She could see the man so clearly in her mind. Though so much older than herself, he was her knight in shining armor—tall, thin, so very austere. His eyes, the most calming, brilliant silver…

"Yes, Mara," the man said, interrupting her thoughts, "your grandfather. I know him as well as I know myself."

Mara glared at him, her eyes narrowing and pulse quickening. "You don't know anything about my grandfather," she said. "Don't ever mention him in these crazy ideas of yours."

Again, he smiled, but she could see in his eyes that he was fighting to keep his composure. "I know him, Mara," he said calmly. "Tall and slender, eyes a burning silver. How many times, Mara, has he promised always to be there? How many times has he spoken to you about your destiny?"

"You don't know him," she insisted. "You don't."

"Clear your mind, Mara. Let it come back to you." He rose from his chair and went to the mantle of the fireplace. "I can already feel you gaining consciousness. You are becoming so much more aware of who you are." Poker in hand, he stabbed at the glowing embers. "It's all right there in your head. You only have to remember."

Blood pounding through her temples, she lowered her head as the migraine rose up against her, sending biting tentacles of pain into her shoulder blades. In a haze, she saw scarlet drops form on the table, and instinctively brought a hand to her nose.

"It's coming now, Mara." His voice swirled in her ears.

Her body lurched forward as her stomach cramped. Flashes of her life blitzed into her mind—incomprehensible, but familiar. Again, she knew that she should recognize it all. A crop circle. Wolves and screaming. A present in the pretty red box. But who were these people? Tall man, silver eyes. Castle and fire. Mountain…

"It's all there, contained in your subconscious mind," he said. "Every bit of who you are and who you used to be."

The pain dispersed and her head lightened. Sweating, she touched her glossy cheeks with trembling hands, as her voice sounded deeply in her throat. "What is it all?"

Suddenly, he was at her elbow, his hand on her arm. "The headaches have always been the signal to your subconscious mind that it was time to move on. They were a way of clearing your head of all that you had come to know, as well as a way to empty it so a new life could be programmed. Every three years you were moved. You have lived throughout Europe, and more recently, the United States. You have been the daughter of an English tea baron and of an Indiana farmer. Step-daughter to a Scottish banker, and granddaughter of a Bostonian lawyer. You have possessed all these identities, Mara, and each time you played the adopted girl, the beautifully mysterious child of Middle Eastern descent, an unwitting stranger in a family committed to your love and protection. And each time you had no recollection of where you had come from, and no awareness that in every case your time there was limited."

"Who are you?" she whispered, slowly collecting herself. "Who are you to know all of this?"

"I am the one," he answered, "who should have been protecting you all of these years. When I first learned of your birth, it was too late. They already had you. I was reduced to scouring every medium of information that I could collect in order to locate you so I could take you in and protect you, but every time I came close to finding you, you disappeared. I lost track of you again, so I would begin my search all over in earnest."

She peered up at him through the tears. "But who are you?"

He drew in a long breath and held it in his lungs. "You can know me only as Michael, for if my true identity were known we would both be in danger."

"Who is responsible for what's happened to me?"

"I assumed you were to meet him earlier today," he said, returning to his chair. "He is known as Mantrella, but he is far more than a name. He is the very silver-eyed man you have known in all of your lives—as father, step-father, grandfather. He is the man responsible for moving you, for keeping you from the world."

"But why?" she pleaded, her voice cracking.

"He believes you to be of a very old bloodline, Mara, one that goes back to the dawn of Christ."

"The dawn of Christ?"

His face softened and he grinned. "Many would claim Mantrella to be mad. I know him to be dangerous. You have no idea the capacity the man has for destruction. He is of the darkest matter, Mara, and has been a threat to mankind since the beginning."

131

Mara tried to clear her head and feigned a slight smile. "Am I to believe that he's the devil?"

He stared at her, his face drawn tight and pale.

"You've got to be kidding," she said, shifting in her chair. "What will you tell me next?"

Looking away, he chose his words carefully. "He has been known as Lucifer, Bearer of Light, and I am he who has been chosen to defeat him." He returned his gaze to her. "You have been marked as a daughter of the Messiah, and he wishes to bleed the life from you."

"I won't believe that a man who has been as good to me as my grandfather, no matter who he may really be, is your devil, *Michael*. How do I know that you're not insane and want to kill me?"

"Because I was not the one who kidnapped you, imprisoned you, and shot at you," he answered directly. "Soon you will believe me."

"Soon? What's next for me?"

He stood and straightened his gray suit coat. "All you have learned in your faith, in your movies and books, about the devil is true, Mara, and he is hunting you. Believe me or not, it is no matter. I will protect you just the same. After all, there is only *one* true God, no matter how people throughout the ages have referred to Him. The very Creator of all of mankind is the very will that is in me. I only have your best interest at heart." He paused as the door opened once more and a servant entered with a silver platter of fruits and cold meats. "What is next for you is to eat. You're weak, and you have a long journey ahead of you."

She watched him move toward the door. "Where am I going?"

Stopping in the doorway, he glanced back at her. "Home," he said. "Each of us has multiple destinies and must choose wisely which we will meet. I know which of yours will keep you the safest. When you have reached it, you will go home, where you belong."

Mara opened her mouth to speak, but he was already gone, as was the servant who had placed the platter of food in front of her and dropped a serviette into her lap. As the door slowly closed on her, she stared at the platter, a mutation of her beautiful face reflecting back at her and into the silence of the room.

***

Michael shortly dismissed the servant who followed him out of the dining room, wishing to be left alone as he walked to receive his most recent guest, especially one as important to him as the girl.

"It would be so easy to kill her," he muttered, marching through the hollow corridors, the soles of his leather shoes clicking off the tile floor. "To kill them both and be rid of this whole affair. But then I risk waking

Him. Damn you, Mantrella. Whatever you've done to keep me from physically harming them, I'll soon undo it." He smiled, suddenly arrogant. "For now, I cannot make myself raise a hand against her, as precious and dangerous as she is. A singular beauty, my Mara." Clenching his hands into fists, he stopped abruptly and gazed off, lost in thought. "But what can it be?" he questioned the silence. "How did Mantrella ever become so powerful as to shield her—and *him*—from the wrath of destiny?" He grinned. "After all, I am the hand of destiny, am I not?" He straightened the knot of his tie and ran a hand through his hair. "I am but the finger of God."

CHAPTER 27

CATHOLIC DIGEST—As if the world was not suffering enough tragedy, horror unfolded in the Holy City today as UN peacekeeping forces infiltrated St. Peter's Square and initiated a seemingly unwarranted full-scale attack on innocent civilians.

Observers on location report seeing an explosion in the center of the square, followed by an assault of tear gas. As the victims attempted to flee the scene, they were fired on by UN soldiers.

The current death toll stands at 33, a number that includes three of the UN's troops. Sources are still not sure what caused the vicious actions of the troops, and it has been reported that General Rami Abdul, acting Supreme Commander of the UN peacekeeping forces, has been detained for questioning.

The President of the United States, along with England's Prime Minister, has requested that the United Nations come to session in order to "sort out the details of a situation that has gone tragically wrong." With information relating to the attack extremely limited, no word as of yet has been released as to whether the UN will meet to discuss the issue...

***

When no answer came, Andrew knew he was no longer in the care of the Watchers. He hoped Nilaihah and Moloc were all right, but he doubted it. As his head finally cleared, he began to wonder about the necessity of everyone having to behave so dramatically. *Abductions and disappearances,* he thought—when maybe a simple *Hey, can we talk to you?* would do. Even though Andrew desired some kind of resistance, he also sought information. He was now caught in a world where nothing was as it appeared to be, a world in which irony had been redefined to an infinite degree. Was Mantrella telling the truth? Was he really so important to humanity?

The elusive and very alluring Mara was another enigma.

Who was she, and why did he feel that he would give anything to find her? These, and a thousand more thoughts assaulted his mind and his sanity.

The air was cold and the helicopter drifted in and out of wet gray clouds. Periodic barrages of ice pellets pummeled the copter's sides, sounding like machine guns firing into a wall of sheet metal. Thick fog formed a continuous vortex in the air as the blades sliced through the low clouds. Though the visibility was near zero, the occasional thinning of the mist nonetheless allowed momentary glimpses of the terrain below.

Andrew checked his *Timex*, but the hands had frozen at 8:49. Given the state of his universe, he questioned whether time had not actually stopped, and he considered that his last real moment of awareness might have ended when he had smashed into the dashboard of the Mercedes. The ultimate question, however, was whether he was on the chopper to heaven or to hell. Then he remembered that Mantrella had denied the existence of Dante's *Inferno*. He mused whether, without perdition, salvation even existed. He felt powerless, to him a condition worse than damnation. At least with the latter, he admitted, a fate was sealed and a judgment reconciled. The scales had been weighed and he'd lost—end of discussion.

Just as Andrew had the notion to talk himself into jumping one of the escorts and grabbing a gun, the helicopter broke through the mist and was greeted by the brightness of a late afternoon. As the sun pulled his gaze to the window, he had the feeling that something had intervened to prevent what probably would have been a suicide attempt to retake control of his life, yet he had no time to dwell on this thought; his attention faltered as he spotted their intended destination.

His friend Eli jokingly referred to Andrew as *Mr. Britannica*, a name that he came to loathe, but it was true that in the oddest of moments, Andrew would espouse information that only an encyclopedia normally contained. On dates, drinking, at the movies, he would relate pieces of obscure information no one really wanted to hear. Even Andrew was not totally sure of the source of all this information; they were bits of fact that he just *knew*. He was exceedingly well-read, but sometimes the depth of his memory surprised even him.

Now the information had begun to flow. What he saw below was the world's largest brick castle—the ancient Teutonic Knight stronghold of Malbork.

He had made it to Poland after all.

Construction on the castle had begun in 1309, when the Knight's Middle East fortress fell in 1271. The Knights, who promised to struggle against the enemies of Jesus, were invited by Duke Konrad Mazowiecki to protect his lands from the Prussians and Lithuanians. More recently, the castle, located on the Nogat River, was restored after suffering considerable damage during World War II.

Many portions were now open to tourists. However, given that the castle contained a labyrinth of secret corridors linking thousands of rooms, many areas were still off-limits. Many such corridors were the locations of mysterious sightings of ghosts and what were purported to be extraterrestrial lights. There had even been claims that aliens had used the underground caverns as a base of operations. Andrew knew that such claims only boosted the tourist trade, but superstitions aside, Malbork was one of the greatest fortified complexes in Europe. Despite war damages, magnificent interior decorations had been preserved, including the unique vaulted ceilings, collections of old weapons, china, amber ornaments, and blue clay pottery.

Moreover, the castle was also known as "The Fortress of Mary."

As this last bit of trivia faded from his conscious memory, the helicopter made a soft landing in a courtyard behind the tall brick walls, out of view from the surrounding community. He felt as if he were entering the belly of the beast.

When Andrew stepped off the chopper, he quickly realized that there were no tourists, most logically because the castle was *Zamykany dla Napraw—Closed for Renovations*—as the posted signs read in Polish, offering translations in English, German, and Russian.

Amid the high wind of the blades, two armed men dressed in black uniforms motioned for Andrew to follow. He was ushered through a pair of large wooden doors of the older High Castle. The receding sounds of the helicopter's engine convinced him that his stay wouldn't be brief.

As his escorts' boots clomped over the stone floors, he was reminded of the precision beat of goose-stepping Nazi soldiers. An unexpected, almost trivial thought occurred to him as the rhythm of synchronized steps lulled him into a daydream—*If Nilaihah was some kind of vampire, how was she out and about in the daylight? Shouldn't she have exploded into a fiery ball of dust when exposed to the sun?* He was only vaguely aware that they had passed through another set of doors and had come to a halt.

"Because they are creatures of light, not darkness, and because they actually feed upon the rays of the sun. The myth of their nocturnal nature has been a ruse to hide their true feeding habits."

Andrew slowly turned to confront the source of this information, and fell to his knees in both awe and fear.

CHAPTER 28

Never before had Mara experienced such absolute silence. Nothing around her stirred. Not even the embers of the fire, slowly burning to black, crackled or popped in the hearth. There was only silence — silence like she'd never known — thick with a loneliness much heavier than the ache in her temples.

The cold meats and fruits on the platter hadn't appealed to her. Actually, she was sick to her stomach, and even the thought of food promoted the notion of vomiting. Shoving the platter across the table, she went to the mantle and stared into the subtle glow of the embers. She could feel no heat coming from the hearth, but the room was still comfortable. Mara welcomed the cool air wrapping its soothing tentacles around her slender body.

Not even the coolness could temper the thoughts drilling through her head. She should know what was happening to her; she should somehow understand it. The answer to all of it was just out of reach.

If only she could stop the throbbing in her head — the pains in her shoulders and neck. If only she could find some release from the migraines, from the lonely confusion in her brain, from...

Her body slumping against the fireplace, she clutched at the mantle to keep herself from falling. *Coming again.* She felt a warmth in the back of her throat and tasted blood, tasted the bitter liquid of her own swirling existence. Mara closed her eyes and steadied herself against the mantle as the visions came — the glimpses.

I can already feel you gaining consciousness... You are becoming so much more aware of who you are...

The visions slipped in and out of her conscious mind, moving like ripples on a pond. None stayed for any length of time, making so few of them intelligible, yet she could feel each one deeply in the core of her being, knowing that it belonged to her, was part of her — if only she could remember.

Suddenly, she saw him — the one in her dreams. The man from the session, once there, then gone, who had stared at her, gasping, from the rear window of the limousine... Then he disappeared, replaced by a darkness so real it frightened her.

Mara opened her eyes and gazed across the stone room. She could still see the pictures dancing in the cold space before her, gently floating through the room and dissolving, like ghosts slipping into the sunlight. So many thoughts — so many things to remember.

An image of her grandfather rose from the tabletop, his silver eyes shimmering as he smiled widely at her. She reached for him, but he could not be touched. Instead, fire rose behind him and his expression turned dark, eyes burning, mouth twisted in laughter. Beside him, a minion, one whom she recognized so clearly now…A whisper wormed into her ears, carrying on its silken wings the quiet name — *Andrew*.

***

The emerald green aura surrounding Michael's body shifted to a burning yellow, then to a red so hot that fire appeared cool by comparison. His saffron hair swirled in a self-contained wind and seemed to hold the faces of a million screaming souls. If Andrew had any doubt that his life had entered a battle between competing forces, all doubts were now removed. Before him was proof of the Eternal Struggle. Mantrella was real, and so was Michael.

He could barely stand to look into Michael's blinding brilliance, but he was compelled to witness him. It was not until the radiance at last faded that Andrew could finally make weak eye contact with the powerful host, and he felt himself drawn to the menacing figure, as if his very soul was being bound within his flesh.

"Rise," Michael commanded. "I can sense that you already know who I am, and it is time that you understand the reality of your situation. The world is at stake."

Andrew stood, palms and face wet with perspiration. While he heard Michael's words, his mind was still trying to grasp the fact that he was indeed in a reality that would determine the future of all humanity. Though he was fairly convinced that Mantrella was a force of considerable power, he was still uncertain about some of his claims. At least now he was sure that an event of biblical proportions was in the making.

With a sweeping hand, Michael gestured for Andrew to accompany him as he walked down the corridor. "I know that you have been in the company of Lucifer," he said, "or should I say *Mantrella*, and that he has filled your mind with a great many tales rancid with lies and half-truths. That is his way, to tell a story that contains enough truth to make the whole seem plausible. Many will believe almost anything."

A silent force made him follow, the steely edges of his mind pulled to Michael's magnetic presence. Remaining a few steps behind his host, he could no longer see Michael's eyes, and the pressure on his spirit lessened. He took advantage of the momentary reprieve to make a quick study of the man.

Michael was tall, at least six feet, and his features were in a constant state of subtle flux, making the man's facial appearance difficult to define, since they varied minutely every few seconds. His height slightly increased and then decreased; the color of his hair alternated between red, saffron, and a more golden yellow, always just a bit out of focus.

Andrew followed him into a large great room, decorated with medieval armaments and banners from the orders of knights. Michael sat at an ornate oak table, the legs of which were carved with angels and whose surface was so polished it reflected the elements of the room in sharp detail. He motioned for his guest to sit at the opposite end. As Andrew moved cautiously to the chair and slowly sat down, it appeared as though Michael's flickering image had stabilized, and the dizziness caused by the wavering appearance quickly dissipated.

"We have much to discuss," Michael began. "I know that Mantrella has filled your head with *garbage*. At this point I suspect that he has painted me as evil incarnate. You must understand that Mantrella is *the* master of deceit. I am here on behalf of God and have man's best interests at heart."

"You really are..."

"Yes, I am the Archangel Michael. Your soul hangs in the balance, dangling between heaven and hell, and with due consideration on your part I believe that we can tip that balance in favor of salvation."

Andrew felt his pulse quicken, an instinctual reaction to uttered fallacies of religion and faith. If there was one certainty that he maintained, it was that there was no hell, and that any god worth his salt would not create such an unfair system of existence.

Michael sensed the offense and decided to avoid immediate confrontation. "Mara is here." He said.

The proclamation disarmed Andrew. "When can I see her?"

"Now."

No sooner had Michael spoken than a large set of double doors opened behind him and a pair of imposing guards escorted Mara into the room. Andrew pushed himself out of his seat and stood, dumbfounded. He stepped toward her, extending his hands. When Mara's eyes fell on him, her intuitive smile and deep-seated affection gave way to fear and suspicion. Instead of accepting him, she staggered backwards, shielding her face in her hands.

"Mara, it's me. Don't you remember me?" He asked, he pleaded.

Her voice quavered. "I know who you are; I just don't know *what* you are."

A grin slithering on his lips, Michael relished the mistrust that he had managed to implant into Mara's bewildered mind. As far as she knew, Andrew was a tool of the devil, ready to ravish the virgin maiden and unleash a demon child into the world.

Lowering her hands, she purposely avoided his eyes, though she angled her head in such a way as to make an indirect glance at her alleged beseecher. Her thoughts reeled and her head spun with disorientation. Flashes of previous lives with Andrew invaded her memories. Her heart was pounding. Only the alertness of one of the bodyguards kept her from collapsing altogether onto the stone floor.

"Take her to her room," Michael demanded.

One of the guards scooped her limp body into his arms, and as quickly as she had come, she was gone. Andrew, in confusion, turned to Michael for an explanation, but the host simply shrugged his shoulders, and the young professor felt as if he was being mocked.

"She is very tired and very sensitive," Michael offered indifferently. "She merely needs time to rest. I am sure that once she sees that you have come back into the fold, her reaction will be different. You need to rest as well. We will have plenty of time to discuss matters in proper detail later." His form was in flux again, like a flickering television picture.

Another guard entered the room.

"Take our guest to his quarters and be sure he is not disturbed until morning."

Andrew looked at the guard, then returned his eyes to Michael, but the host had vanished.

Exhaustion overtook every fiber of Andrew's being. The guard motioned, and Andrew obediently followed his lead. He soon found himself on a sprawling bed within the rough stone walls of a medieval chamber. Mere moments later he surrendered to the oblivion of a deep sleep.

Andrew awoke with a new sense of energy. He didn't know how long he'd slept until the guard, who'd brought him breakfast, informed him that he had been asleep for close to three days. It was now nearly eleven in the morning and he was told that he had a meeting with Michael at noon. As a matter of fact, he would have these noon meetings with Michael for the next few weeks.

During these times of religious debate, Andrew only experienced a few brief visits with Mara, who was secluded in another wing of the castle. They were never left alone, and he was never permitted to go to her chamber. At least on this front Andrew was encouraged. While Mara maintained an air of suspicion regarding him, she occasionally stared at Andrew as if she were recalling some past relationship. At these moments, she would smile at him, as if the memory brought pleasant thoughts, and she would speak in a civil, if not endearing manner. Their conversations were always closely monitored and abruptly ended by Michael. Andrew began to suspect that his host was using the random visits as a way to mock him, as an experiment by which he could prove to Andrew that Mara was *his*, and that even in Andrew's presence the archangel suffered no threat of losing his hold on her.

Indeed, Michael's arrogance was at play as he danced in the fire, only to prove that he could not be burned. But the conversations of the captives was continually dampened to the level of trivial chatter; Andrew had not yet managed to reach Mara with his words, nor had he the chance to sway her in one way or the other. Unfortunately, Michael was highly successful in ensuring that each visit with Mara ended in the same way for Andrew. She would suddenly close down, as if some outside force had cut her thoughts from her mind. Each time Michael's grin grew to wicked proportions as Andrew was forced out of the room, as guilty in her eyes as ever.

Conversely, the private meetings with Michael were intense and exhausting. To Andrew, these sessions became a battle for his soul as he put his theological knowledge to the test with one who had been responsible for much of the world's religious dogma.

Each time his host entered the meeting room the level of ambient light increased. Not that Michael glowed, but his presence somehow increased the illumination of the area that surrounded him. When he left, the level of light always diminished. At first Andrew was hesitant to argue with Michael. He was, after all, an archangel, with an imposing sense of authority and knowledge, but as he pushed dogma, Andrew grew confident.

Michael hit every sore spot in Andrew's philosophy, and he found himself able to hold his own with his opponent. Michael told him that man was inherently sinful and that the only path for salvation was an unwavering belief in Church doctrine and sincere contrition. He said that man was on the verge of the Apocalypse, and that evil had infested every aspect of humanity's being. Moreover, he claimed that Mantrella, also known as Lucifer, had pulled out all the stops and was responsible for the current turmoil that rocked every corner of the globe. Through lies and deceit, Mantrella was attacking the Church with the goal being its destruction. If successful, Mantrella would have a clear path in his quest for complete domination and the establishment of a kingdom, with him as ruler and god. He refuted Mantrella's claims that he was the Christ, and insisted that the notion that man was meant to evolve to some kind of godhood was merely a play on humanity's ego. If man were to accept this theology, it would mean that humanity abandoned the Creator and would have to suffer the consequence—Armageddon. While some of the Church Fathers may have gone astray with the help of Satan, the basic tenets of Church doctrine were sound and guided by the will of God. If man continued on his sinful journey, the only alternative would be destruction, save the few faithful.

There were several moments when Andrew almost bought into Michael's ideology. He was very charismatic and persuasive. However, the whole idea of a vengeful god, inherent human sin, and the requirement to blindly follow Church dogma disrupted Andrew's sense of fairness and logic. An omniscient deity would know the frailties of its creation. It would know that human perfection would be a work in progress, and as any father would no more kill his child for making mistakes, it made no sense that a god would eternally punish its creations for mistakes it knew in advance they would make. The god of heaven and hell was not a god Andrew could worship. As a matter of fact, it was illogical that any real god would even demand worship. This idea personified god and gave it human emotions and desires which would hardly be godlike qualities. In Andrew's mind, with such a god it really would be better to reign in hell than to serve in heaven.

Andrew wanted no part of a deity that demanded servitude. This was not the god of Jeshua, or of any other prophet. This was a god that relished the power of life and death and held such power over the heads of its creations. And how did such a god wield so much power and keep its creations in line? An army of angels would certainly help. Keeping its creations ignorant, the only real sin, certainly aided its aims. The creation of a false enemy and a scapegoat also added to this elixir of servitude. No, Andrew concluded, there was something definitely wrong with the state of heaven.

The sessions continued and sometimes became heated discussions of differing views. Somehow, from somewhere, Andrew found the courage and the will to oppose Michael. Recognizing his and Mara's captive state, he was careful not to push Michael to a point of blind rage. Instead, whenever he saw that Michael was nearing anger, Andrew would capitulate and feign agreement. He was always sure to end the meetings on a positive note, with a promise to further evaluate his ideas. He didn't want to incur angelic wrath, for he was certain it would mean the demise of both himself and Mara. And yet he could not understand why Michael continued these debates. What prevented the archangel from writing him off as a perpetually lost sheep and simply leading him to the slaughter?

Three weeks after the first of the many meetings, Andrew woke to find his chamber door open and the outside corridor empty of guards. Never had he been allowed out of his room without permission, and never without a personal escort. He had immediately understood that the right to roam freely over the castle grounds would not be granted to him, so he had been kept locked in the chamber and under close guard. Meals were brought to him, and each time he left the room he returned to find the bedding changed, clean clothing in the dresser drawers, and fresh toiletries in the bathroom.

But now he could pass uninhibited through the doorway and step out into the corridor. *Why?* He was not so befuddled as to ignore the possibility of a trap.

They are watching me, he thought. Michael would never let such an error be made accidentally. He moved down the corridor cautiously, more than once scrutinizing the shadowy recesses of the ceiling and upper walls, in search of cameras and other surveillance technology. He found nothing, yet he was still not convinced that a guard had unknowingly forgotten to lock him inside the chamber. It seemed too easy. Nonetheless, he made few mistakes in trying to find his way through the castle and to Mara's chamber. He had prepared for this moment beforehand, committing to memory details as minute as the color of an area rug, so that one day he could retrace the steps to her and finally try to break her free of Michael's mind games.

The south wing represented the most newly renovated section of the castle — the place where Mara was held in relative luxury. The walls and corridors didn't feel as cold and medieval to him as the wing in which he was housed did. The heavy timber doors were newly lacquered, the floors clean and polished, and the bulb in each golden sconce shone brightly. There was a sense of warmth here.

Andrew knocked lightly at her door. He waited, and when no response came, he knocked again. Still, no one answered. On a whim, he tried the knob and found that it turned easily, clicking the bolt out of its plate and allowing the door to slide silently open.

"*Mara*," he whispered forcefully. He didn't want to startle her, for he already knew that the sight of him would be fear enough.

No answer.

He moved deeper into the room, taking in the twisted and folded sheets of a bed that had recently been slept in, the gilded pictures and marble accents. Things were out of place — chairs turned away from tables, clothing on the floor. It was an apartment definitely occupied.

To his left, he caught movement out of the corner of his eye, and he turned to meet Mara coming out of the bathroom. For an instant, time stood still as the air moved around him in a gelatinous cloud. His eyes scanned her body, absorbing the dark skin and finely shaped legs, hips, breasts. She stood in shock, mouth open, green eyes wide and glassy. She was absolutely beautiful — and absolutely naked.

"What are you doing?" she gasped, reaching behind her for a towel and quickly wrapping herself in it. She stumbled against the casing of the bathroom door.

He put out his open hands cautiously. "Mara," he said calmly, "all the doors are open. The place is empty. I've finally got the opportunity to talk to you — alone."

"I don't want to talk to you."

He stepped closer to her. "You have to listen to me. This is not what you think it is; Michael is not who you think he is. Soon it will all make sense to you. Just let me explain."

She skittered over to the bed and threw herself under the covers. "If I scream, they'll come and take you away."

Andrew pulled the chair from the vanity and positioned it at the side of the bed. She watched him suspiciously, the green of her eyes dark and piercing.

"I know that you think I'm evil, or whatever term Michael used to turn you," he began slowly, softly, "but you know better, Mara. Somewhere inside of you, you know me."

"I don't," she uttered, beginning to cry.

"Yes, you do," he answered. In a move that made him tense with anxiety, he reached for her hand, afraid that he might not be able to make such intimate contact so early. But she let him take her hand, and he squeezed it gently. "Remember, Mara. That's all you have to do. I first saw you at the channeling session in Boston. It was me in the back of the limousine, watching as the very people who were protecting me tried to free you from Michael's claws."

"They shot at me," she snapped.

He shook his head. "They were shooting at *him*," he corrected her. "I'm the one that you've been looking for, even though you never had a clue that you were."

"I've seen you in my dreams…," she whimpered. "You've haunted me. But you and my grandfather…"

"Are the ones who have suffered so greatly to find you again," he said. "This Michael, the one whom you've come to place so much trust in, isn't who you think he is. He's a trickster, a manipulator. A liar. He knows he holds your soul, Mara. He's been playing with us since the moment we arrived here. Can't you see that he's bastardized so much information that he's created this web of illusion to catch you in?"

"So who's to be believed?" she asked. "I haven't known who I am in a very long time. Do you have any idea what it feels like to be me right now? I have no past. I have no identity." She yanked her hand from his. "I have no one."

He took her hand again. "You have me—you know you do."

She met his eyes.

"I'm going to get us out of here."

"And if I don't go?"

He stared at her for a moment, and he could feel her heart pounding. "Then you'll never know who was right," he said at last. "Get dressed. I'll wait for you in the hallway."

Andrew left the room, not knowing if he'd convinced Mara to leave with him or not. It was an awful feeling, a pit in the very core of his being. His mind ached, and an overwhelming veil of depression descended on him, but most importantly, he was scared—as scared as he had ever been in his entire life, he guessed. It was uncertainty that unhinged him. There was something more than just a frightened, lonely, confused girl back in the bedroom. He knew in his soul that she was the very reason for his existence.

When she touched his elbow he was leaning over a table in the hallway, open hands pressed against the smooth top. He hadn't heard her approach, but it didn't matter. She was there with him, and he had to get them out of the castle.

Carefully, he led her through the corridors, hoping he was going in the right direction, yearning for an exit sign, a window low enough to open—anything that would gain them freedom to the outside world. Andrew hadn't yet considered what they would do once they escaped. There wasn't enough room in his mind for the pressure of that yet.

They quickly made their way out of the south wing and entered what he believed to be the center of the structure. He recognized the area and knew that he was very close to the rooms where he and Michael had had their countless meetings. Just as he was about to turn Mara toward the corridors that faded off to the east, he noticed crystal shards of light streaming through the seams of a pair of oak doors. He knew that they should run in the opposite direction and try to find a way out in the eastern wing, but he was drawn to the doors and their radiant light. Releasing Mara's hand, he left her standing at the crossroads of two cold hallways. For a moment he stood in the light, feeling it vibrate through his body. He moved closer, pressing his ear against the thick wood. His face went white and his hands clenched into fists as he closed his eyes and listened.

CHAPTER 29

Andrew stood outside the oak doors, tears of anger winding down his unshaven face. *How could this be? How could God's so-called angels have so much hatred toward humanity?* Despair turned to anger, and anger to righteous outrage. Adrenaline coursed through every fiber of his being as he grabbed the door handles and burst into the room.

The doors flung open, and fists ready to dole out punishment quickly rose to cover his eyes. Light of such brilliance and purity drove Andrew to his knees and face down onto the floor. His body, once twitching with anger, now seemed to melt like wax, and his mind and soul sank into an abyss of despair. Gradually, the light began to fade and he found himself staring at the most beautiful Persian carpet he'd ever seen. The threads shimmered in strands of gold, silver, and copper, interlaced with unimaginable hues of purple, crimson, and lapis blue. Nose to the carpet, there was no discernible pattern, but each fiber took on a crystalline sparkle where his own tears acted as miniature magnifying glasses. Andrew slowly raised his head, a sudden awareness forcing him to his feet. He stood, with his attention drawn to the middle of the room, his mind a whirlwind of emotions.

In the center of the chamber was a great round golden table, surrounded by thirteen throne-like chairs. Crafted of the richest mahogany, each headrest was inlaid with a silver symbol or sigil. Seated in twelve of the thirteen thrones were "beings," the only word that Andrew's mind could grasp to describe them. He could not tell if the forms were male or female. Each had a body without any real physical boundaries. Translucent, and surrounded by a golden glow, their basic appearance was almost holographic, but there was no question that they were not projections; they were real. As the forms turned to Andrew, their glow began to soften and their bodies took on a more solid presence. At the last stage of their transformation, they appeared as typical medieval depictions of angels with wings of emanating bands of light. The halos, spiraling vortices of energy, steadily withdrew into their heads.

"What is the meaning of this, Andrew?" Michael demanded as he rose from his throne. The others remained seated, expressionless, and staring blankly at him.

Andrew scrutinized each of the angels and found that his emotions fluctuated as he shifted his attention from one to the other, and he saw that faint hues of distinct colors surrounded each of them. The spectrum of the rainbow and all shades in between gave the appearance of a wheel of fire. His intellect went into overdrive—*Twelve thrones, twelve tribes,*

twelve apostles, twelve Knights of the Round Table, twelve signs of the Zodiac.
Then his eyes fell on an empty throne—the thirteenth. He studied the
sigil on the headrest, and while his mind didn't know the exact meaning,
his heart grew heavy with loneliness and futility.

Michael's expression betrayed neither sympathy nor pity as he gazed
on the confused and bewildered intruder. Rather, he wore a look of
contemptuous disgust. Yet even Michael's sneering face didn't detract
from his natural beauty, anger, and wrath, all made attractive by his
radiance and sheer force of presence.

Andrew believed that Michael's majesty had to be one of the reasons
why the archangel was most favored. He was vexed with a sense of
shame. There was no logical way in his mind that something so perfect
could be behind something so wrong. No longer able to comprehend
Michael, his eyes were once again drawn to the floor and the tapestry.
Then, as if his heart had been ripped from his chest, Andrew yelled out in
anger. While beautiful beyond the capacity of mortal hands, the weave
on the floor was that of a closed rose bud. Without truly knowing why,
he knew that the rose should—*must* be open.

"What in God's name are you doing?" Andrew's voice trembled and
his blood ran hotly through his veins.

"And what do you think you know about God's name?" Michael
answered calmly.

Andrew hesitated, groping for a response. He knew that he was
talking about a god other than Michael's, but he didn't have a clue as to
where to even begin such an argument.

"I heard your plot for humanity's demise," he uttered at last,
struggling within himself for strength and courage. "Killing the pope,
bankrupting the world economy, disposing of world leaders, reinventing
the crusades, using your *miracles* to confuse and demoralize. These are
the kinds of things you blame on the devil." He straightened his back
and tensed for retribution. "The real devil stands before me!"

There was no time for Andrew to question from where the audacity
came to accuse the head of the angelic hosts of being the real evil in the
world, but he had, and it was a sudden relief, though he had reverted to
religious dribble in the charge. There was no devil. Mantrella's words
rang eternally true. It was always a matter of perspective, and this notion
of individual perception was causing the current dilemma. He had to
make some sense of a universe gone astray. Perhaps he had entered an
alternate reality in which the fallacy of good and bad was a mirror image
of opposites.

If he could not trust God, who could he trust?

No longer did he feel even an inkling of safety. He regretted that he
had doubted Mantrella. If he hadn't been swayed by Michael's lies, he

may already have discovered how he was going to get himself and Mara out of this mess. He knew now that the halo was the enemy, never to be believed—forever to be mistrusted.

Michael laughed at him, declaring that if Andrew thought the archangel was the devil, then all the centuries of lies had been worth the effort. "If you still believe in the devil, with all of your education and guidance, then we have done our jobs well enough."

"How much blood is on your hands in the name of the evil that *you* created?" Andrew seethed as he replayed history's countless crucifixions, burnings, tortures and wars—the millions and millions of deaths directly attributed to a fictitious devil and a non-existent vengeful god.

"And what are a few million of the likes of you?" Michael asked as his own rage began to grow. "Do you really think that humanity deserves to become godlike? The god that we created for you was in *your* image, full of self-righteousness and ego. *Bow down, worship*, and *obey* is all that your kind understands. Your Fisher King would have you think that you have a destiny greater than ours, but that will *never* be."

Stepping so close as to violate any field of personal space that the archangel might covet, Andrew locked his stony eyes on his opponent. "You're afraid, aren't you? You and the rest of your kind fear what we may become." Andrew felt charged with Paul's bolt of lightning. Mantrella, he knew, was right. "If we become like gods, there won't be much of a need for messengers like you, will there?" He smiled viciously. "Bye-bye angels. Job's done—you're not needed anymore." He laughed in Michael's face. "All this time you've put fear into *our* hearts and minds, when it's really *you* who's afraid. Keep us ignorant and at each other's throats, and man will never awaken. That's why you killed the pope. That's why you committed murder in Armana. That's the reason for the crucifixions and the crusades and the holocausts. God forbid anyone should shine the light of truth on the dark religions of your creation. And here we are again, the world on the verge of religious genocide, economies in chaos, science with its sights on the genetic code to expunge the godseed from the helix so you can re-create the ever-sleeping ape-man."

Overcome with energy and adrenaline, Andrew's fury erupted and he lunged at Michael, though he knew the attack would prove futile. His vision of wrestling with an angel, like Jacob of biblical lore, was dissolved in an ear-piercing howl. The first came from the courtyard, but soon the entire castle reverberated with bloodcurdling wails that forced Andrew to press his hands over his ears. As the howls subsided, they were quickly replaced with the screams and yells of battle.

"Just in time," Michael said, "but it is no matter. We have Mara, and unfortunately for humans, it still takes two."

A flash of light slammed into Andrew. The percussion threw him against a wall of amber ornaments and blue pottery, sending fragments of ancient ceramic in all directions. It wasn't until Andrew had recovered his sense of equilibrium that he saw that only a reddish after-image remained where Michael had once stood, and that the table was empty. For an unsettling moment, all was silent, then an explosion of glass sent crystal shards through the armory.

A creature, half man and half wolf, crashed through the window and landed several feet from Andrew. Though the image was shocking, he knew that he was in the presence of a Watcher. Seven feet tall, the beast was magnificent. Unlike their portrayal in horror movies, this *werewolf* was beautiful to behold. Glistening silver fur covered its head and back, and its flowing tail was as long as its body. The chest and arms were perfectly sculpted muscles, reminiscent of powerful Greek athletes, its eyes, large orbs of green surrounded by a mask of black fur. The man-wolf glared down at Andrew, and he knew this creature.

"Moloc?"

Called by the howls of its kind, Moloc turned from Andrew and burst through the thick oak doors, blowing them off their hinges, and disappeared into the cloister. To Andrew's relief, Moloc still lived.

Continued bays and screams drew Andrew to the shattered window. From his perch in the High Castle he could see the Watchers—both men-wolves and vie-pyres— traversing the battlements, coursing the high walls, and streaming over the pre-gates into the courtyard. On the receiving end of the Watchers' fury were humans that were being easily dispatched. Rather than having their limbs torn from their bodies, those who encountered the likes of Moloc—the Dogs of Isis—imploded. When clawed or bitten by the beasts, the victims sank in on themselves like grapes exposed to intense heat, then they dehydrated and crumbled. In contrast, those who met vie-pyres exploded. As the lily-white beings fell on their prey, the victims' energy was sucked from the body. The vie-pyres approached their targets, raised their hands and arched their backs as they inhaled a rainbow of colors that poured out of the humans, from head to abdomen. Finally, the bodies burst like rockets at a fireworks display.

The scene was mesmerizing, despite the reality of death. Andrew peered across the river at the surrounding apartment complexes, wondering if the town's residents had even reacted to the noise and bursts of light. Perhaps they had become complacent with any disturbances emanating from the castle, interpreting them solely as more manifestations of the UFO phenomena that had caught the attention of the world. He thought that since angels seemed to come and go in flashes of light, it was little wonder that Malbork was the focus of rumors of alien infestation. He concluded that angels were the real aliens of folklore and science fiction.

He stood in awe as the sights and sounds of this unearthly battle took on a netherworld appearance. The human contingents of the warring factions were doomed from the outset. Their bullets had virtually no effect on Mantrella's minions. The lead slugs merely made temporary holes of light that quickly closed, and despite the slaughter, no blood was to be found. The nature of the humans' deaths left only ashes, scattered by the cold winds. Yet it was a curiosity that the angelic forces of Mantrella and Michael avoided each other, as if their energies created a natural repulsion. In the few instances where contact was made, both combatants vanished into a kind of swirling black hole, reminiscent of the yin-yang symbol.

Another man-wolf smashed through a second window, sending Andrew to the floor in an attempt to escape the sharp glass that whipped through the room. The beast crashed through another set of wooden doors, sending splinters everywhere.

Alone again, he stood and once more the tapestry on the floor drew his attention, and he suddenly remembered.

"Shit!" he gasped. "Mara."

He was only a few steps behind the man-wolf, racing down the cloister, oblivious to the death cries of the others as he sprinted toward the Main Refectory, where he somehow knew he would find her. He ran on, sheltered by the vaulted ceilings and columns, the large windows blurring by him, all of which had been shattered. A loud noise spun him on his heels, and he halted at the nearest gaping hole in the stone wall. In the courtyard, a helicopter rose unsteadily from the green common. In its window he saw Mara staring at him, her large green eyes pleading for rescue.

CHAPTER 30

The helicopter faded into nothingness, and Andrew stood staring at the empty sky, recalling his first brief encounter with the captured woman He loved her, and he was certain that he had always loved her. Unlike an earlier time, when the idea of reincarnation was nothing more than a hopeful myth, he was now a true believer.

Burned into his memory were those eyes, pleading for intervention, as she was spirited from his grasp. While he saw her frequently at the castle, they were never left alone, making physical contact an impossibility. In the end they had been duped. Michael had come close to convincing them Mantrella was indeed the Great Trickster of religious myth. Now Andrew was closer to a realization of the truth. Rather than sitting eternally under the Tree of Life and living a life of eternal boredom, humanity was given the opportunity to know and experience the "whys" and "wherefores" of existence. The desire to know brought man into the cycle of birth, death, and rebirth.

The creation of the Veil was the moment of humanity's mass amnesia. The precipitating event that sent man in every culture and at every stage of evolution in search of what they lost—contact with their Creator. Andrew concluded that the only way to gain wisdom was from experience. The only place to gain experience was to enter the world of illusion—the physical world. Here, he thought, man had to submerge himself in a realm of time where he grew old and died and was reborn in order to add to his cumulative experience. Only in a heightened state of consciousness could he briefly glimpse behind the Veil. In a condition of cosmic awareness man transcended time, though this level of awareness was brief in order to maintain a physical existence. Andrew figured that the angels had no desire other than to maintain their existence. As a result, they had come to resent man's destiny. The great temptation and the Fall were only half-truths at best. Man was tempted by knowledge and the promise of wisdom. But the Fall was voluntary, and he dared to tread where the angels feared to go. He became a willing participant in the Great Work, and God began to experience its nature through the consciousness of its creation. Lucifer was the enabler, which angered the angels. Oddly, angels wouldn't enter the cycle of life, and as a result, they now feared that very cycle. He considered that perhaps their exposure to humanity had given them little desire to do so, and consequently they had come to fear and resent the path of human evolution.

Was man truly destined to partake of both the Tree of Life *and* Knowledge and thereby become as a god? Perhaps the true Trickster was the mythological slayer of dragons, and true evil was just an acronym for ignorance. It was no wonder that the keepers of the Rose had to veil their existence. While Adam may still sleep, he was the driving force in man's physical reality.

Andrew couldn't believe how his whole cosmology turned back on itself. Angels and demons did exist, but not in the way fairy tales told of them. The Church was created to control and confuse the masses and to keep man in a constant state of fear and ignorance. And the biggest demon of them all was actually man's savior, who sought to allow the annihilation of the physical in order for humanity to achieve its godhood.

He felt a cold hand gently caress his shoulder, derailing his mental train of thought.

"We must leave before the trail goes cold, Andrew," a welcoming voice whispered.

He turned toward the nurturing touch of Nilaihah and wrapped his arms around her. In the lingering sadness, he was happy to see her again. Coming back to himself, he released her, remembering what she was. He could have sworn that her alabaster skin blushed pink with embarrassment.

"I'm sorry," he said. "I thought you might be dead. I saw Moloc, but..."

Nilaihah raised a hand to stop his ramblings, and with a pleasing smile she said, "Thank you for your concern." A slave to her own nature, even among her own kind, little emotion was expressed. "However," she continued, "we need to leave this place and find Mara. Time is growing short."

She pivoted gracefully and headed for the courtyard, with every expectation that Andrew would follow. He wanted to pursue her comment about time being short, but he realized the conversation would have to wait. He saw Moloc meet Nilaihah in the outer corridor, nodding to each other in simple acknowledgement. In unison, they turned back to Andrew and their expressions commanded his immediate presence. As he followed them, he couldn't help but notice that while many had died this day, all that remained of their earthly existence was a few piles of ash quickly dissipating into the down drafts of the arriving helicopter's swirling blades.

CHAPTER 31

As the helicopter left Malbork, Andrew suddenly thought of the napkin and the telephone number that the stewardess Kathleen had given him. Stranger things had certainly happened since his encounter with the beautiful girl, and his gut told him that more fantastic events were to come. Still, the woman's purpose in the web growing around him was unclear, and he wondered if her brief appearance in his life was just another part of a deliberately crafted plot to involve him in something that he would have rather avoided. But how had she known about Eli? And how could anybody have predicted that Andrew would ultimately need his mathematician friend? If anything, one idea was becoming gravely clear to him: Nothing happened by chance.

He asked Nilaihah if there was any way that he could contact a friend of his in the States. She produced a cellular phone, and after pressing a few buttons, surrendered it to him. She also provided a set of earphones so he could hear his friend's voice over the roar of the chopper's engines.

Moments later, a connection was made and Eli's phone began to ring. "Hello."

Andrew was glad to hear a familiar voice. He'd been gone for longer than a month, and he felt like he was trapped between realities, neither of which, ironically, seemed real.

"Thank God you're home. It's so good to hear the voice of a friend," Andrew said.

"Andrew? Is that really you? You *son-of-a-bitch*! Where the hell have you been? Are you home? Are you all right? Are you still in Italy?" Eli sounded happy to finally hear Andrew's voice as the questions and concern flowed uninhibited from his mouth.

"Slow down, Eli. I'm fine. I'm just leaving Poland."

"*Poland*? What the Christ are you doing in Poland?"

"It's a very long story and I don't have time for details. I'm calling from inside a helicopter and I'm not sure how long this connection will last."

"What the…"

He was becoming aggravated because he knew that time was of the essence,.

"Eli, please," he insisted, "I really need you to listen. I promise, I'll tell you everything as soon as things calm down. I need you to do me a favor. I don't have a computer handy, and I need you to do some research."

"You mean that computer in your head crashed?" Eli asked lightly in feigned disbelief. "*Mr. Britannica* is missing a few pages, is he?"

"Eli, I'm serious," he answered with finality. "This is very important. I need you to find as much information as you can on the Tarot."

"Have you blown a mental cork?"

"*Eli!*" he snapped.

"Okay, what do you need?"

He took a deep breath. "I want you to find any parallels between the Hebrew alphabet and the twenty-two major arcana. Find the meaning of the letters and relate them to the symbolism on the cards. Look at it both from zero to twenty-one and one to twenty-two. There are twenty-two letters in the Hebrew alphabet, so the matching is not straight up. There's a blind in there somewhere. And look at it backwards, too. In Hebrew they read and write backwards, right to left, so string the meanings backwards and come up with any possible interpretations. Also, see if you can find out if any of the pictures have any relationship to real places, parts of the world, continents, and so on."

Confused, Eli said, "I don't get it, Andrew. What are you really trying to find?"

"There's a code there, Eli." He was vaguely aware of Moloc and Nilaihah's eyes on him, and he lowered his voice.

"What kind of code? Like the DaVinci thing or something?"

"It's bigger than the DaVinci thing, Eli. In fact, it's kind of 'the code of codes.' At a minimum, it may contain a composite record of all of the ancient codes. I don't have time to explain all of this, but you know how to research, and given your Jewish roots, I know you can speak Hebrew. Separate the wheat from the chaff. Find as much original documentation as you can. Look at the fringe sites, too. There's a lot of stuff that people think is off-the-wall that's a lot closer to the truth."

"I'll do what I can, Andrew. I know you wouldn't ask if it wasn't important. How am I supposed to get back to you?"

"I'll call you. I'm not even sure where I'm headed." The reality of the thought made him shudder. "Anyway, thanks Eli. My life could depend on what you find. I've got to go."

"What do you mean, your life could depend on..."

The phone went silent, the connection lost.

***

The helicopter made its way across the Polish landscape, flying just above the trees. The clear, crisp day clouded over and soon white flakes hid the houses and countryside below. The winds increased, but the helicopter seemed to move in a bubble of its own. The rushing air had little effect on the machine, and the blinding snow appeared to avoid its path altogether. When they left Malbork and he called Eli, the drone of the spinning blades made it difficult to hear, but now Andrew was wrapped in a cocoon of silence, as if the helicopter and its strange crew were somehow not even a part of this world.

He studied Nilaihah. She was quite beautiful in spite of—or maybe because of—her alabaster complexion, dressed in a tight red leather suit like Terry Goodkind's *Mord Sith*.

"I have a lot of questions," he said.

"I thought you would," she replied in her cool voice.

"When you and Michael's people were fighting, something really strange happened. It was kind of like a vortex was created when you clashed, and then both people disappeared. Did they die?"

"We do not know," she said flatly. "Those of Mantrella and those of Michael are like matter and anti-matter. When we come into direct physical contact and wound or get wounded, both combatants seem to get sucked into a miniature hurricane. It is difficult for us to be in the same place at the same time. We do not know what happens to us when the opposites are reconciled. No one has returned from such an encounter to tell us."

Experience told him that when she stopped speaking about a subject, he wouldn't receive any further information. Instead, he asked a different question.

"How did they get me away from you that day in the limousine?"

"They utilized pure humans. They blew out the tires and used a gas to make us unconscious. We are sorry that it took so long to find you. They have ways of covering their tracks, as we do, but eventually they leave a scent." She smiled at Moloc, who simply nodded in agreement.

Though Moloc often seemed oblivious to conversation, he never missed a beat. Still, he was not the spokesperson of the duo.

"A lot happened at Malbork," Andrew offered. "Even though I was allowed to see Mara, we were never left alone, at least not until the end. For a while, Michael had me questioning Mantrella. I wondered if he was, indeed, the Great Deceiver. The world seems a little messed up, Nilaihah. I still don't understand why." Andrew looked pleadingly at Nilaihah, searching her emerald-green eyes for answers.

Nilaihah returned the stare. "Recall the story of the prodigal, Andrew," she began. "He is the son who goes out into the world as mankind. He leaves in order to find an experience which will lead to knowledge, understanding, and hopefully, wisdom. The son who fears to venture out is symbolic of the angels. The fatted calf is prepared for the prodigal, but not for the son who refuses to leave home. Man will become as gods; the angels will not. In man, the principles of physical creation are perfected and he embodies the blueprint of the Great Plan; the angels do not. When your evolution is complete, you will rise so far above their order that their purpose will be mute. I believe they feel that if they can keep humanity in a state of chaos and prevent the fulfillment of the dream, they might preserve their place in the universe forever."

"How—*when* is all of this supposed to happen?"

"I cannot give you that answer, Andrew. Not because I do not want to, but because I do not have the answer. Mantrella knows, but he keeps many mysteries to himself."

Andrew turned his attention to the maelstrom outside. The snow was so thick that he could no longer see the ground, and he had no reference point as to where he was in space.

"What do you know of the Tarot?" he asked.

"Depend on your companion Eli for that information. It is not my area of expertise. Mantrella has said little on that subject. I do know that it contains much of what was lost and hidden. It is a guide to the ancient wisdom and tells of what will be, when all is done. It is a map, but to what I do not know. It has never been a concern to my existence, so I have not pursued the matter."

The pilot cocked his head and interrupted the conversation to announce that they would have a layover in France until word was sent from Mantrella to move on. He informed them that there was heavy winter gear in the compartments under the seats, and that all of Europe was in the midst of an out-of-season storm of the century. Andrew immediately thought of the Stephen King movie of the same name. The film also happened to include a vampire.

He shifted his glance to Nilaihah, who turned to him and smiled. As if reading his mind, she opened her mouth wide to show him that there were no fangs. Andrew began to laugh, and even Moloc let out a deep guttural chuckle. The laughter continued as the pilot made ready to land. Lately, he had questioned all that he thought he knew, but he was certain that he had come to really like Nilaihah and Moloc, and to count on their company. They were his source of safety.

Yet he had no idea how the pilot was going to land the helicopter in this raging whiteout.

CHAPTER 32

WORLD LINK PRESS — The residents of Malbork, Poland were once again treated to a surreal light show at the famed Teutonic Castle.

While closed to the public for general repairs, multi-colored flashes were observed by local residents in the early evening hours. The light show was seen along the ramparts and from every corner of the castle grounds.

Historically, Malbork has been the sight of strange events and occurrences, ranging from the purported presence of ghosts of Teutonic knights to roaming balls of light. Residents of this suburban town are convinced that aliens have used the castle as a base of operations from which to spy on European defenses. Local officials have denied these rumors and stress that all such reports have a logical explanation.

They contend that last night's lights were merely the result of a freak lightning storm and the passing of a low-flying helicopter.

***

Eli's conversations with Andrew always made for interesting debates and he loved to taunt his best friend. While Eli recognized that God truly geometrized, he would never admit this to his esteemed colleague. He thoroughly enjoyed taking an opposing view, just to see Andrew go off on a tangent. He pretended that it was science versus theology, but in his mind, that was far from the truth. The only meaningful secret he'd ever kept from Andrew was his research concerning the mysterious Bible code that in many ways had been inspired by his philosopher friend. Working in the original Hebrew, he was using a number-based alphabet to decode the text in an effort to find hidden messages in the Old Testament. While he was not ashamed of this project, he was waiting for a breakthrough before informing Andrew of his efforts. Having known the gifted professor for the past fifteen years, he knew better than to present theories to him unless he had his "ducks in a row," as it were.

Eli was concerned for Andrew. The dire and cryptic call from Poland unnerved him, though the assignment with which he'd been charged was intriguing. He vaguely knew the Tarot existed, but that was the extent of his knowledge. Andrew calling it the "code of codes" was all too ironic. He wished now that he'd told his friend of his involvement with the Bible code. Nonetheless, Eli began his research in earnest since Andrew had been so insistent, and he gathered his initial ideas and information from the best and most logical place he could think of — Andrew's den.

Living only two blocks away, Andrew often asked Eli to look in on Nevyn, reminding him the presence of the dog was, after all, his doing.

Eli had no problem with this occasional duty, since he and Nev got along well enough. He enjoyed teasing the rapidly growing dog he called "Bubba." He wasn't really sure where the name had come from, but each time he said "hello" to Bubba, Nev would give a low growl as if to respond, "Call me that again and you'll be minus your manhood." Sometimes, for the sake of convenience, Nev would have to stay at Eli's brownstone if Andrew was on an extended absence. The dog usually went willingly, seeming to enjoy the change of scenery.

But this trip—Nev refused to leave the apartment. When Eli tried to put on the choke chain, a task he'd performed dozens of times before, Nevyn bared his fangs and wouldn't let Eli near him. It wasn't until he put the chain back into the closet that Nevyn's mood changed. He could pet the dog without reaction, but if he touched the chain, Nev quickly became the *Hound of the Baskerville*.

Eli ultimately decided that he wouldn't try Nevyn's patience, mostly because he was afraid of the dog. Instead, he made many visits to the apartment to care for his canine friend. Jen minded little, telling her husband that she knew he and Andrew were basically insane and that she was used to their odd behavior. She spent as much time as she could at the apartment with Eli, feeding, walking, and generally caring for Nevyn, yet she feared Eli's new project, and she wasn't exactly sure why.

For many nights, Eli went to the apartment alone, in search of answers.

Nevyn, consequently, began to read Eli's intentions. When Nev had to go out to relieve himself, he allowed the use of the choke collar. If Eli got the notion that the dog had settled enough to take him to his place, the teeth and attitude returned. He didn't understand what was on the dog's mind, but he had a feeling Nevyn was on guard to some elusive danger. Perhaps the dog had picked up on his master's current precarious situation and felt the need to be at home.

At any rate, Eli made some interesting progress on the Tarot project. In fact, he was becoming most fascinated with the Tarot numerology and its application to his own code project. He was amazed at not only the information contained in the twenty-two major arcana, but also at the fact that so much information historically had been hidden in a variety of codes. He thought that the whole issue of secret codes begged the question of the need for the secret, as well as of the secret's author. If those who wrote the codes had told the truth in the first place. there wouldn't have been the perceived necessity for the codes. Eli figured there had to be a reason for all the cloak and dagger, that reason was probably buried, obviously, in a code. Regardless, he enjoyed toiling with and exposing the unknown.

Working on Andrew's laptop, Eli separated the wheat from the chaff with regard to the Tarot. He sorted, collated, and cross-referenced, until he finally culled all the data he'd collected to key concepts and translations. He rid his analysis of fake decks; traced the ancient origins, brought the symbology forward, examined what societies, sects, and organizations were connected to the symbols, and most importantly, examined the numbers, letters, and meanings associated with various sequences of the cards. What began to emerge was a series of patterns that Eli found astounding. He discovered worlds within worlds and meanings within meanings—all paths of enlightenment.

The correlations and correspondences were almost infinite. Card twenty-one, *The World*, could be reduced to a three by adding its single numbers, 2 and 1, which correlated to *The Empress* card. *The Devil*, card fifteen, became a six by adding 1 and 5, correlating to *The Lovers*. When arranged with the twenty-first card as the first, he noticed the androgynous being surrounded by spirals of what could be DNA. When twenty-one was reduced to three, he recalled the Law of the Triangle, which brought all into manifestation. The cards could also be arranged into the *Qabbalah's* Tree of Life and its shadow, the Tree of Knowledge. Information was presented in all planes depending on the layout, with horizontal, vertical, and diagonal lines having different meanings.

While totally intrigued by the *gematria*, he began to focus on the interpretations of the Hebrew letters. This was a project that he'd put aside several days earlier so he could focus on the numeric. Now he wanted to decipher the letter sequences to see what hidden messages they might reveal.

All the while Eli worked on his research, Nevyn lay at his feet. On Saturday, at around 8:15 pm, Eli was startled when the apartment door flew open and Jen came rushing in with a pizza and a six pack of *Gristmill Ale*. Nevyn had no reaction to her sudden entrance, remaining at Eli's feet.

"Christ, Jen!" Eli exclaimed. "I thought you weren't coming over here while I was doing this research. Didn't you have plans with some friend of yours?"

"In case you haven't noticed, there's a raging blizzard out there," Jen replied heading for the kitchen. Nevyn caught the scent of his favorite food and rose to follow her.

"Just a minute, Bubba; you always get your share," Jen said, and the dog let out a low growl. "Sorry, Nev, I forgot how much you hate that nickname." To make amends, she opened the pizza box, tore off a strip of crust, and tossed it to him. The peace offering was enthusiastically received and devoured.

She opened two beers, grabbed the pizza box, and headed for the sofa. Eli, who had gone to the window to check out the heightening winds of the Northeaster, sat beside his wife and took a piece of the pepperoni, extra cheese pizza.

"So, how goes the research?" Jen asked.

"Kind of early for snow, isn't it?"

Jen wiped the tomato sauce from her mouth with a napkin. "Some weird front or something is moving through," she answered. "It's all over the news."

"Oh," he said absently. "Anyway, it's very fascinating."

"The snow?"

He glanced at her. "The research. There's really a lot of stuff in the Tarot, once you get past the bullshit." He'd taken only a single bite of the pizza, and was now tearing off pieces and feeding them to the dog.

"I don't know," she said, cheeks fat with warm dough. "I don't like the idea."

He reached for a beer and took a sip. "People got so hung up on fortune telling with the cards that they totally missed the point. It's kind of like astrology. The energies of the heavenly bodies affect all of us and influence our behavior, but there is no way you can use them to plot your future. The cards won't tell you who you're going to marry or when you're going to get laid, but that's how people use them. The cards are a kind of purloined letter. They tell a story in pictures, numbers, and sounds that would blow your mind. You can find them everywhere, but hardly anyone really knows anything about them. And then you get these idiots that just make up decks and call them 'mystical' when they don't even know the meaning of the word."

"People really suck," Jen said inching her hand toward his groin.

He was bending his head to kiss her when Nevyn bolted upright and growled at the door. Eli stood and held his hand out to signal Jen to stay where she was as he moved cautiously toward the foyer. Nev stayed near the end of the couch continuing his low, constant grumble.

Peering through the peephole, he saw nothing. Eli shrugged and returned to the living room, only to find, to his own terror, that where Nevyn had stood was now a creature as tall as the ceiling. The man instantly thought *werewolf*, but the image didn't fit the Hollywood stereotype. It was too beautiful. Though it scared the shit out of him, he was no less entranced by its beauty and perfection of form. His eyes drifted to Jen, who had passed out with not so much as a yelp.

At a loss for action, any options he might have considered were quickly removed as the door behind him blasted inward. The explosion sent him flying toward the sofa, where he came to rest beside Jen. His vision blurred and the room began to spin. Eli fought to stay conscious. All he remembered of the ensuing seconds was the sound of men's voices, the crack of gunfire, and the screams of those who were torn apart by a relentless animal.

Losing the fight, Eli's world went dark as he joined Jen in a state of mindless oblivion.

When Eli awoke, he wasn't sure if what had happened was real. Blinking to clear his vision, he surveyed the apartment. Splinters of the door were scattered through the foyer and living room. Bullet holes riddled the walls, and furniture littered the floor—but there was no blood. Although his last conscious memory was of the screams of the dying, no bodies were present.

The noise of chewing drew his attention to the end of the couch. Nevyn lay on the floor with the box of pizza. He turned his head to Eli as he swallowed the last piece of crust, tail wagging as if to welcome his babysitter back to reality.

CHAPTER 33

"Eli?"

"Andrew? Where the hell are you? You're never going to believe what happened at your place. I hope you're on your way home," Eli said in earnest.

"I'm in Ussat-les-Bains."

"Where?"

"Montsegur," Andrew replied.

"That sounds French."

"That's because I'm in France," Andrew said.

"Why the hell are you in France? I thought you were on the trail of something important. Sounds like you're on vacation."

"I'm hardly vacationing, and I'm nowhere near Paris. I know it's been a while since my last call, but I'm involved in something that is taking on cosmic proportions. What happened at my apartment, anyway?" Andrew asked.

"For starters, you have a new front door. The old one was shattered into hundreds of pieces when it blew up," Eli answered emphatically.

"How the hell did my front door blow up? Are you okay?"

"We're fine. Neither Jen nor I were hurt. We were having pizza a few nights ago when someone blew up the door and came into the apartment. The strange thing is I'm not exactly sure what they wanted or what happened to them." Eli became increasingly agitated. "Then Nevyn turned into a frigging werewolf or something."

"A werewolf?" Andrew's voice lacked surprise. "Did you find any ashes on the floor?"

"How did you know there was ash on the floor?" Eli's blood pressure had sky-rocketed, along with the volume of his voice.

"After what I've been through lately, nothing would surprise me, but Nevyn isn't a werewolf It won't mean anything to you right now, but my dog's what is referred to as a 'Watcher.' You shouldn't fear him, Eli. He's a protector."

"Andrew, you're really getting me worried. You need to come home. I think you need treatment...or I do. What in God's name is a 'watcher'? Have you gone CIA on me? Have you become a spy without my knowledge?" Eli was rambling, coming close to an anxiety attack.

"I'm safe, Eli," Andrew assured him. "And I'm not CIA, but they may have been the ones who tried to break in. There's so much I want to tell you, but not over the phone. Just understand that a Watcher is a kind of angel—a protector. Trust me; you have absolutely nothing to fear from Nevyn. As a matter of fact, you couldn't be in safer hands. It might not be a bad idea if you and Jen stay at my place until I do get back. I'm pretty sure that you won't be bothered again now that they know a Watcher is with you."

"Who are 'they'? You think the CIA might have tried to get in?"

"Eli, I swear that I'll share *all* that I've discovered when time permits. I have to go to the Sabarthez cluster shortly. How is the Tarot project coming?"

"What the hell is the..." He hesitated. Then he added, "The project's coming along fine. I've been cross-referencing data with my Bible code project, and..."

"Bible code project?"

"Just something I've been working on."

"And I didn't know about it?"

"I wasn't about to give you any ammunition for our arguments."

"Well, that's a good idea, anyway. I know all these codes have a connection, and if anyone can find it, it's you."

"When are you coming home? We really need to talk."

"Eli," Andrew said, "I really don't know. I'll try to touch base more often. I feel that things are coming to a head and we should be able to talk in more depth soon. I just need to be sure that no matter what, you'll come through for me. I can't promise that you won't end up in danger, but I'll make sure that whatever happens, you'll be safe. I have to go now. I'll call as soon as I can." The phone crackled. "One last thing, I want you to get my journals out of the locked bottom left-hand drawer of my desk. The key to the desk is in the capstone of the little pyramid on the fireplace mantle."

"You've never let me touch your journals before."

"I know, but now you'll have to. I want you to read them and then burn them. I think that's what the intruders were after. You'll have a better understanding of this whole thing, and we can talk about it more the next time I call. By the way, don't do any computer analysis while you're on-line. Get whatever data you need, then unplug. It'll be harder for anyone to monitor you that way."

"Now you tell me," Eli exclaimed. "Jesus, Andrew, what the hell do you have me involved with, anyway? Andrew? *Damn it!*" he cursed as the phone went dead. He felt a rub against his leg and looked down to see that Bubba had curled up at his feet.

***

Andrew was nervous. While the night sky was clear and shimmering with a billion points of light, the near-zero temperature only added to his shakes. Nilaihah was dressed in a black leather suit that sharply contrasted with her white skin. In the darkness, her head appeared to float as if it were detached from her body. Moloc was also in black, and as invisible against the night sky as his partner. The threesome was headed for the Cave of Bethlehem, the ancient spiritual center of the Cathari. Andrew was familiar with Cathar lore. He knew that few records existed anymore, since they had been burned, along with most of the Cathars. However, it was widely understood that their beliefs were based on a form of Manichaeism mixed with Druidic teachings, a touch of Moslem Sufism, and Jewish Cabbalism.

Unfortunately for the Cathars, they rallied the poor to resist the abuses of the Church and the nobles. The Church may have been more tolerant, but unpaid tithes taxed the pocketbook, and this offense could not go unpunished. And so, in 1209, Simon de Montfort began the crusade against the Cathars with a fanatical vengeance. When the Council of Lateran established the Inquisition in 1215, a further reign of Church-sponsored terror resulted in a death toll of over one million people. In 1244, the Cathar bastion of Montsegur fell, and the 205 faithful walked to their death in the Church's waiting fires.

There was still speculation that several Cathars escaped with their secret treasures, including sacred books and the Grail Stone, but nothing had yet been found to confirm the theory. Andrew once believed that the mystical Cathars were extinct, but now he knew differently. He was about to climb the Path of Initiation and partake of *The Consolamentum*.

Nilaihah and Moloc brought Andrew to the entrance of the stone cave and bid him to enter. Hesitantly, he took his first step and then stopped, realizing that his new friends continued to stand their ground.

"No, Andrew," Nilaihah said, "you must take this journey alone."

Andrew breathed deeply and tried to steady his nerves as he entered the darkened cave. What awaited him was a *parfait*—a perfecti or master adept. It was he who would soon lay his hands on Andrew's head and transmit what was supposed to be the purifying light of initiation into the core of his being. When Andrew stepped further into the cave, he saw the *parfait* off to one side. He was dressed in black, which seemed to be the color of the night's events, and wore a sash around his waist. Any thought that the Cathars were a defunct sect of mystics quickly evaporated from Andrew's mind. They may have been masterfully hidden, but they were alive and well, nonetheless.

As his eyes adjusted to the dim lighting, the arrangement of the cave became clearer. To one side was a square niche which contained, according to Nilaihah, the Holy Grail. In the center of the cave was a granite stone, or altar, on which lay the *Gospel of John*, the most mystical of the books of the Bible, save for *Revelation*. Hewn into another wall was a pentagram—a sacred and ancient symbol demonized by the Church. There were no lamps or torches in the cave, yet there was a weak source of light. It finally dawned on Andrew that the source of the light lay in the stone floor and walls, glowing in flowing currents of *telluric*, or earth energy.

Andrew's last cohesive memory was of the *perfecti* motioning for him to approach the altar and kneel. Afterwards, he remembered only fragments of the initiation that followed.

"Wheresoever two or three are gathered in my name, there I am in the midst of them."

"Ye are the Temple of the Living God...I dwell in them and walk in them..."

"...and he shall give you another Comforter, that He may abide with you forever; even the Spirit of Truth, whom the world cannot receive, because it seeth Him not, neither knoweth Him; but ye know Him, for He dwelleth with you, and shall be in you."

"Know ye not that ye are the temple of God, and that the Spirit of God dwelleth in you?"

"Go ye and teach all nations."

"Go ye into the world..."

"They shall lay hands..."

"Heal the sick..."

"He that believeth in me, the works that I do he shall do also."

"These signs shall follow them that believe..."

Though he felt himself to be in a state of unconsciousness, he could hear his own voice responding to the ritual, *"I have this will...Parcite Nobis..."*

The final words to circle in his mind were, "*Adoremus, Patrem, et Filium et Spiritum Sanctum.*"

Andrew felt a sacred thread being wrapped around his torso and a black gown draped over his body. The *perfecti* then gave him a kiss of peace, the final act of the initiation.

As he left the cave, Andrew saw a white dove flying overhead. Both Moloc and Nilaihah were seated on the ground in a Zen-like position of meditation. As he approached them, they rose and bowed their heads to him.

"Your soul is now released from bondage, Andrew," Nilaihah declared solemnly.

For the first time in his life, Andrew felt truly free.

CHAPTER 34

The drive back to Hotel Villa de Rosa transpired in silence. Andrew was processing the series of images he'd received when the *perfecti* had laid hands on his head. He could hardly comprehend the flow of energy climbing up his spinal column. At one point he'd thought his head would literally explode when the charge reached his brain. While much of the detail of the experience was now imbedded in his subconscious, Andrew vividly recalled screaming in agony as the kundalini force cleansed his mind of all the dross of human existence. He was now aware of the degree to which basic and universal truths had been distorted as people used extreme means to achieve their own ends. He discovered that so much of the Cathar beliefs had been twisted. The inner circles of the *perfecti* believed that the Supreme Being created twin forces of reality and unreality—positive and negative—but negatives or unrealities were not seen as evil unless one was blinded by them. To the masses, this polarization became the battle of good, Light, or God, versus evil, Darkness, or Satan. The illusionary Veil took on substance, as those who sought power used the illusion for their own selfish needs. For this, millions would perish, and the core of the atrocities would remain constant, continually showing itself as the Church. He could not believe that the Church would allow, even encourage, the holocaust, just to prevent the possible birth of a new messiah. In their ignorance, they didn't even recognize that Jesus was a Gentile, not a Jew.

Moloc pulled the Mercedes into the hotel parking lot. Without uttering a word, they went to their adjoining rooms, Moloc and Nilaihah in one, and Andrew in the other. Nilaihah insisted that the connecting door remain open so she could more easily watch over Andrew.

Shortly after he had gone to his room, he appeared in the connecting doorways.

"Are you two asleep?" he asked quietly.

"We do not sleep very much," Nilaihah said from the darkness.

"Could I ask you something?"

Nilaihah and Moloc joined him in his room. Moloc stood near the door, the lamplight from Andrew's room washing over his hulking form, and Nilaihah sat on the edge of the bed, beside her human friend.

"I need to confirm an impression," Andrew said, his thoughts turned inward.

"I will do my best, Andrew," she said softly.

"I have wondered why Mantrella, with all of his power, has us running around Europe in search of Mara and fighting battles. I figured that if such beings truly exist, why not just snap a finger and change things?" He knew that this was not precisely a question, but he wasn't certain what he wanted to ask.

"Andrew," Nilaihah replied, "Mantrella will not force his will upon anyone. He wanted you to have his version of events. He knew that Michael would take you, and he wanted you to have the Archangel's version, also. Did not Mantrella tell you that it was not about humanity, but about each individual?"

Andrew clearly remembered the conversation. "Yes."

"You are on a great journey of self-discovery," Nilaihah continued. "Of what value would it be if you were simply brainwashed into believing one side or the other? Mantrella knows that free will must prevail, and right decisions will be made if the facts are known. He will not lower himself to Michael's level and use fear and propaganda as a means to an end. The ends never justify the means, Andrew. You are experiencing your personal precipitating events. As the truth is revealed, it will be up to you to use that truth if you will ever truly be free."

"Thank you, Nilaihah. You answered the question that I wasn't sure how to ask. The way of Mantrella is the way of responsibility. I can see why most choose the easy road. Do you…"

Moloc raised a hand to end the conversation, cocking his head to one side as if straining to hear something.

"Malta," Moloc said.

"What?" Andrew asked.

"We must go to Malta," Moloc repeated gruffly. "Mantrella has said so."

"Now that you have *seen the light*," Nilaihah explained, "Mantrella will use more direct means of communication. You must learn to clear your mind of extraneous thought and open yourself to direct contact. You no longer have to go into a sleep state to talk to Mantrella." She rose and moved toward Moloc. "We had better fly."

***

Soon they were soaring over Malta in a private jet, and Andrew still had much on his mind. New concepts emerged and old dogma had been purified in the fire of his Cathar initiation. He made no attempt to mentally communicate with Mantrella, partly out of fear of failure, and partly because he needed to sort things out on his own. After confronting the Yin and Yang forces of the universe, he needed to find his own internal balance.

"Things are really never as they appear to be, are they?" he questioned Nilaihah.

"No, Andrew, they are not," she answered.

"Why do people put so much trust in ideas and institutions that they know so little about?"

"It makes them feel safe, Andrew. It means that they do not have to take responsibility for their actions or shortcomings. By letting others worry about the true nature of existence, they can continue to play the role of being humans, which they find exceedingly difficult. If *others* are dealing with the spiritual, they are then free to focus on the illusionary physical world that they call 'life'."

"I'm sure you're right, Nilaihah," Andrew answered absently. "No, really, you are definitely right. Having eyes, they don't want to see. The promise of 'Don't worry, we'll take care of it' has so imbued the human psyche that I don't think they could deal with the truth if they had to."

"This is why there have been so many cover-ups and resulting conspiracy theories," Nilaihah added. "Anything that might rock the spiritual or reality boat is hidden because people tend to panic. If governments were to admit to their dealings with aliens or to their involvement with assassinations or the true extent of environmental degradation, people would start committing mass suicide."

The jet banked south to make its approach to Valletta, the capitol of Malta. Andrew once again was lost in contemplation as he focused his attention on the beautiful Mediterranean sky and the setting sun. He liked being in the air. From this vantage point everything looked so peaceful below. The drama of everyday life, with its trials and tribulations, was absent in the space above. *Perhaps if people could fly*, he thought, *things would be different*...

A question suddenly arose from the depths of his befuddled mind.

"Where exactly is Adam?" he asked abruptly.

"Wherever you look, there Adam is." The voice was deep and heavy. At first he thought it was Mantrella, invading his thoughts, but he turned from the consolation of the window to see Moloc's black eyes on him.

"He may be big and brutish, but he is not shallow," Nilaihah said lightly.

"Pardon me if I sound confused," Andrew said, "but are we talking about the birth of a messiah or Rosemary's baby? I mean, what about this plan for Mara and me, and the whole genetic code idea?"

Moloc grunted, and Andrew felt his own ignorance flush into his cheeks.

Nilaihah answered, "For someone with your education, you are yet tied to the myths that blind most."

Though her comment was delivered without malice, Andrew still felt the sting of it. He'd spent his life exposing and questioning the fallacies of conventional *wisdom*, but here he found that in spite of his training, mass-marketing of dogma had claimed a fertile patch in the garden of his mind.

"Andrew, you must understand this," she said evenly, demanding his full attention: "Adam is *dreaming* himself into existence, and someday he will enter the physical world."

The words—the concept—slapped him as if with an iron hand. "And Mara and I..." he uttered, but he couldn't complete the question.

Nilaihah gave him a warm smile.

"We're about to land, so please fasten your seatbelts," the metallic voice of the pilot sounded from the intercom.

***

Andrew's neurons were numb. They simply wouldn't fire as his mind fell toward a deep freeze. Nilaihah ignored his pleading glances, and he concluded he would have to struggle with his questions concerning Adam on his own. Only one viable image pulsed in the growing glaciers of his brain—finding Mara.

As the party exited the jet, they were met by three jeeps and a truck that was no doubt used to carry army troopers. A gray-haired man in fatigues stepped out of the lead jeep and approached them. On closer inspection, Andrew saw that the stranger was one of Nilaihah's kind, his skin a milky-white.

"Nilaihah," the man said with recognition. "We must hurry. They have her near Mnajdra. We do not know how long they intend to stay, for they have boats at the ready."

176

"Nico, it is good to see you again," she said, gently brushing his cheek with her fingertips.

"Your touch always clears the head," Nico replied as the tension drained from his stiff shoulders, "but the pleasantry must wait. Mantrella was adamant that we try to keep them from leaving the Islands."

"Then we must hurry. This is…"

But Nico had already turned from her and begun his return to the jeep, saying behind him, "I know who he is." He glanced back at the human, their eyes locking for only an instant, and Andrew sensed that the two of them were bonded in the tides of time. There was an old familiarity from a place in ancient days, and in some distant time he had called this man "friend."

Andrew sat in the front seat beside the gray-haired man, while Nilaihah and Moloc climbed into the rear, behind the mounted machine gun. The vehicles fell into line behind Nico, the obvious leader of this small but lethal assault team. When they entered the countryside, the rocky terrain and aridness reminded Andrew of Greece. Periodically, they drove past ancient megaliths and stone temples that could be seen in a hazy fog on the horizon.

Malta, he mused, was the site of a strange civilization whose ruins predated Stonehenge and the Great Pyramid of Egypt by over a thousand years. He recalled that the temples in Ggantija were the oldest freestanding monuments in the world. Steeped in goddess worship, the islands were a center of mystical practices known collectively as the "Sacred Island" of the Mediterranean world. He wondered if the temples and megaliths were a product of Atlantean influence, and the Goddess but another name for Eve. He remembered many of the theories regarding the great stone works. To some, the monuments marked the constellations. To others, the ideas ranged from being boundary markers or celestial calendars to sites of worship and beacons to an alien race. But to Andrew, the ruins seemed to be obvious places of worship, meditation, and contemplation, though the giant stones remained an enigma. Perhaps they were placed around the globe as some kind of spiritual reminder to keep people focused on the mysterious. Either way, their presence had forced many to raise mystical questions about life in general, and to that end, the stones' mere existence served a profound purpose.

The questions for Mantrella are endless, he thought.

As they continued along the dusty roads, Andrew turned to Nico and asked, "Why Malta?"

"The *Knights*," Nico replied in disgust.

"The Knights of Malta?"

"They are the devils of the Church, if you'll pardon the reference," he said.

"I know of their existence, but I have to confess ignorance as to their purpose," Andrew admitted.

"That's the way they like it," he answered. "They are the Sovereign Order of John of Jerusalem. To be a member you had to be a Catholic and have had prior military service. The Emperor Charles V gave Malta as a fief to the Order in the 1500s, but their history goes back to St. Paul. The current history is more important, however. They were tied to the 'Rat Run' after World War II. They helped high-ranking Nazi officers defect from Germany to escape punishment as war criminals. The Order's highest award, the Grand Cross of Merit, was given to General Gehlen, Hitler's henchman in Russia and Eastern Europe. He slaughtered thousands of Jews and Slavs. Juan Peron in Argentina was a Knight and he laundered Nazi gold through the Vatican Bank. They created the Bilderberg Group during the Cold War to *guide* world affairs, and they have had links to right wing revolutions, the Mafia, and the death of Pope John Paul I. You can only guess that they played a role in Peter's death. They are also closely linked with the Vatican's Opus Dei. Some have tried to link them with the Rose Cross, but this is not so. When Napoleon, a Grand Master of the Rose Cross, conquered Malta, he booted the Knights out. Even he knew the game they played. As with most of these Church secret societies, they hide under the name of Jesus. *Pro fide, pro utilitate hominum*—as we are united in Christ, we are united with one another. This kind of bullshit is what gets all of the benedictions of the popes. Peter refused, and we know what happened to him."

"Now I see why you call them devils," Andrew conceded. "It seems that no matter where you turn, the Church reaches its tentacles into just about everything. The bad just far outweighs the good. To see the world, you have to look at it through a mirror; everything is the opposite of what it seems."

"A good philosophy to live by," Nico replied. "Now it's time to send those bastards to see the namesake they claim to serve."

***

The plan was simple: attack, kill, rescue Mara. No scouting, no stealth. A direct charge requiring anything that needed to be done. On a handheld radio, Nico called his troops. He spoke in a language foreign to Andrew, but he got the gist of the message when the vehicles aligned laterally with theirs.

The gray-haired man pulled a 9mm from his holster and asked Andrew if he knew how to use a firearm. Andrew shook his head. Nico quickly instructed him, before handing him a belt of clips and showing him the button to push and how to insert a fresh round. He smiled, and with his free hand patted Andrew on the shoulder.

The vehicles crested a small rise, and Andrew saw the ruins of the Temple of Mnajdra. He also saw men scurrying to several boats anchored on the rocky shore. Within seconds, gunfire was heard from the temple and from the vehicles to either side of him, the noise deafening. Adrenaline coursed through his body as he gripped the 9mm with both hands.

Within a hundred yards of the temple, the vehicles came to an abrupt halt in clouds of dust. Nico's people jumped from their vehicles, save for those who manned the turreted machine guns. The mounted weapons unleashed a curtain of cover fire as Nico, Moloc, Nilaihah, and the rest surged forward. In response, the enemy made its way down the rocks and began to board the boats. The humans were the first to try to make their escape, as they knew they were the most vulnerable. Those like Moloc transformed on the run. Creatures in the shape of Anubis clashed with the Dogs of Isis along the rocky coast and bursts of energy at their deaths exploded everywhere. Humans were shot. Even Nilaihah used an automatic weapon to fell her prey.

Andrew spotted Mara on the dock, locking eyes with her. He raced to intercept her and her captors before they reached the waiting vessel, whose engines roared in neutral. At the water's edge, he felt Moloc beside him, and his confidence rose. The two rushed onto the narrow makeshift dock jointly seeking the same prize. Moloc was faster and got ahead of him. He looked back and saw that an enemy's AK-47 had a line on Moloc. Andrew knew that the bullets would have little effect on his beastly companion, but his human heart urged him to save his friend just the same. With little thought, he moved to take the bullets targeted at Moloc. A fiery pain seared through his shoulder, then his chest, then his right leg. As he fell off the dock, he glimpsed a jackal-headed creature catch his friend from behind and sink its teeth into Moloc's neck. Moloc thrashed, and with all of his strength, he managed to sever the head of his assailant, who burst into a bright ball of energy.

Everything moved in slow motion as Andrew hit the cold water of the Mediterranean Sea, landing on his back and sinking. He gazed toward the surface at the reflection and wavy image of the sun, its brightness turning crimson red in a cloud of his own blood.

But before he completely faded into nothingness, he heard the familiar voice call his name.

"Andrew," Mantrella whispered.

Andrew responded in his mind: *I'm dying…*

"In a way, you are dying. Baptism is a kind of death. You have received baptism of spirit, and now water. Fire is next. We will meet in Mexico…"

"Mantrella? Mantrella?" He could see the darkness coming, and the words surfaced from the depths of his rapidly dying thought, *Heloi, Heloi, lama sabachthani.*

As the remaining part of his brain sought the origins of these words, a thick black arm grabbed him by the hair and yanked him from the cold sea. A forceful compression of his chest brought water belching from his lungs. Kneeling over him was Moloc, light emerging from his neck where he had been bitten. Nilaihah was beside him.

Barely able to whisper, he pulled together what remnants of strength still floated in his soul, uttering, "I'm sorry I let you down. If you get to Mara tell her…tell her…"

Moloc's huge hands pressed into Andrew's chest with the force of a jackhammer. His body convulsed as the electric current twitched through every muscle fiber.

In the shriek of a banshee, Nilaihah screamed, "Moloc, no!" But it was too late. The tear in Moloc's neck began to grow and his body flickered like bands of heat rippling from desert sands. Andrew, slowly regaining consciousness, realized that Nilaihah's mournful cry was not for him, but for her other half, and he fed from the reserves of energy that were being replenished by Moloc's jump start.

"No, Moloc…Stop…" Andrew yelled weakly, as he tried to squirm from under Moloc's powerful hands.

"You gave your life for me. It is now my turn to give mine for you," Moloc answered, his brow creased in pain. He removed his hands from Andrew's body and tried to grin in satisfaction. His body shimmered faster now, and he turned to Nilaihah, his love for untold centuries. "When the tide next comes in," he said, extending a hand to her, but before their fingers could touch he flickered out of existence.

Nilaihah's hand remained suspended, seeking a touch that was no longer there.

CHAPTER 35

Andrew gradually returned to full consciousness. He had felt Moloc's healing touch and his body tingled with electricity as muscle and tendon were repaired. He looked into Moloc's eyes and he suddenly realized that he was giving the last of his life force to rebuild what should have been Andrew's bullet-ridden corpse. He wanted to tell Moloc to stop, to let his body and mind fade into the peacefulness of oblivion, but the words would not come. The healing energy was so intense that he was unable to form the sounds. He saw Moloc look to Nilaihah, and the gentle giant's expression spoke of great love and a final goodbye. He heard Nilaihah scream, and her cry sent a wicked chill to the core of his very soul and echoed through the universe as a lament to all lost loves.

Moloc had simply dissolved into a small pile of ashes.

Soaked to the skin, Andrew wormed in the discomfort of his wet clothes. He sat up on the makeshift dock and clutched his knees to keep from falling over. It was then that he heard the howls. All of Moloc's companions had raised their heads, and their wails reverberated to a mournful pitch in a crescendo of farewell. Andrew began to cry. He looked for Nilaihah and found her gazing back at him, the sadness on her face aching in his heart.

"I'm sorry," Andrew uttered, his voice pleading for forgiveness.

For a moment she continued to stare through him, then she answered, "I thank you, as does Moloc. No one has ever put their life on the line to try to save one of his kind. You cannot know how deeply this touched his heart. Giving you his energy did not kill him. He would have died from the bite. He would have had more time, but his transition was certain. He felt that the least he could do was to heal your wounds. He told me you were a true friend—for a human." She looked away, at the rolling sea. "He said one day we would be together again. Moloc never lies."

"Couldn't Mantrella have healed him?" Andrew asked. He wiped the tears from his swollen cheeks.

"No. The lawmakers are not above the laws. It was beyond even his power to prevent the passing of Moloc. Truly, there is a season," she said. Before the wind scattered all that was left of Moloc, Nilaihah scooped a small bit of ash and placed it in an amulet that she wore around her neck—an equal-armed cross with a raised rose in the center. It was the rose that opened, and now it contained the last earthly remains of a good friend.

Nico approached, bowing slightly to Nilaihah. She returned the gesture, but no words were spoken. Andrew knew words weren't necessary, and for a brief moment he could almost hear the thoughts pass between them.

"Mantrella has said that we will have a layover. The time is not yet right," Nico explained. He turned to Andrew. "I am sorry that we failed in our task, but we will have another go at it shortly. I believe that the next time the tide will be in our favor."

"Moloc's loss was for nothing," Andrew said bitterly.

"Do not think such thoughts," Nilaihah said as she clutched the amulet. "All that happens is for a reason."

"I'm so sick of that cliché," Andrew retorted, straining to his feet. "Whenever something goes wrong in this world, that's the standard response. I'm fucking sick of it. For *whose* reason do these things happen? Certainly not mine or yours." Andrew picked a stone from the dock and threw it into the ocean "If there is a reason for all of this, why can't we know *why*?" he asked more evenly now. "Why does everything have to be shrouded in some secret mystery to be shared by only a select few?"

Nilaihah took a deep breath in exasperation. "Sometimes the reasons are not shared because the very act of sharing them would change the outcome of events. If you knew the reason for everything as it happened, you would stagnate. Man is not yet all-knowing. If he were, there would be no purpose for any of this. Not having all the answers at one's fingertips puts us on the path of discovery. It is how we evolve. I do not know why Moloc had to pass at this precise moment, but I will begin my search for answers. The journey is more important than the destination."

"*Ancora Imparo*," Andrew uttered.

"Exactly," Nilaihah said. "Even Michelangelo said, 'I am still learning.'"

Nico interrupted. "Mantrella has sent us a gift to replenish our stock." He opened a wooden box and exposed rows and rows of neatly stacked bullets.

Andrew looked into the crate. "I thought bullets were useless against angels and ... your kind."

"Normal bullets *are* useless," Nico explained. "These are special, created with the five elements. We tried them years ago at a hospital when our missions first began and found them to be quite effective."

"Five elements?" Andrew asked. "I thought there were only four elements—air, water, fire, and earth. And what happened at the hospital?"

"The fifth element is spirit. I do not know how Mantrella does it, but he adds spirit to the bullet. He says that it is very difficult to do. It drains him of energy and they can only be made during certain solar cycles. The hospital story will have to wait."

Nilaihah reached into the box and grinned. She picked up one of the bullets, tipped with a raised pentacle insignia, and said, "As always, I will make special use of these, and I want Moloc's share. There will be retribution."

"We had better get going," Nico said, sealing the box of fresh ammunition. "We will take accommodations and rest. Mantrella suggested that our time here should be brief, but that a few days to heal and regroup would be in order."

"We're not to go directly to Mexico?" Andrew questioned.

"No." he said with a grin, "we are to stay here a few days and then we will be instructed as to our next move. You are to contact your friend Eli."

Frustration mounting again, Andrew asked, "Why didn't Mantrella tell me all of this?"

"Your mind was too cluttered with thoughts and emotions," Nico offered. "Sometimes humans are cursed with thinking too much."

CHAPTER 36

The meeting was held high above nowhere, in a place that was no place. It was at the point that was not a point, between the light and the dark, in the timeless space between time and no time. At one side there appeared to be light, and at the other side there appeared to be darkness. Within the light, a dot of darkness emerged. Within the darkness, a spot of light emerged. And they existed suspended in the Veil.

"It is ironic that in a universe without time it moves so slowly."

"Truly spoken, my brother."

"I know a rose is a rose, but shall I call you Mantrella, or do you prefer another?"

"*Samael* is fine, Michael."

"The old name is a good one," Michael responded.

"We are at that crossroads once again. Do you think they will take up the challenge? They have never been this close, and it would be a shame to start again."

"We stand as the two pillars between which they must pass. Whether they will reconcile the sun and the moon is anyone's guess. Now the seeds are joined. You know we oppose this. Adam would have been better left alone. In his dream state he can do no harm. He could have played with his imaginings eternally. We bowed to the potential, as long as it stayed potential."

"And there lies the dilemma," Samael noted. "This has been the source of our conflict, my friend. Of what value is the acorn if it is not planted? Why just imagine the oak when you can see it grow, touch it, and partake of its majesty?"

"And what of its pain and misery? It must suffer the elements and the constant attack on its very being. It must endure the misery of its annual death with no guarantee what the next season may bring. This is what you have brought to Adam the false dream that he may be as a god. How can you possibly trust what he may become?"

"Adam desires more than a dream for existence. You would keep him a prisoner in his own mind. He chose to partake of life, to experience it to its very core. Through this experience he has gained understanding, and the collective wisdom is growing. The hundredth monkey approaches, and the Tree of Life that you guard with your flaming sword shall soon be breached. They shall be as gods, for that is their design. The dormant gene shall emerge. What you buried in the Red Sea of blood will sleep no more."

They looked at each other, knowing that the meeting had come to an end and that the age-old rivalry would never be reconciled. But there was no animosity. There never really was. Each had his part to play on the universal stage of the planes. Each played his part well, and as long as reality existed, they knew that this would be their endless role.

With a gracious nod to one another, the pattern of their meeting place began its eternal dance, and the spiral swirled until it could be seen no more.

CHAPTER 37

Andrew and his companions stayed at the Preluna Hotel in Sliema. Their holdover lasted only three days, during which time Nilaihah said nothing. Andrew figured it was a period of mourning, but he missed discussing the nature of the universe with his odd friend. He decided instead to take the opportunity to do a little more exploring of ancient Maltese sites and temples. Nico went with him wherever he traveled as a kind of bodyguard, since they had been warned that their continued presence would only be tolerated for a short time. Nico didn't say who issued the warning or who they were warned against, but there were times when Andrew knew not to pursue questions.

He went to the temples in Ggantija and the rock-cut tombs at Zebbug and Xaghra. He journeyed to the large stone figures at Hagar Qim and the temple at the same site. At the Hypogee of Hal Saflieni he saw the sepulchers that contained over 7,000 bodies, and in almost all of these megalithic wonders he saw the presence of the goddess. Wherever he looked, he noted statues, pottery, and other symbols of ancient goddess worship. The irony of such a history, contrasted by the male dominated Universal Church and its knights, didn't escape his contemplations. He also remembered that Napoleon was a Grand Master in the Order of the Rose Cross. Yet when the Frenchman had conquered Malta, he immediately exiled the Maltese Knights from the Island. The complexities of these secret societies astounded him, and he concluded that they, too, represented varying sides in the struggle for man's soul. Perhaps the goddess still had her champions.

On day three, at one of the great stone megaliths, Andrew felt a tingling sensation throughout his body. It reminded him of being near the Van de Graf generator at the Science Museum in Boston. The air seemed filled with a subtle static charge and he could hear the faint murmur of a hum. The closer he got to the stones, the louder the hum and the greater the static discharge.

"It is time to go," Nico said at his shoulder.

"Can you feel that?" Andrew asked him. "There's a vibration. If you listen, you can almost *hear* it."

Nico nodded. "We really must go."

Within an hour, Andrew and company were aboard a private jet, headed for the Azores. Nico joined the group and had several private conversations with Nilaihah. Soon the jet flew silently into Azore airspace and landed on Pico Island.

There was much debate and controversy concerning the legend of Atlantis, its location as much a mystery as its existence. Varying theories put the lost civilization in Cuba, Central America, the Yucatan, Crete, Antarctica, the South Pacific, Sardinia, Bolivia, or finally, the Azores. If one followed the works of Edgar Cayce, the Azores were the last remaining vestiges of Poseidia, the last of the sunken remains of Atlantis. It was claimed that Plato's *Timaeus* and *Critias* placed Atlantis west of the Pillars of Hercules and that the pre-ice age Azores fit the bill for the great Atlantean empire that extended its authority throughout the ancient world from Europe to India and to the Americas. It was said that a line of fallen angels—the *Nephilim*—created a race of pre-humans as slaves. These creatures interbred with Adam and Eve, and the new gene pool and subsequent DNA combinations created modern man. The offspring of the *fallen* were said to be evil, and great battles occurred between the varying races. The two trees in the Garden of Eden—the *Tree of Knowledge of Good and Evil* and the *Tree of Life*—were said to represent the two strains of DNA that compete for dominance over the earth. The seed of the *woman* and the seed of the *serpent* had therefore become surrogate fighters in the war between God and those who opposed Him. Much of the early fighting was said to have taken place in Atlantis, which included not only the island continent, but also its worldwide empire. This, some speculated, was why so many myths and symbols were shared among highly divergent cultures that supposedly had no ancient contact. With vast technological resources, the Atlanteans may have surpassed that of modern civilizations; a theory that flew in the face of modern man's ego and its archeologists. Yet one idea remained fact: several secret societies referred to Mount Pico of the Azores in many of their rituals. These same societies claimed knowledge of the lost Atlantis.

Pico Island was the second largest in the Azores. A part of Portugal, Mount Pico was actually the tallest mountain in that nation, and it reached over 8,000 feet. Its population of just over 240,000 was predominantly Catholic. Until 1534, the Azores fell under the jurisdiction of the Grand Prior of the Order of Christ. Andrew once again found himself in the belly of the beast. He began to think Mantrella was indeed twisted, but, he considered, perhaps the old *purloined letter* trick was a valid means of hiding, especially in the modern age of techno-spying. After all, who could believe where they finally found Bin Laden?

Sitting on the veranda of a mansion that looked out toward Mount Pico, Andrew took a sip of a sweet Portuguese wine. *I have to call Eli*, he thought. Responding to the notion, Nilaihah came out into the cool late evening air with a cell phone in her hand. When she handed it to Andrew, the phone was already ringing.

"How do you—never mind. You never cease to amaze me, Nilaihah," he said.

Without answering, Nilaihah smiled and walked down the steps, disappearing into the vineyard.

Eli's voice sputtering "Hello" into the phone drew Andrew's thoughts from the spectral image of Nilaihah as she moved out of sight.

"Eli."

"It's about time," Eli said. "Where are you?"

"I'd rather not say over the phone. Let's just say I'm in the remnants of Atlantis," Andrew replied.

"Atlantis? Are you are okay?"

"I'm fine."

"Good." Eli paused. "Nevyn is fine, too. Any closer to knowing when you'll be home?"

"I'm sending you a ticket," Andrew informed him. "You'll have to come alone. I don't want to put Jen in harm's way. You will be meeting me..."

"In Mexico?"

"How did you know that?" Andrew interrogated. "Did Mantrella..."

"Who?" Eli asked.

"Eli, how did you know I was sending you a ticket for a flight to Mexico?"

"Have you been following the news?" Eli answered.

"What's going on? What does the news have to do with you knowing about Mexico?"

"Have you ever heard of tree circles?"

"What are you talking about?"

"You were in this place called Malbork, right? In Poland?"

"Okay," Andrew said, his mind struggling to draw a connection.

"In a forest in that very town appeared a huge tree circle. Not a crop circle, but a *tree circle*. It covered five acres of forest. The trees were bent to the ground like corn and wheat circles, but these were frigging trees.

They were lying down like they were made of rubber or something. They formed a gigantic goddess symbol like the ones in some of your research books. It's incredible. Since there were reports of alien spacecraft over the town, the buzz is that UFOs caused the circle."

"No shit!" Andrew replied. "The signs are showing up everywhere."

"I'm guessing you were in Malta, too," Eli continued.

"We left there a week ago."

"Well," Eli went on, "it was about then that the megaliths began to *sing*. Not the way we'd think of singing, but more of a hum. It started in Malta, but according to the news, megaliths everywhere are humming. Plus, if you get near them, your hair stands on end because of the static electricity present. Scientists are saying that it has to do with solar flares and something about magnetic lines, but you and I know that's bullshit. Something really big is going on, isn't it?"

"Maybe it is, Eli, but what does all this have to do with Mexico?" Andrew pressed.

"You really should watch the news. You used to be on top of what was happening in the world. I won't even go into what happened in Rome. Anyway, remember back in '91, when Mexico City came to a full stop because of all of the UFO sightings? Of course you do. Well, what's going on there now makes '91 look like amateur night at a Trekkie convention. So I just figured that Mexico would be your next stop. These things tend to follow you rather than precede you, but I'm only making an educated guess. Am I close?"

"Yes," Andrew conceded, the pit in his stomach growing deeper and deeper.

"Andrew?"

"I'm still here," he said at last. "I'm just trying to sort all of this out. How's the work on the code coming?"

"I thought you'd never ask. You mentioned Atlantis, and from what I can gather, the Tarot originated in Atlantis. Not the actual deck, but a pictorial concept or a transferring of ideas and thoughts through the use of images. They, whoever *they* are, say that God speaks in images. Many of the images in the Tarot are Atlantean based, and the images carried over to ancient Egypt. There are even Atlantean images in temples at Chichen Itza in Mexico. As the Church turned to dogma, organizations sprang up to carry on the true meaning of spiritual truths through the use of images as a code to keep them from being barbecued. The symbols on the cards speak to the subconscious mind, and they release insights into not only ancient history, but also into the future. I've still got some more work and sorting to do, but I'd say that the Tarot cards hold numerous keys to unlocking—or rather *activating*—genetic codes that currently lie dormant in human DNA. For example..."

"You need to finish your work by the time you get to Mexico," Andrew interrupted. "I don't want to discuss this over the phone."

"You're right. I should be able to wrap things up fairly quickly. When is the flight scheduled?"

"You'll get the ticket and instructions by courier. If you're not home, Nev will take care of safeguarding things until you can read my note," Andrew answered. "I won't be calling again, so please follow all my instructions to the letter. I'll see you soon, my friend. Give my love to Jen and give my puppy a big hug." He closed the cellular phone and placed it on the porcelain floor of the veranda.

Andrew hoped that he wasn't putting his friend in any real danger. He decided that he needed to talk to Nilaihah. He went into the vineyard searching for the one person who could calm his fears., He found her sitting on a stone bench beside a luxurious fountain. In the center was a woman on one knee, holding an urn. The water flowed from the urn into the pond, creating a familiar image that he couldn't quite place.

"Nilaihah, do you have a moment?" he asked quietly.

"Certainly."

Trying to gather his thoughts into some coherent order, he asked, "Is there really evil and evil people?"

"Andrew, what am I to do with you?" she replied sadly. "Think of *Notan*, a Japanese art form that uses black and white paper. In order for an image to appear, you must place white on black or black on white. If you put white on white or black on black, nothing is created. The two are required to create the work of art. Contrary to appearance, there are no evil people. Bad people, yes, but evil people, no. Your people are fond of bringing up the name of Hitler as a truly evil person, yet how many opportunities did he provide for people to make right choices? How many chances did he give people to do the right thing? If his father, the German people, Chamberlain, or even the Church had refused him, history would have been vastly different. He provided many lessons for this world, but still the cry has not been heard. The Jews said 'Never again,' but the rest of the world has not listened. Bosnia, Africa, Iraq, the Sudan, and scores of other places have been the scenes of genocide. In these places, they saw that the lesson Hitler offered went unheard, so they repeat the very same lessons. All of these offenses are opportunities for man to grow and evolve, yet the voices have remained silent. If humanity had said 'No' to Hitler, maybe he would have become a great leader." She spoke with an air of introspection, as if she, too, were pondering all of the lost lessons and opportunities wasted on deaf ears.

Andrew decided to take her comments to heart and to explore their validity later. "Have you heard anything about the humming megaliths?"

"You mean the singing stones? Yes, I hear them. Even Pico is singing."

"You can actually hear them?" Andrew asked. "Why can't I?"

"You could if you really stopped thinking. Too much…"

"Mind," Andrew said. "What does it mean?"

"I am not very sure, Andrew," she answered. "The last time I heard the stones sing was during the fall of Atlantis." Nilaihah hung her head in great sadness. Andrew reached out and took her hand, and together they watched the fountain in silence.

***

290 miles northeast of San Francisco, in the radio-quiet Cascades north of Mount Lassen, two scientists had turned the 350 telescopes of the Allen Telescope Array to a specific point in the night sky. Only hours before, the pair of researchers for the privately-funded organization SETI—*Search for Extraterrestrial Intelligence*—began receiving pulsing signals from two of the telescopes in the field at the Hat Creek Observatory. Now, having modified the coordinates of each of the telescopes, every dish was receiving the same sound.

Dr. Jill Klein sat anxiously behind the monitor of SETI's central computer station, blips of color reflecting off the shiny surfaces of her sweaty forehead and cheeks. *Heartbeats*, she thought. And the idea, strange as it seemed, continued to stab at her cold, scientific approach to reality.

"What have you got?" Tom Asper asked. He had joined the SETI team only months before, and suddenly felt not only excited, but also blessed at being the only other person at the observatory on what could prove to be a historic night.

Dr. Klein shook her head, staring at the computer screen. "It's amazing," she answered. "Finally, a signal, like the beating of a heart."

"I'll call it in," Asper said, moving toward the phone.

"No," Klein insisted, turning to him. "Not yet. Let's see what the system makes of it. It could be anything." But she didn't believe her own words. They had definitely discovered something, she knew it. Yet feeding off the ignorance of her green colleague, she could buy enough time to investigate the phenomena more closely as the computers worked to decode the signal, hopefully before any private sky-listeners picked up the sound on their homemade devices and began broadcasting it over the Internet.

Tom Asper pulled up a chair and sat beside Dr. Klein. Together they watched the streaming data on the computer screen as the mainframe attempted to interpret it. Abruptly, the monitor blanked, then lit again. Against a bright white background, lines of binary code revealed themselves in black text, and Dr. Jill Klein scrambled to translate in her notebook the seemingly random presentation of ones and zeros:

```
01001001
0110000101101101
0111010001101000011001011
0100001001110010011010010110011101101010000111010001100101
011000010110111001100100
0100110101101111011100100110111001101001011011100110011111
0101001101110100001100001011100010
```

"Code," Asper breathed. "Something is transmitting a binary code."

Klein nodded emphatically. "Yes, it is." She smiled, still scribbling as she assigned letters to every eight numbers and painstakingly worked to decode the message. "This is scientific history," she declared. "We'll be famous."

Asper laughed. "Next they'll land on the White House lawn," he joked.

But she wasn't listening. Instead, she dropped her pen and sat gaping at the words she'd written in the notebook. Tom Asper moved closer to her as he read the message: *I am the Bright and Morning Star.*

CHAPTER 38

When Mantrella's private jet landed, Eli could hardly believe the crowds of people that had gathered to witness the continuing UFO events. Rumors were rampant with regard to the nature of the sightings. Many claimed that the sightings were not UFOs, but rather images of the Virgin that seemed to hover around churches. Thousands came to be healed by the Virgin or to hear if She would proclaim new prophecies, since Rome had not yet been able to elect a successor to the papacy. This was a growing concern in the Church hierarchy due to the recent announcement by North American bishops and cardinals that they were appointing an acting *Pope Pro Tempore* to oversee matters in the Americas. European clergy were considering a similar move and talks of schism appeared in all of the major world newspapers.

Mexico stayed loyal to Rome. There was even talk of electing a Mexican pope, but so far, efforts to choose a successor to Peter had failed. With the recent UN fiasco in the Holy City, Catholics everywhere were at a loss as to how to proceed and who to support as their spiritual leader, so sightings of virgins, angels, and spacecraft drew the hardcore to Mexico.

Eli was lucky that his mode of air travel was a chartered plane. If not, there was little chance that he would have found a seat on a commercial airliner. Even so, when he finally entered the airspace of his destination, the flight experienced a four-hour delay in landing. If it hadn't been for low fuel, the plane would have undoubtedly been diverted to Guatemala. Many commercial flights were sent to other Central American airports in an effort to relieve the congestion.

Exiting the plane, he found the climate uncomfortably humid and sticky. The terminals were packed with sweat-ridden bodies, and he felt like he was going to be sick. Yet he had noticed a peculiar phenomena — the air was yellow and still. It was the kind of weather that immediately preceded a hurricane, but no hurricanes were in the forecast. As he struggled through the terminal in search of the limousine Andrew had promised, he was bombarded by what he thought to be every crazy person that walked the earth. Signs read, "The End Is Near," "Welcome, Our Space Brothers," "Repent," "This Is All A Government Conspiracy," "Read Revelation," "Welcome, Satan," "The Russians Are Coming," and hosts of other messages intended to offer some explanation for recent events in Mexico and the world.

Everywhere Eli turned, strangers harassed him with questions in dozens of foreign languages. His pat response soon became *"No hablo español,"* though he wasn't even sure if what people were asking was in

Spanish. Caught in the current of sweating bodies, he didn't know what direction to take in order to exit the terminal. Having only carry-on luggage, per Andrew's instructions, he stood clutching his bag, wary of losing his valuable research to *banditos*.

Suddenly, the squirming mass of people to his left grew silent and the sea of bodies parted. The split in the crowd unzipped toward him until finally he saw the reason for their actions in the form of a seven-foot-tall black man with wide shoulders and bulging muscles. The gargantuan towered over him and said deeply, "Eli, you are to come with me."

Eli stared at this singular mass of humanity, certain that if he tried to run, the long arms of the beast would grab and crush him. So he did the best he could do—he froze.

Then the giant added, "Andrew sent me. Come."

The mention of Andrew's name thawed his frozen muscles and released the tension in his vocal chords. "Are you the man Andrew said would meet me?" Eli asked timidly.

The giant smiled, before turning abruptly and walking away. Eli had no choice if he wanted to get out of the airport, so he followed in the wake created by the human steamroller. As he walked, he noticed that all whom they passed gave the sign of the cross.

They made their way through the terminal, out to a black Mercedes idling at the curbside. The hulking man opened the rear door and motioned for Eli to enter. Eli did as he was directed, nervously sliding onto the back seat. When his guide took the driver's seat, the left side of the vehicle sank toward the asphalt. Eli couldn't imagine how the man was able to fit into the seat, and he wasn't sure that the shocks would hold under the weight of such a colossal being. Nonetheless, the driver steered the car away from the curb, and like the crowds at the airport, traffic automatically pulled to one side of the road or the other to get out of the way of the tilting black Mercedes.

Since the driver offered no conversation and Eli was too frightened and exhausted to initiate one, he fell asleep. He had no idea how long he'd slept, but he was rudely awakened when the car came to an abrupt stop and he was jerked forward. For a moment he was disoriented. He felt the vehicle balance itself and heard a door slam. Suddenly remembering where he was, he quickly checked for his bag and was relieved when he found it safely on the floor of the car. His body was assaulted with blazing heat and humidity as the driver yanked open his door and the air conditioning quickly dissipated into the torrid air. Slowly exiting the vehicle, bag in hand, Eli stood before a beautiful red building with a sign that read *"Hacienda Santa Rosa."*

Standing at the doorway, with outstretched arms, was Andrew.

Eli's mounting uneasiness drained from his body when he saw his best friend. He raised his arms and ran toward the steps, bag in hand, smiling widely. In his happiness, he was oblivious to the small army of gargantuan look-alikes that were strategically positioned around the *hacienda*. His complete focus was on Andrew. When he at last reached his friend, he gave Andrew a bear hug with such strength that Andrew gasped for breath. Eli released him and stepped back, studying Andrew's face. He realized that his friend had changed; Andrew's hair had streaks of gray and his eyes shimmered with an unmistakable glow.

"My, how you've changed, Grandma," Eli said lightly, "but thank the gods it's you! I wasn't sure if the cretin that met me at the airport was really sent by you or…" Eli suddenly became aware that more beasts like his driver were watching the reunion from vantage points around the building.

"Are you okay?" he asked slowly, taking in the eyes that were on him. "Where did you find these guys?"

"We'll get into all that later," Andrew answered. "For now, let's get out of this miserable heat and get you settled." He took Eli by the arm and led him into the *hacienda.*

Eli was impressed with the colonial grandeur of the facility. Deep rich earth tones and antiques from the 18th century abounded. Andrew opened the double pecan wooden doors to his suite and ushered Eli into the lavishly decorated living area. Tropical plants were in every corner, as well as on shelves and tables. Eli saw a man and a woman sitting on the couch, talking. He dropped his bag and gulped. He'd never seen a woman so beautiful and so—white.

"Good god, girl, you need some sunlight!" Eli quipped, immediately realizing that the words had bumbled out of his mouth. He always spoke first and thought last, and this frequently caused Andrew much consternation, both at staff meetings and in public. The woman turned and looked at Eli. Her eyes blazed, and he thought that the glare would strike him dead on the spot. Eli tried to back-pedal. "I just meant that you were a little pale. I mean, you're very beautiful and I love that outfit and…"

Laughing, Andrew tried to ease the tension. "Enough, Eli, she understands your reaction. Your best bet is just to say 'Hello.' Eli, this is Nilaihah and that is Nico."

Nico was grinning, though he hadn't the nerve to laugh at the woman's expense. Instead, he stood and came to shake Eli's hand. His iron grip nearly crushing Eli's fingers, he said in a bellowing voice, "Nice to meet you, Eli. Don't mind Nilaihah; her bite is worse than her bark."

Eli caught the subtle reversal of the words in the phrase and looked once again at the pale beauty. Nilaihah approached him, and he gradually backed up toward Andrew. As she came ever closer, he was overwhelmed with the power of her presence and the mesmerizing effect of her eyes.

"Nice to meet you, Eli," she said sweetly, and it struck him that her voice would make the Sirens sound like bullfrogs.

"Very interesting to meet you, too," Eli uttered, after a jab from Andrew who was still chuckling.

Nilaihah returned to the couch with Nico, and the two resumed their conversation as if they were the only ones in the room.

Andrew touched Eli's elbow. "Let's go into the sitting room, where we can talk."

Without hesitation, Eli followed his friend, glancing back over his shoulder to take another look at what he truly felt was quite the odd couple.

***

They sat at a finely-turned Teakwood table as Eli unpacked some of his research, as well as his laptop.

"Tell me what you've found," Andrew began.

"Okay," Eli said, drawing in a long breath. "Try to follow me here. There are one sextillion, one-hundred-twenty-four quintillion, seven-hundred-twenty-seven quadrillion, seven-hundred-seventy-seven billion, six-hundred-seven million, and six-hundred-eighty thousand ways that the twenty-two Major Arcana of the Tarot can be arranged."

"Jesus!" Andrew gasped.

"Hold on," Eli answered. "The number of pictorial images that can be created is almost infinite. They spell out words in Hebrew that can be correlated to the Old Testament, and they reveal meanings that would blow your mind. Every color, symbol, image, and even sound invokes mystical states of understanding. The printed images can be traced back to the 1200s. That was when the Church really began to assert its power. Mystics from all cultures needed a way to communicate and preserve ancient wisdom. To do this, they devised the Tarot deck, which could transcend the language barrier. Adepts from Israel, China, Tibet, Europe, and you-name-it convened to form a mystical system, based on numbers, letters, and even sounds to convey the wisdom that was lost in Atlantis and from the destruction of Alexandria. 'A picture is worth a thousand words,' became the means by which the adepts circumvented the Inquisition and other persecutions."

Andrew nodded approvingly. "Go on."

"One of the basic principles is *numerology*. Using the numbers from zero to ten, a Star of David is formed, using six concentric circles tangent to a seventh, which is the basis of all creation. The Great Pyramid and various symbols used by the secret societies are all tied into this system of numbers. All of this numerology relates to the *vault* of the Order of the Rose Cross and is closely connected with the Freemasons, and all of this is tied to the *Qabbalah*, which is tied to the elusive Great White Brotherhood. The images in the Tarot are universal and timeless. They are common to and transcend culture, language, and time. They speak to some hidden seed that is dormant in all of humanity. Christ, Andrew, the cipher of this code would take lifetimes to complete!"

"We've run out of lifetimes," Andrew responded indifferently. "What is this about a seed?"

"This is really good stuff," Eli said excitedly. "Throughout the Major Arcana are various *seed* symbols. The *Death* card has a seed in the upper left corner. The symbol for the Hebrew letter *Yod* is everywhere. This seed symbol is indicative of potency, and not actuality. It speaks to what can be, if the mystery of the ages is solved. And then we have card twenty-one, *The World*. In it, an androgynous being holds two spirals, symbolic of the double helix of the human genome. In *The Tower*, card sixteen, *Yods* are in two groups—a cluster of thirteen and a cluster of ten. The cluster of ten forms the pattern of the Tree of Life in the *Qabbalah*. It is all indicative of suppressed ideas *and* suppressed genetics. If you look at *The Devil* card, there are five *Yods* beneath a torch that gives off no light. This relates back to card five, *The Hierophant*, sometimes called *The Pope*, in which two forces, or postulants, kneel before a set of keys, all of which point to some hidden information in which *genetic codes hold the future of humanity*."

Andrew didn't grasp the meaning of Eli's words intellectually, or even numerically—he grasped them intuitively. He asked, "And what of human history and the future?"

"That gets really interesting," Eli said. "Remember, the Tarot speaks in images and numbers. The cards tell of a *force of consciousness* that is not only the cause of existence, but also of existence itself. In its imagination it creates an entity, *The Fool*, which embarks on a journey of discovery. It is in control of all of the basic elements of the universe—fire, air, water, and earth. It creates a flow of consciousness, and in a paradoxical way impregnates itself to bring forth all manner of creation. It thinks of the idea of order, establishes the notion of duality, and separates itself from itself. It must create a vessel within which to pour its creative ideas, and thus positive and negative, the notions of male and female, emerge. It is not yet manifest. It is a seed in potential. It is in complete control of the forces of nature which emerge from its thoughts. It is the Wheel of Fortune, in complete balance and in total control. To manifest a physical world, it must create a duality. It must reverse its thinking. In a way, it must die spiritually to create a new beginning. But always the seed that is the core of its being remains, but is soon forgotten. In its dream state, it becomes trapped by its own illusion and its own creative forces. It becomes the inverted pentagram, immersed in the dream of the manifest and it forgets how to awaken. It must somehow remember how to shatter the illusion and to reconcile the opposites that it created in its dream state. It must evolve in order to return to its state of Edenic bliss. It seeks to know from where it came, but a Veil is created that is difficult to penetrate.

"There are forces that enjoy this state of confusion and ignorance and thrive on the forgetfulness. In a way, the scriptures are accurate in saying that one must be born again, but this is by no means the Christian version of rebirth. To become as a child is to ignore the teachings of the ignorant and to view the world through the eyes of innocence. The hidden seed in the genome tries to emerge throughout history in the form of avatars and teachers, but those who owe their existence to the dream twist the ideas and prevent the prodigal ideas from remembering that all is but a dream. Within the genome is the pattern of the pentagram, in which the slumbering humanity, through knowledge, understanding, and the gaining of wisdom can awaken to its true nature and destiny—spirit in control over the four building blocks of the manifest world. The *life force*—the serpent—is the hidden teacher that is buried by lies and deceit. The cards speak of a fall, but it is an act of its own will. It seeks to understand and to experience the totality of potential creation. This is the nature of the Primal Cause, and the seed does not fall far from the tree."

Andrew stared at his friend. "So," he said, "there's a message in the cards of something trying to dream itself into existence so it can ultimately experience itself." He remembered what he'd been told about the sleeping Adam.

"Take card fifteen, the so-called *Devil*, with the loose chains around the necks of a man and woman," Eli continued. "The restraints are an illusion. The ties don't bind. The one and the five reduce to six. The sixth card is *The Lovers*. Here are the symbols of the Trees of Life and of Knowledge. Both forces are guided by the Sun, or the ultimate spiritual force. The apples are the five senses, and the flames are the twelve powers, represented by the Zodiac and by the twelve disciples. All of the numbers stand alone, but must also be reduced for correlations. For example, a way to arrange the cards is like this." On a blank piece of paper, Eli drew:

```
              0
    1  2  3   4  5  6  7
    8  9  10 11 12 13 14
    15 16 17 18 19 20 21
```

"The cards, arranged in this manner, give clues to relationships and forces that act on man and humanity. Each row represents a plane of existence or thought, and one, eight, and fifteen share a special relationship, as would three, ten, and seventeen, and so on. If you then arrange the cards in the form of the *Qabbalah*, a whole new set of information emerges." Next he drew:

```
              0
              1

        3           2
        4           5
              6
        7           8
              9
             10
```

"Now repeat the pattern with eleven at the zero position and twenty-one at the ten position and you have a mirror image. The above zero to ten is not manifest, and the eleven to twenty-one is the manifest. The correlations and implications are mind-blowing, Andrew."

"Yes, they are," the man agreed.

"There is an important point to make to show you where some of this goes. This comes straight from Paul Foster Case, who founded B.O.T.A. He said that the 'name of the serpent which tempted Eve is NChSh and the number of the word is 358, the same value as MShICh, or Messiah.' He goes on to say that 'The Devil is God, as He is misunderstood by the wicked.'"

Andrew felt a shiver run down his spine. All he was told seemed to be coming together through his friend Eli. This was just what he needed—some outside source whom he trusted with his life to validate the information he'd been fed. The voice of Mantrella whispered in his head, "Andrew, the time is near, and your friend must go."

"Eli, you are the new John the Baptist," he said. "You must finish your research and spread the word. You have to leave now. When you return to Boston, there will be information that will speed your efforts, as well as instructions on how you are to proceed." Andrew stood, gathered Eli's papers and computer, and put them into the bag.

Stunned by the hasty dismal, Eli said, "You can't be serious. I just got here and there is so much more to go over. We're in this together, my friend, and I'm not going anywhere."

Nilaihah entered with Nico and grabbed Eli's bag, while the man took Eli by the arm and escorted him out of the room. Though he struggled, there was no way for Eli to counter Nico's sheer physical force.

"Wait a fucking minute!" he yelled back at Andrew. Nico stopped in the doorway.

"I'm sorry," Andrew said apologetically, "but for your own safety you must go. Much will be explained in the letter that is awaiting you in Boston, and stay tuned to the news. I love you, Eli, and I pray that this isn't the end—for either of us." Apprehensively, Andrew turned his back on his friend, and Nico pulled Eli into the corridor escorting him to the front door of the *hacienda*.

"Sariel, your driver, waits," Nico informed him coldly.

Dumbfounded, Eli slowly descended the few steps and walked toward the idling limousine. A man approached him, donned all in black. As they passed each other, their eyes locked, and in the few moments of what could only be described as mental telepathy, many thoughts were revealed to Eli.

"Have a safe trip, Eli," the stranger said. "So much depends on your tenacity and courage." Then the man disappeared into the *hacienda*.

Once inside the limo, Eli's head reeled with mysterious information. "Who was that man?" he demanded of the bulky driver.

"Mantrella," Sariel responded simply. "The *MShICh*."

CHAPTER 39

GEOGRAPHIC CONSPIRITOR—People have been mumbling threats of Armageddon and the End of Days for weeks now, and perhaps with just cause.

Globally, world economies are in shambles. Even in the United States, corporations that have maintained superior profits since the market crashed in 1929 have gone under. As the currency of countless countries drops below the value of gravel, hurricanes, typhoons, earthquakes, tsunami, and other natural disasters plague the earth. Defying all logic, circles of trees are appearing in our forests, and complex, otherworldly geometric designs are forming in wheat and cornfields, rice paddies, and lettuce patches.

Recently, the SETI (Search for Extraterrestrial Intelligence) Institute claims to have received a message from outer space that is nothing short of Biblical, though no official statement has been released on exactly what that message is. Communication from another planet would prove timely in these days of continual UFO sightings and mass hysteria over the threat of aliens among us.

Will it ever end? Only time will tell.

***

For a long time on the trip to the airport, Eli was silent. His mind was still trying to process the mental images he had received from the enigmatic Mantrella. His thoughts were a jumbled mix of pictures of ancient civilizations, surreal worlds whose achievements surpassed modern-day societies, great battles between strange looking beings, floods, and destruction, yet two particular images haunted him.

The first was of ancient Egypt and the pharaoh known as *Akhnaton,* or "the Son of the Sun." The pharaoh acceded to the throne in 1383 B.C. Going against all of those in power, particularly the high priest in Thebes, he proclaimed that there was only one God—the *Aton.* While symbolized by the Sun, it was not the Sun that he worshipped, rather it was a universal force that spread its light equally on all creation, rich or poor, good or bad. He built the city of his dreams, *Tel El-Amarna.* Here the Religion of the Disk took root. In his temple there were no commandments, no sacrifices, no promises of reward or punishment, no concocted miracles, and no hint of evil. It was here, amidst the glorious garden and open courtyards of light, that this renegade king proclaimed a God that was not a person, but rather the power and source of all things. It was a God that was all things and devoid of good and evil, devoid of the concept of immorality. This was a religion and a philosophy of Truth: *maat.* The religion had no dogma. Akhnaton's God was the energy that not only pervaded all of existence, but also was all of existence. It was the visible and invisible, material and immaterial—a pantheistic monism.

Akhnaton hadn't tried to force his views on others. He didn't destroy the temples or the priests of those who held sway over the masses. He didn't expand his empire nor properly defend it because he lived his life according to his beliefs, of which war was not one of them. He was the pharaoh who initiated Moses into the *mysteries,* and in brotherhood, let his people go.

The Son of the Sun died at the age of twenty-nine. Some said he was poisoned; others said that he walked with God. On his death, the beautiful city of light, Armana, was destroyed, and his religion was wiped from the stones, pillars, and tablets. The powerful priests removed from the people's memory the very existence of this messenger of Truth.

The second image that disturbed his mind was that of a being whose beauty exceeded imagination. As he tried to examine the image more closely, the limo suddenly veered to miss a burro standing in the middle of the road. The sharp turn slid him across the seat, bumping his head on the window.

Having been jolted from his visions, he yelled, "Shit! We have to turn back. I have to tell Andrew about the goddess and the birth."

"Believe me, he knows of the goddess," the driver said.

"I'm talking about the goddess images in the Tarot. If you read the cards in reverse, you're presented with a double helix and a new kind of being. The being comes out of its gray coffin of ignorance from the watery depths of consciousness. Somehow, Gabriel has something to do with this, since he heralds the arrival. Ironically, he flies the red cross standard of the Templars. Even more important is the fact that somehow the single child becomes two, male and female, children of the sun. The goddess spreads truth over the land and the tower of ignorance and deceit is destroyed. Then…"

Sariel interrupted Eli with a jamming of the brake. "We're here. You must leave now."

The driver quickly got out, opened Eli's door, and pulled him from the car. Before Eli could say another word, the limousine sped away from the masses of people still clogging the airport. Abandoned, Eli numbly made his way through the terminal, constantly bumped and shoved as he went against the flow of the human sea. People continued to pour off the planes to get glimpses of the mysterious night sky lights, an event that completely escaped Eli's attention. Caught up in his own thoughts, he managed to find the terminal just as it announced the departure of flight 144 to Orlando, and then to Boston.

As Eli was about to step onto the boarding ramp, he felt something sharp seize his arm. He yelped in pain, only to find the source of the attack—Nevyn.

"Holy shit, Nevyn! How the hell did you get here?"

The wolfhound wagged his tail, but with his fangs firmly gripping Eli's arm, he forced the man from the terminal. Several times, Eli tried to release himself from the stinging vice, but Nevyn wouldn't relent. The people jostling around him didn't seem to notice the large animal that was attached to his arm, and he realized that in some way the creature appeared invisible to all but him. The dog pulled him to a remote terminal and onto the tarmac. A private silver jet, with engines idling in standby mode, awaited him. Nevyn led Eli up the steps and into the jet, then, finally releasing his arm, pushed him into a seat. Eli rubbed the quickly fading bruises on his forearm, then buckled his safety belt. The man now secure, the dog ceased his guard and lay quietly beside him in the narrow aisle.

An hour later, Eli was fast asleep. Over the Gulf of Mexico, flight 144 was soaring toward Orlando at an altitude of 32,000 feet. Without warning, the plane carrying 124 passengers burst into flames, sending pieces of its occupants down toward rusty Gulf oil rigs mindlessly pumping crude to feed an ever-collapsing world economy.

CHAPTER 40

The entrance structure of the *Parque Nacional* was dark and silent, the welcome center, public restrooms, and gift shops hollow in the absence of the regular season's tourists. Their footsteps echoed hauntingly off the cement floors as they passed blindly through the building, at last emerging into the jungle heat and brilliant moonlight and out onto the gravel pathways of the ancient city of *Chich'en Itza*.

Mantrella walked in the wake of Andrew and Nilaihah, positioning himself into a protective station between the two ahead of him, and Nico and nine shock troopers behind him. None spoke. With the exception of Andrew and Mantrella, all were armed and on full alert, anticipating a violent reckoning at any moment.

Once into the open air of the Northern Precinct of the city, called "New Chich'en" by archeologists, Andrew stood in quiet awe of the magnificent stone structures rising like giants before him. Nilaihah left his side and joined her comrades as Nico silently motioned for them to fan out across the sprawling square in quiet patrol.

At the center of the precinct stood the Pyramid of *K'uk'ulkan*, a radial pyramid with four stairways climbing to a two-story temple—a dream-chamber—at its summit. The Spaniards had named the pyramid *"El Castillo"* —"The Castle"—during their conquest and subsequent raping of the Mayan people. To the east of the great pyramid was the Temple of the Warriors, where the council of the ancient *Itza* people once met to rule the kingdom—where their whispering voices still echoed in the ceibas. The Venus Platform lay to the north, at the mouth of the *sak beh*—white road—the causeway to the Sacred Cenote, where offerings to the gods were thrown into the murky waters sixty feet below. The final massive construction in the precinct stood to the west of the *Castillo*, and was the Great Ballcourt that represented the crack that formed in the top of Creation Mountain. It was a crevice that gave man access to *Xibalba*—the Underworld, the home of the gods and ancestors, often through blood-letting ceremonies such as human decapitation.

K'uk'ulkan, the Feathered Serpent, figured into Mayan legend as a great king, and later, a god. Called *Quetzalcoatl* by the Aztecs, he was believed to have ruled *Tollan*—"Place of Cattail Reeds"—and to have been the cause of that capital's eventual ruin. In shame, he and his loyal followers left *Tollan* and journeyed east, promising to someday return. Conquering the peaceful Mayan of the Yucatan Peninsula, *K'uk'ulkan*

created a new great empire, and introduced practices of warfare and human sacrifice. *Chich'en Itza,* like many great cities of the era, contained symbols that recalled *Ah Puh*—the "Place of Reeds"—a sacred location of origin where people first learned the arts, writing, and the ways of civilization as they came to know them. And so the capital city of *Chich'en Itza* was established by the *Itza* as a "Place of Reeds" over eleven-hundred years earlier, in order that the founders could claim their ancestral rights back to the beginning of time. Masks with long snouts and flowered headbands appeared in many places throughout the settlement, preserving the image of *Itzam-Ye,* or *Mut Itzamna,* the gigantic bird that sat at the very top of the Mayan World Tree, *Wakah Chan.*

Mayan mythology saw *K'uk'ulkan* as the quetzal-feathered snake god who aided in creating Earth and humanity. He taught man the precepts of civilization, as well as the skills of agriculture. More importantly, he was the god of the four elements—fire, earth, air, and water—as well as a culture hero who brought forth law, agriculture, medicine, and fishing. As water, he was a fish; as air, the vulture; as earth, maize; and as fire, the lizard. Born of the ocean, it was said that he returned to it and would one day rise at the End Times as the overwhelming source of positive and negative energy, a belief that closely tied him to the Yin-Yang symbol of the Orient.

As the Great Ballcourt came to represent supernaturally the fissure that opened into space and time from the Underworld, the Pyramid of *K'uk'ulkan* came to signify Snake Mountain, a place of origin established at the beginning of the world at *Ah Puh.* Each of the structure's stairways had ninety-one steps, and when combined with the single step onto the chamber platform at the peak, 365 days of a full calendar year were represented. The pairs of thick limestone railings bordering the stairways were capped at the ground, with great gaping serpent heads representing the god *K'uk'ulkan*, which became living undulating serpents at the equinoxes when a show of light and dark cast shadows of the pyramid's blocks up the balustrades. Andrew had always been fascinated with the undulating snake effect, and he knew that hundreds of people each year came to witness the incredible phenomenon. The pyramid itself was constructed in nine stepped sections, symbolizing the regions of the dead, and raising the structure to over seventy-eight feet into the dense sky.

The most fascinating element of the great Pyramid of *K'uk'ulkan*, Andrew believed, was the fact that the existing construction had been superimposed on an earlier pyramid. Deep within *El Castillo* was an inner chamber, accessible through a door at the base of the north staircase, which led to a tunnel, at the end of which was another staircase leading up and into the pyramid. In the heart of Snake Mountain was the Temple of the Red Jaguar, which housed the bejeweled throne of the jaguar painted red with jade spots, and a strange statue of a *Chac-Mool*. *Chac-Mool*, a type of stone altar, was the figure of a god lying on his back in a sit-up position with his head up and turned to one side, and his hands holding a dish over his stomach. The dish was believed to be the offering plate on which human hearts were placed as sacred objects of devotion to the gods. In the 19th century, an antiquarian by the name of Augustus Le Plongeon excavated Mayan sites on the Yucatan Peninsula and published volumes on the history of the people. Thought of as nothing more than an eccentric who based most of his findings on elaborate tales and information that he had concocted, he ultimately uncovered a statue that he claimed represented a king of Atlantis, and thus dubbed it *Chac-Mool*, meaning "Red Jaguar" in Mayan.

Mantrella laid a hand gently on Andrew's shoulder, lifting him from his momentary trance. "Eerily beautiful, isn't it?" he asked. "I remember it so well. The power I absorbed from these sacred grounds was unlike any that I had gained from countless other places." He stepped away from Andrew, moving toward the great pyramid. "The feathers always tickled me, though." A twisting grin crossed his lips at the humor. "Come," he continued. "There is much left to do."

Nico and his soldiers congregated near the western corner of the pyramid. The leader spoke softly in the foreign tongue to Nilaihah as Andrew and Mantrella approached the base of the northern staircase. Glancing back at the Venus platform, Mantrella smiled. "The white road," he said in an easy breath. "How many innocent people did they kill in my name?"

Andrew studied the man's angular profile. "How many did you demand that they sacrifice?"

Mantrella considered him for a moment, searching his heavy eyes as the full moon rose sneakily from behind the Temple of the Warriors. "I only demanded that they discover the light," he answered calmly. "The same force that seeks to oppress you sought to paint the Itza gods as brutal and sadistic. I offer no excuses—only the truth."

A balmy wind moved roughly over the brown grass of the square, and Andrew watched as the soldiers slid behind them and waited, staring up at the pyramid's temple.

"What are we..."

"He's here," Mantrella whispered. "I can feel him."

A tiny point of light emerged in the doorway of the temple, and with a stiff arm, Mantrella forced Andrew back as his body grew warm and unstable. "There he is," he said. "Come, Michael."

The glowing dot slowly grew larger until at last it completely filled the doorway and radiated out into the precinct, bathing the monuments and buildings, the reliefs and platforms, in silver light. Mantrella arched his back in the illumination, spreading his arms to both sides, as his body shook and ripples of cool, blue energy streamed from his clothes and pores. Straightening himself, he pushed back the silver light with the power oozing from his limbs and torso until halfway up the northern staircase the two forces created a sparking wall, a pulsing band of matter and anti-matter repelling each other. A figure took form at the top of the pyramid, the features vibrating into clarity, as Michael was born of his own glory.

"I'm so happy we could all be here together," Michael called down to them, his voice crystal clear through the opposing energies. "I'd only hoped that the reunion could have happened on slightly different terms. But I have you, regardless." He smiled wryly, and the ground began to hum.

Mantrella glared up at him. "Who really has whom, Michael?" he asked smugly.

Raising his hands to the sky, Michael spoke harshly. "Now it ends. Your plans of allowing Adam to dream himself into existence have failed. Andrew and Mara will *not* give birth to him. It is better for humanity this way. Besides, they're not worthy, old friend. Can't you see that mankind is not yet responsible enough to become a god? The notion that they could even be half as good as us is a cosmic joke."

"You take from them what is not yours to take, Michael," Mantrella yelled into the fizzing air. "The scripture you taught them to follow is the very plan that keeps them like bugs feeding on a corpse of lies. 'Fear God!' you commanded them. And what an awful God you gave them! But when the God of War could no longer suppress man's intellect and spiritual urges, He laid his bow and arrow in the clouds and you struggled for a different way to control him."

Michael howled in laughter. "I control them still! See this, brother!"

"The first mistake was made when the blue-eyed god Gabriel turned from you and let his own desires bring him into union with the Virgin," Mantrella continued. "In desperation, you used my prophet, the Son of God sent to pave the way to a new age of enlightenment, as an example, nailing him to your crooked symbols. But he lived, didn't he? Then you martyred him, calling him 'the Messiah' and twisting his words to reflect the feces that you wished to spread. Once again, it seemed that you had won them over to your side. I know now, Michael, that the time for the ascension simply hadn't been right, and that your victory would only be temporary."

"I expected so much more from such an *earthly* angel," Michael retorted.

Mantrella grinned at him. "Under their noses, you put forth in *Revelation* your deceitful plan to keep your own power. You would slay the serpent and cast him into a fiery pit. Little do they know that the serpent you have been killing for thousands of years is the very wisdom and knowledge they seek. But I have returned as promised, and I will raise mankind so they may achieve the proper purification that fire brings."

"A messiah will indeed come, brother," Michael answered. "But he will not be you."

"A pawn to crucify again? A weakling to corrupt and bastardize?"

"Of course. Then we'll build again."

Seething in disgust, Mantrella lurched forward, driving his aura further up the staircase and pushing the electric barrier closer to the archangel. "You'll rebuild your temples of servitude! You are no brother of mine!" The words pounded out of his throat. "The destiny of mankind will destroy you! The great Archangel Michael and his faithful counterparts—Fate will render you obsolete, and Gabriel, Raphael, and Uriel will follow you into the dust!"

With the greatest part of his might, Michael shoved his silver light back toward Mantrella, and the wall shifted again and the ground rumbled. "Your precious humans must remain in darkness and wallow in their ignorance. Their churches have edged too closely to enlightenment. Let Peter be their lesson! The upheaval of the world, blossoming at their doorsteps like an infested lotus, has turned brother against brother, father against son, nation against nation. Your Dogs of Isis will soon devour each other as their eternal partners suck the life from their souls. I have already begun to plunge man into chaos so he will seek a new light and guidance as he falters back into ignorance and embraces the doctrine of any false prophet that can glean some fragment of sense from his misery!"

Suddenly, from the dream-chamber, Mara burst forth, heaving her body past Michael. Enveloped by the silver light, she shielded her eyes from the blinding glare and stumbled toward the staircase.

"Here is your grail," the archangel announced.

Mara lowered her hands as her eyes adjusted to the radiance. "Liar!" she screamed, stepping away from Michael. "Everything you told me has been a lie!" Her brilliant green eyes glowed against the luminous background, as she set her jaw in anger and loathing.

Michael smiled viciously at her. "Then go to the truth, Mara." He pointed down at Andrew. "Embrace your destiny."

Unsteadily, she made her way down the narrow steps of the staircase, desperately struggling to maintain her balance. Both the archangel and Mantrella watched her silently as she came finally to the barrier where the forces of their being met in violent resistance to each other. Andrew ran for the steps as Mantrella commanded him to stop. Nico and his men moved toward him, but he was already in the cool blue waves of energy, and clawing toward Mara.

At the sparking wall, he reached out for her, daring to touch the burning surface. "Take my hand, Mara," he yelled into the driving wind. From the nine stepped sections of the pyramid on either side of the stairway, Michael's minions rose in human form, spreading their luminous wings under the full moon. Plunging her hand through the force field, Mara grasped Andrew's hand and fell toward him. Fingers closed to fists, Michael jerked his arms to his sides, yanking the two into the air where, in a flash of orange light, they disappeared.

"No!" Mantrella screamed, sucking the power back into his body.

The silver light settled onto the stone like powder, and the throbbing wall vanished. Falling to his knees, Mantrella tried to regain his strength as Michael steadied himself against the wall of the dream-chamber, he too was exhausted.

Gunfire crackled through the darkness, and the pyramid began to spark as the lead from the shock trooper's automatic weapons ricocheted off the limestone slabs. Some of the minions burst into white light as they were struck by the bullets. From every crack of Snake Mountain, more of them emerged to confront Mantrella's soldiers, screeching into the moonlight as corpse-like monsters with wings of skin and bone. Nilaihah raised her weapon and picked one of the creatures out of the sky with a single shot to its forehead. As it fell at her feet in a ball of fire, Nico's men began to morph into wolves.

"We'll never survive their numbers," Nilaihah called to Mantrella. "There are too many of them."

Soon the moon was blackened by the horde of creatures that had taken flight into the night sky, but then the surrounding forests erupted into unnerving howls, and the boundaries of the northern precinct were invaded by the Dogs of Isis. Hundreds of wolves rushed into the square, slashing and leaping at the creatures. The great battle had begun. Wolf and winged creature clashed together in an eternal struggle. Positive and negative energy swirled all around the ancient capital city.

Mantrella, still on his knees, looked up at the spent archangel. "What have you done?"

Weakly, Michael began to laugh. "They're inside the mountain now," he answered. "I believe, my shining brother, you must concede to the power of the Lords after all."

Dropping his head, Mantrella closed his eyes, his body rigid with anger. A milky haze shimmered around him, protecting him from the game of life and death playing itself out in the square behind him with explosions of light and whirling ash. Though he and his rival were, for the moment, drained of their power, Mantrella knew that he still had a little extra to offer. He would not lie down now—not when he was losing.

From deep within, he called up the forces of his many beings. Currents of electrical energy flickered through the waters of the planet, split the air, and quaked inside the earth, for an instant threatening to implode the world. Fire came out of the ground in a ring around him, stretching its stinging fingers into the night sky. The image of Mantrella seemed to fade away. Then, in a sudden thunderous crack, the fire slammed back into the ground, revealing in its wake a magnificent warrior. Mantrella's once tall and slender figure had transformed into a broad, hulking body covered in emerald armor. The open-faced helmet he wore recalled the knights of the Middle Ages, though the surface of it pulsed with glowing symbols of his existence.

Michael stepped toward the edge of the platform and grinned. "I'd guessed that Baphomet was far beyond your grasp at this point," he chided, "but I haven't seen this form since…"

"Since I departed from your presence at the beginning of time," Mantrella roared. From his side, he withdrew a shining sword of silver and gold and rushed the pyramid, moving quickly up the staircase. Along the way, he slashed at the minions who darted into his path, slicing them in half and reducing their heinous forms to fire and ash.

Once he was on the platform, he seized Michael by the shoulders and threw him against the limestone wall of the chamber's northern doorway. The archangel smiled at him as Mantrella raised the sword high above his head.

"The eternal struggle begins," he said, seething with the earth's adrenaline as the dragon's breath raged in his silver eyes. "Adam, forgive me for the deed I am about to commit in the name of your existence."

***

In the darkest caverns of the pyramid, three angels sat quietly at a golden table, its edges round and smooth. Collectively, they gazed at the ceiling that bore Maya glyphs, communicating instructions of passage through the trials of *Xibalba* to the souls of the dead who would need the guidance. Without a word, the three focused their thoughts, while their physical bodies, only temporary in form and shape, buzzed in and out of clarity. The floor of the pyramid shifted, sending a wave of vibration into the core of the mountain. Though missing their first and final energy source, they understood that they could affect the chaos on the other side of the stone walls without him. Gabriel began to glow in a shade of blue. Raphael's form shimmered red, and Uriel's, yellow. Between them, a throbbing sphere of silver light formed, rose slowly from the table and hovered at the ceiling. A moment passed and the air went icy. The ball of light dropped toward the table again before changing course and suddenly blasting into the ceiling.

Above, Mantrella forced his blade through the air. Michael, bracing himself for the cut, pressed his body against the wall. His energy was low, and he knew that he didn't have the time to reform. He would have to take the strike, though it would release him into the Veil. He would return to finish this. It was only an inconvenience that it couldn't finally end now.

But then Mantrella was gone—vanishing into the pale light of a pregnant moon.

CHAPTER 41

The brook murmured softly in his ears, but the dream remained disjointed and chaotic. He could see, deep within his mind, the angel struggling to be free, wanting to be released. The two needed to be saved so the dream could end and he, too, could be free. He would have to help them, somehow, to speak out across the ages and into their world. Restless in slumber, the naked man's body quivered and he rolled over onto the smooth wet stones of the shore. Though his lips trembled, the ghostly thoughts of his mind took no spoken form. Instead, through the milk of his dreams, he whispered, "Fear not, for I am with you always...even until the end of time..."

***

In an outer tomb, without a door or passageway from which to enter or exit, Mantrella existed, dormantly encased in gold in the deepest regions of the Pyramid of K'uk'ulkan. Three days after he had been sucked from the temple platform and imprisoned in precious metal, Venus rose on the horizon, and the Bright and Morning Star was released from his sepulcher as it melted into the stony ground.

Slowly, his eyes opened and he sensed the stifling darkness around him. He became aware of his true self—his identity. His armor was gone, having retreated back into itself, and returned its energy to the elements. Now he stood wrapped in a russet cloth, his skin tingling with the heat of a growing anger building in the pit of his being. His head fell back, and he erupted into a ferocious roar that quaked through the stone and echoed out into the universe.

Hands closing to fists and body stiffening with rage, Lucifer stepped toward a wall of the outer tomb, blowing a hole in the limestone. Powerfully, he marched out of the room and down a revealed corridor, continually met with the obstacle of a heavy sealed door. But he would not be daunted. Instead, he pushed on, the doors exploding open, one after the other, as he drove his being toward the heart of the pyramid, knowing all too well that what he had sworn to protect and fulfill was waiting for him in another hidden chamber.

When the dust settled from the final explosion and the Angel of Light stood heaving in the prison chamber, his aura glowing into the darkness, he saw a pair of onyx slabs on stone foundations, and he knew them to be the coffins of Andrew and Mara. Raising his hands over his head, he split the suffocating air as he pulled open the fabric of reality and retrieved a sword of blue light.

Blade pulsing in his grip, he laid the weapon on the first of the coffins, declaring "Here is your purification by fire." Like his own prison, the onyx began to melt, first into gold, then into white light, and soon the prostrate Andrew appeared, naked and unconscious. Next, he approached the second coffin and performed the purification as he had with Andrew. When the white light finally dissipated into the rough stone walls and Mara, lying as Andrew had, emerged from its wake, he brushed the strands of black hair from her dark face with a single finger.

Releasing the sword, it vanished into the darkness, and he set his hands on Andrew and Mara's forehead.

"Wake, my children," he commanded them gently. "The destiny of the world is yours."

A sheen of mist fell over them, and with a wave of his hand Mantrella parted the haze to reveal two humans awake and clothed in silk robes.

Within the massive structure, stairways collapsed and tunnels closed in on themselves, restricting their movement and making their release seem impossible. On instinct alone, Mantrella led Mara and Andrew from their tomb, through a long corridor and up a staircase. A solid stone wall marked the end of the corridor, but Mantrella lashed out with his fists and blew it into pieces. Immediately, the yellow light of a new dawn streamed into the suffocating tunnel, and Andrew held an open hand to his brow as he squinted into the fresh sunlight. Mara, eyes slightly closed, breathed in the infant day.

"Come," Mantrella said. "There is much to be done. For now the archangels are sure in their victory, but we still have a dream to complete before the god awakens."

Mara's eyes met Andrew's, recognition on her beautiful face. She nodded once, and he smiled at her, happy that she was safe and with him at last. *He would not let her go again,* Andrew thought. The reason for their existence together was now so very clear, and Mara finally realized the same.

Mantrella ushered the two through the hole and out into the square of the northern precinct. Looking back, Andrew realized that they had emerged from the pyramid at the base of the western staircase, and he wondered just how many levels below the earth the inner chambers of Snake Mountain went.

A whistle broke the stillness, and the three looked across the square to see Nilaihah running toward them from the Ballcourt, a 9mm holstered under her arm and an uncharacteristic smile woven through her lips.

"You made it," she gasped as she approached. Nico's army peered out at them from their places of cover all around the ruins. She stood before Mantrella, her white skin glistening with the slightest hint of perspiration. "We could not approach the pyramid," she explained. "It was too heavily guarded and our ammunition was dangerously low. There were too many minions ascending from the stone, so we dropped back and took cover. Our plan was to wait for the right moment to storm the pyramid and rescue you. We would have waited forever, if we had to."

Smiling down at her, Mantrella placed a hand on her shoulder.

"We saw you as soon as you came out," she continued. "We'd hardly had time to make our move since the explosion and your release happened almost simultaneously."

Andrew stepped toward her. "He blew the wall. That's how we escaped."

"No," she answered. "The explosion didn't come from the wall. Moments ago, a brilliant sphere of light rose from the peak of the pyramid, then exploded into the sky. Four trails of fire streaked forth from the blast, and each went its separate way toward the cardinal points, forming in the sky a burning cross. Then you came out of the pyramid—all of you."

Mara glanced at the top of the pyramid and saw the rubble smoking at its peak, where the dream-chamber had once stood. She looked at Andrew, but he had also noticed the destruction, and gazed up at it.

"We must go," Nilaihah warned. "There's word that the public has become aware of the commotion here. I fear we haven't the time to consider all of this now."

Mantrella nodded and gestured for Nilaihah to lead Mara and Andrew to safety. He followed closely behind, stopping only long enough to observe Venus shining on the horizon. Looking up, he acknowledged the remains of the cross of fire, now merely wisps of smoke in the air, being swirled out of their symbol by a warm Gulf wind. Silver eyes glistening, his lips twisted into his signature grin as they filtered out of the square and through the welcome building, quickly entering the air-conditioned cabins of waiting SUVs.

***

LA MANCHA—Earlier today, Federales just outside the town of Piste, in the province of Yucatan, surrounded the Parque Nacional containing the ancient Mayan ruins of Chichen Itza. The government troops reacted in accordance to national safety and preservation regulations as hundreds of thousands of people flooded into the town to see strange lights in the sky.

In the wake of millions of sightings and supernatural phenomena occurring over Mexico City and other parts of the country, witnesses of strange lights over the ruins have speculated that the end of the world may be closer than anyone ever thought.

"Early this morning," sources say, *"a powerful explosion of light took place over the peak of the famed Pyramid of K'uk'ulkan, launching four balls of fire into different directions. People in the area contend that the streaks of fire made the sign of the cross. Others say that it was simply a large X in the sky."*

Mexican state officials have refused to comment on what could have taken place early this morning in Chichen Itza. Opponents suspect top secret government testing might have somehow backfired and caused the explosion.

In an effort to allay any mass hysteria, NASA is taking full responsibility for the commotion and subsequent outbreak of fire, claiming that its recently launched weather balloon—the high-tech Silver Bug, which was released from Key West only three weeks ago—was programmed to self-destruct in the same manner in which eyewitnesses are claiming the ball of light did.

"Silver Bug no longer remains on our radar screens," NASA spokesperson Angela Contina said. *"We are certain that the explosion above the Pyramid of K'uk'ulkan represents the end of the Silver Bug program, and nothing more."*

"I, Jesus, have sent My angel to testify to you these things in the churches. I am the Root and the Offspring of David, the Bright and Morning Star."

—Revelation 22:16

WAKING GOD BOOK TWO: THE SACRED ROTA

PROLOGUE

They meet in a place that is no place, in a moment outside of time...

"Why have you called this meeting? We have nothing to discuss."

"Oh, but we have much to discuss. You may think that you have won, but you are deluding yourself."

"You have never lacked confidence, Greatest of the Archangels, but you must know that, at least in this world, you are on the cusp of extinction."

"You are blinded by your own folly, and that will be your downfall, again. Just because you have Andrew and Mara, you think that you will give birth to your god seed. But I warn you, if you permit conception, you will be destroying your beloved humanity."

"Will you never admit defeat? The seeds shall unite, and Adam will rise to lead Israel to its destined place among the gods. You cannot stop this."

"Would you permit inception knowing that all humanity, saving my loyal few, would perish? You said yourself in Mexico that I had revealed my plans, and you were right. The seals will be opened unless you abandon your pretentious little Adam."

"You wouldn't."

"I would and I shall. You have never appreciated my will to survive and to maintain dominion over your petty little flock. To show you how serious I am..."

A book appears in the firmament, and on the book are seven seals. The lamb, in Mantrella's image, opens the first, and the seal is broken—

And I saw, and behold a white horse: and he that sat on him had a bow; and a crown was given unto him: and he went forth conquering, and to conquer...

"How dare you! You tread where none should go! If we were not in this place, I would..."

"You would try and fail as you always have. And as for treading, it is you who are being the fool. Cease your meddling or more seals shall be opened."

***

Amsterdam, the Netherlands

The old office was rarely utilized, most members being under the impression that its purpose was virtually defunct. Those who did know of its infrequent but continued use were of the "Inner Circle." Michael almost never attended these sessions. Only the most urgent of issues drew his attention, which was why today he was in attendance at a special meeting that he himself had called. Consequently, none dared to be absent. Regardless of their wealth and power, a call from Michael was the equivalent of an order from the Almighty.

Giovanni, Lord Brathmore, Otto, and John G. were seated at one end of a conference table built to seat the forty combined members of the Advisory Group and the Steering Committee. The walls of the windowless room were impenetrable to the most advanced eavesdropping devices, and the only furniture in the space was the table, its high-backed chairs, and a podium. The walls were unadorned, the polished blackness of their marble composition reflecting images of the members in a surrealistic darkness. There were no statues or art work of any kind. Although a red carpet lay under the table, the gloss-white floor was in sharp contrast to the otherwise dimly lit room. There was no paper, nor were there any writing devices of any kind; members were not allowed to record anything lest a quick note, name, address or idea might find its way into the media or into the hands of some other undesirable seeker of information. Moreover, the normal entourage of U.S. Secret Service and private security guards was absent. With a major event about to occur, Michael had no need for such nonsense.

A red orb appeared at one end of the sparse room. The Inner Circle members understood the meaning of the light, but even though they had come to expect this manner of grand entrance, they continued to be awestruck each time it happened. The orb grew in size and brilliance, until the group had to shield their eyes as the crimson radiance, reflecting off the polished walls, was like looking directly into the sun. Within seconds, the room returned to its normal obscurity, but the afterglow still burned in the members' retinas.

"Greetings," Michael said as he made his way to his faithful followers.

The four stood, bowing to Michael, who indifferently motioned the group to sit. They knew not to ask questions or to speak until Michael precipitated the conversation.

"Are we on schedule?" he asked.

"All those you designated and more have been tagged with RFD's," Giovanni replied. "We know their whereabouts at all times. We have checked the audio chips and they are functioning well. This second generation chip is a marvel. I wish we had had it earlier. It is one thing to know the location, but it is quite another to hear their conversations." The grin sliding across Giovanni's deeply tanned face communicated a sense of satisfaction for the small, very thin old man.

John G., however, squirmed. He did not want to say what he knew he must. Nonetheless, he cleared his throat. "I am sorry to say that Mantrella has become aware of the Adam Gene Project." He averted his eyes from Michael in expectation of a tirade, or worse. "One of Mantrella's men was working in the lab. Before we caught on to him, he managed to download the data on the mitochondrial DNA serum."

Unconcerned, Michael said, "And how are the vaccinations going?"

"All who might be of consequence have had the gene disrupted," Otto offered. "The masses will be neutralized within the year, minus a few isolated strays."

Michael smiled in approval and the Inner Circle finally relaxed. "There is little that Mantrella can do. Who would turn down a cure from the AIDS pandemic? Already hundreds of millions have perished. If the religious strife were not enough, few will refuse the opportunity to be spared from the mutated virus. They fear the plague more than the clergy."

"Lord," Brathmore said, "we are losing much in this turmoil."

Michael turned on the man, eyes blazing. Brathmore fell to his knees in maddening pain. The others moved back from their comrade in fear of touching Michael's anger.

"You know nothing of losing," Michael whispered. As he spoke his eyes cooled and the pain in every molecule of Brathmore began to subside. Michael felt absolute contempt for the petty desires of humans. He needed them, but he also hated them. The thought that he once bowed before the archetype, an event he vowed never to repeat, turned his stomach.

Regaining his wits, Brathmore uttered, "I am sorry, my Lord. You have always done us well. I did not mean to doubt. Forgive me." Brathmore prostrated himself before Michael, who smiled at the supplication.

"Fear not for your worldly treasures," Michael insisted. "I will soon reveal the Joshua Tree."

Otto and the others were shocked by the Archangel's announcement.

"How did you get the Priory to reveal the name of the Joshua Tree?" Otto questioned.

"They have been betrayed," Michael answered evenly. "I have had an insider since the beginning. He will be making the announcement. He will use DNA from Mary to prove beyond any doubt that David is of the lineage of Jesus. The world is ready to buy into just about anything that will offer some hope of salvation from these terrible times. And who better than the next Secretary General of the United Nations?"

"Does Mantrella know?" asked Giovanni.

"He will learn of it shortly in the news, along with the rest of the world," Michael promised, erupting into bitter laughter. Although uneasy, the Inner Circle joined in the jubilation.

They had no choice.

***

Eli's flight from Mexico to Boston's Logan International Airport was uneventful, offering clear weather and little turbulence. Nevyn slept the entire flight on a padded birth that seemed designed for the dog's proportions. When they first boarded the plane, the dog had curled at his feet, but once in the air, he decided to seek the comfort of what was apparently his personal bed.

Haunted by Mantrella, every time Eli closed his eyes in an attempt to sleep, he saw those silver gray orbs boring jumbled images into his head. He somehow knew that the information would organize itself, but it was disconcerting to have someone else's thoughts operating in his brain. He was not sure if he feared Mantrella; actually, he decided that he did not. He was uncomfortable, not afraid. He knew that his choices were very limited with respect to the use of his own discretion and this new knowledge that kept rolling like a movie in fast forward across his mind. Exactly what he was to do had not yet been made clear. Andrew had told him that the instructions waited at home, but he was not sure whether he was in any hurry to know the mission. The reference to John the Baptist was not encouraging to this Boston Jew.

His thoughts turned to his best friend. *What in the hell had Andrew gotten himself into?* Everything in Mexico happened so fast. He had hoped to have more time to spend with his friend and he'd figured they could spend days on the beaches of the Gulf musing over his findings. Instead, his expectation for a leisure holiday turned into a whirlwind tour of the Twilight Zone. The airport in Mexico had been a zoo filled with alien hunters, UFO watchers, and religious fanatics. He was picked up by a likeable but gigantic man who would have made wrestling federation stars look like ninety-pound weaklings, then he arrived at a hacienda filled with dozens of leviathans. On the bright side, he had met one of the prettiest women in the world, though it appeared that she had never been allowed to be in the sun; in a snowstorm she would never be seen if she were naked. The thought actually aroused Eli. After spending almost no time with Andrew, his friend basically kicked him out. Then his path crossed someone named Mantrella, a man with godlike qualities, who had been invading his thoughts with strange images, symbols, and incredibly interesting ideas ever since.

Eli was both anxious and nervous. He was anxious to get home bring Jen up to date on Andrew and his bizarre companions, no matter how hard the story would be to believe. Luckily, Jen's willingness to listen and talk about every aspect of Eli's life and work was why he had fallen in love with her. The fact that she would engage Eli in his rather boring discussions concerning mathematics and code theories was what really cinched the union. Anxiety aside, he was nervous. He knew that a letter was waiting for him from Andrew that would finally put him on the inside loop concerning the peculiar events of the past year, a place in which Eli both wanted and didn't want to be.

A bell rang in the cabin and Eli saw the blinking *Fasten Seat Belts* sign. He looked over to Nev, who didn't so much as twitch. This convinced Eli that the landing would be uneventful. The sky was cloudless and the shimmer off Boston Harbor was blinding. Eli barely even noticed that the jet had landed and taxied to a private terminal. When the plane came to a halt, he collected his few belongings. The cabin door opened and Nev finally jumped off his special seat and followed Eli to the exit.

Making their way through the throngs of would-be travelers, Eli came to an abrupt halt in front of a newsstand. There, a crowd of people had gathered around a TV to read the words proclaiming the destruction of flight 144 from Mexico to Boston, while on the screen flickered images of airline debris floating in the Gulf. This was the same flight that Eli was supposed to have been on but thanks to his canine friend, he was on another flight. Eli glanced down at Nevyn and the dog looked up at him, wagging his tail in what could only be interpreted as an expression of self-satisfaction.

About the Authors

Philip F. Harris

Philip F. Harris was born in Massachusetts and currently resides in Maine. He received his degree in Political Science from The American University in Washington, D.C. and has worked at every level of government. He currently works in special education.

He is co-author of the controversial **WAKING GOD** series, coined a "spiritual thriller," which was first released 6'06 and was re-released in '09 with a new publisher. The Third Edition was released by All Things That Matter Press. His second novel, **A MAINE CHRISTMAS CAROL** was released by Cambridge Books in 2'07. His third book (non-fiction), **JESUS TAUGHT IT, TOO: THE EARLY ROOTS OF THE LAW OF ATTRACTION,** 2nd edition was released by ALL THINGS THAT MATTER PRESS. His fourth book, **RAPING LOUISIANA: A DIARY OF DECEIT** was released by Cambridge Books in 2007. **POLARIZING YOUR LIFE TOWARDS PERFECTION** is published by Cambridge Books. **WAKING GOD BOOK II: THE SACRED ROTA** was originally published by Literary Road Press. See the series, **COLLECTED MESSAGES: GUIDES FOR PERSONAL TRANSFORMATION** at ALL THINGS THAT MATTER PRESS.

Mr. Harris is a nationally syndicated and featured writer for **The American Chronicle** and has a blog called **ALL THINGS THAT MATTER.** He is spiritual growth expert on **SelfGrowth.com.** More information on his works can be found at:
http://allthingsthatmatterpress.com,http://philipharris.blogspot.com, http://wakinggod1.blogspot.com,http://www.wakinggod.com. A certified Holistic Life Coach, Mr. Harris offers guidance to those seeking to take control of their body, mind and spirit.

Brian L. Doe

Brian L. Doe was born in Ogdensburg, New York, and grew up on the shores of the St. Lawrence River. From a young age, he recognized his passion for the written word and committed himself to the pursuit of writing. He received a Bachelor's Degree in writing from St. Lawrence University, and a Master's Degree in secondary education from the State University of New York at Potsdam College. His first novel, *Barley and Gold*, was published in 2001 and again in 2008 along with his second book, *The Grace Note*. He is also coauthor of the trilogy *Waking God* with Philip F. Harris. Mr. Doe is an English teacher in Upstate New York where he lives with his wife and children.

ALL THINGS THAT MATTER PRESS ™

FOR MORE INFORMATION ON TITLES AVAILABLE FROM
ALL THINGS THAT MATTER PRESS, GO TO
http://allthingsthatmatterpress.com
or contact us at
allthingsthatmatterpress@gmail.com

www.ingramcontent.com/pod-product-compliance
Lightning Source LLC
Chambersburg PA
CBHW051640260626
47170CB00004B/1259